MY
WHOLE
TRUTH

MISCHA THRACE

MY WHOLE TRUTH

Mendota Heights, Minnesota

First Edition
First Printing, 2018

Book design by Jake Nordby
Cover design by Jake Nordby
Cover images by Sparking Moments Photography/Shutterstock; Pixabay

Flux, an imprint of North Star Editions, Inc.

Library of Congress Cataloging-in-Publication Data
Names: Thrace, Mischa, author.
Title: My whole truth / Mischa Thrace.
Description: First edition. | Mendota Heights, Minnesota : Flux, [2018] |
  Summary: After killing her attacker, seventeen-year-old Seelie must prove
  in court and in the hallways of her high school that she acted in self-defense.
Identifiers: LCCN 2018020960 (print) | LCCN 2018027297 (ebook) | ISBN
  9781635830255 (ebook) | ISBN 9781635830248 (pbk. : alk. paper)
Subjects: | CYAC: Trials (Murder)—Fiction. | Rape—Fiction. |
  Friendship—Fiction. | Lesbians—Fiction.
Classification: LCC PZ7.1.T526 (ebook) | LCC PZ7.1.T526 My 2018 (print) | DDC
  [Fic]—dc23
LC record available at https://lccn.loc.gov/2018020960

Flux
North Star Editions, Inc.
2297 Waters Drive
Mendota Heights, MN 55120
www.fluxnow.com

*To everyone who has ever had to be
their own hero*

1

The air is dead with the stench of blood.

Mine.

His.

A high-pitched quavering pierces my ears and I scramble backward, convinced he's still alive, he's still going to get up, and he's still going to kill me.

But he doesn't.

It's me. I'm the one making the raspy dying noise.

My wounded leg collapses under me and I drag myself away from the ground-meat mess I fear could still rise up and attack. I tumble headlong down the hayloft stairs, leaving a swath of blood in my wake.

Horses snuffle and stamp their feet in their stalls and I still can't stop making the dying noise.

Using hay bales for leverage, I force myself up into a world that's spinning far too fast. I'm going to faint. But I know if I faint he could still get me, could still kill me. I throw myself at the tack room door and lock myself in before collapsing in a quaking mess against the hollow door.

The lock is nothing more than a push button on the knob and it's so inadequate I start to laugh.

I *laugh*.

Covered in blood, almost certain that a dead man rests above my head, and I can't stop laughing. Then just as suddenly I'm suffocating, gasping short, sharp breaths that do nothing to fill my lungs. My heart is a broken metronome. Each pulse throbs in my ravaged eye and in my leg like a prisoner desperate to break free.

This is panic.

I can't afford to lose it. Some tiny part of my brain knows that and screams for order. I inhale, counting—*one-hippopotamus, two-hippopotamus, three-hippopotamus*—and exhale with the same slow count. It takes four rounds before the stars recede from the edge of my vision.

I wipe more blood out of my good eye and take stock. My riding pants are a mess of crimson. I reach up and drag a saddle pad down from a rack, then press the thick white cloth hard against the angry flesh.

There's too much blood. Blood on my breeches and soaking my T-shirt from the waterfall of my face. I swallow the nausea and press my tongue against the back of my teeth. I will not be sick. I will *not* be sick.

I know my phone is in here. It always is, because even though I should keep it on me when I exercise the horses, I don't. My breeches don't have pockets and I don't believe in storing things in my bra that aren't boobs.

Of course it's as far away as possible, clear on the other side of the room, sitting on top of a container of horse supplements.

But the room is tiny, and between the saddle racks and grain bins, I have enough to lean on. I grab the phone and slide to the floor. My leg vibrates with pain.

In the glossy black of the unlit screen I catch a glimpse of my reflection and my heart jackrabbits away. My curls are plastered to my cheek with blood. I don't know why I do it, I know it won't help, but I hit the button to activate the front-facing camera and use the phone as a mirror.

I'm a figment of my own nightmare.

The dying noise starts in my throat again.

My hands shake enough to dislodge the phone and it tumbles to the wooden floor. I snatch it back up, exit out of the camera, and tap the phone icon. It takes three tries to key the right numbers.

"911, what's your emergency?"

What is my emergency? I'm breathing too fast to talk, to think.

"911, what's your emergency?" the woman repeats. "Hello?"

"I need help," I whisper.

"What's your emergency, ma'am?"

I can't say it out loud, not while panic is a noose around my throat. "I need help."

"Can you tell me where you are?"

"At work. 143 Summers Road, in the barn. The door is locked," I say and I'm crying now, salty tears mixing with salty blood. "Please come. Please come get me."

"I need you to calm down," the woman on the line says. Her voice is soothing and I find myself not wanting to make her mad at me.

"I know, I know, I'm sorry," I say in a rush, because I do know. Freaking out isn't helping. It takes everything I have to speak. "I need help."

"What's your name?"

"Seelie Stanton."

"How old are you, Seelie?"

"Seventeen. Please, I need help."

"Okay, honey, take a deep breath. Another. My name is Maya and I'm going to get you some help. But I need you to tell me what happened so I know what you need. Are you hurt?"

I cry harder. "Yes."

"What happened?"

"Got attacked." The words are tiny, scared things in my mouth. "He had a knife. I'm bleeding a lot. Please come help."

There's a rattle of typing and the woman says, "Someone attacked you with a knife?"

"Yes."

"Where is this person now?"

I don't want to answer. If I don't say it, maybe it doesn't have to be real.

"Seelie, are you safe now? Is the person still there?"

"He's here." Not a lie. I start to hyperventilate, stars roaring toward me.

"Okay, honey, just stay calm. Deep breaths. I have an ambulance and police on their way to you now. You said you were in a locked room?"

I nod, even though she can't see. "I'm locked in the tack room. In the barn."

"Honey, I need you to stay calm and stay on the line with

me. Stay right where you are. Does your attacker know where you are?"

"No." He doesn't know anything anymore. But I don't say it. Can't say it.

"That's good. Tell me about your injuries. The ambulance is only a few minutes away. Stay on the line with me."

"He cut my face," I say and my voice sounds shrill. Panic is pushing in again. "Stabbed my leg. My eye. I don't think it works anymore. Please, I'm bleeding a lot."

"Help is almost there. Can you describe your attacker?"

"It was Shane Mayfield. I know him. Knew him. He went to my school." The words taste like pennies. "It was Shane."

"You're sure?"

"Yes."

Sirens sound in the distance and I sob with relief. The saddle pad is soaked through with blood and I can't help but think it's ruined. Such a mess. I've made such a mess.

"The ambulance is almost there. Keep the door locked until they get there," she says.

"I don't think I can get back to the door," I say, new tears flooding my good eye. "I'm too far away."

Maya is unfazed. "That's okay, they'll get to you. What kind of lock is it?"

"It's just a stupid button, the regular kind like for a bed-room." A lock like that would never have saved me. The sirens are louder now. "I hear them."

"That's good. They're going to take care of you, honey."

"Thank you," I whisper.

"You're welcome, honey. Now when they—"

I hang up on her, even though I know I shouldn't, because I have something to do that's more important than her final instructions. I open my contacts folder and select the group marked "Faction" and quickly compose a text to send to the three of them: **Avengers assemble. Harrington ER. NO PARENTS**. I hesitate, needing to explain more but not knowing the best way. I add **Attacked. Need you.**

The message has barely sent when there's a hard knock at the door that startles me enough that I drop the phone. I pray the text went though.

"Seelie Stanton? Paramedics," a deep male voice announces.

"I'm here!"

"The dispatcher said you can't get to the door. Is that correct?"

"I can't. I'm sorry." I wipe blood and tears from my face. I'm shivering hard and my teeth clatter together when I speak.

"Not a problem. Stay where you are. We're going to break the door open."

The hollow door explodes inward to reveal the paramedic. If anything about my appearance shocks him he doesn't show it. He's a big guy, both tall and broad and he takes up so much of the small tack room that I don't know how he's going to get me out.

His partner passes him a long, narrow backboard.

"We need to get you onto this," he says, placing it on the floor.

"Okay," I say. I don't want him to touch me, so I scoot myself down and onto the board. Ribbons of pain lace up my leg and I yelp. He arranges the straps and grasps the handholds by my head while his female partner lifts the end at my feet. They gently deposit me onto a padded gurney in the barn aisle and wheel me out of my nightmare.

Cop cars decorate the area outside the barn, painting the air with red and blue lights. I know I need to say something. As the EMTs push me by, I reach out for an officer. The gurney stops and he comes over.

"Please call Elaine Burgess," I say. "This is her farm. I work for her. Someone has to be here for the horses."

Not what I planned to say at all.

"Is your attacker still here?" the officer asks, ignoring my request. Three other officers are making their way into the barn, guns drawn.

"He's upstairs," I whisper. Constellations swirl around me and my teeth chatter hard enough that I couldn't say more if I wanted to. Which I don't.

"Get her out of here," the cop says to the paramedic and disappears into the barn.

I hear the heavy boots pounding up the stairs, then shouting.

Not real, not real, not real.

The stars close in and finally the world goes dark.

2

I wake with a start.

If I could kill my brain, I would. My brain is a terrorist.

I mean, I have nightmares a lot, but this one was just uncalled for.

I blink, squinch my eyes shut against light that is far too harsh, and grope for my phone. What time is it?

The realization comes in less time than it takes for my brain to send the signal to move my arm.

The light . . . not sunlight.

Not my room.

Not my bed.

Not a nightmare.

///

There are too many people around me, although I can feel them there more than I can see them. Everyone is moving so fast, calling out orders that sound like a foreign language. Tubes run into the back of my hand, making it burn. I desperately want to go back to sleep so I can wake up and have this all be a dream.

But it's not.

"Ah, there you are," says an olive-skinned nurse.

At least I think he's a nurse, even though he definitely doesn't look like any nurse I've ever seen before. He's young, with a stubble-coated jaw and tattoos covering both arms beneath the short blue sleeves of his scrubs. Eyelashes most girls would be jealous of frame kind eyes, but I don't want him near me.

I think if he touches me I'll scream, and though he doesn't deserve it, I say so. Or try to. My voice has been ripped away; my mouth moves like a dying fish but no sound comes out. I try to clear my throat but the words strangle me.

"You're okay now," he says, smiling. "My name is Aram and I'm the physician's assistant. You've been in shock, but we're taking care of you now. Do you remember what happened?"

I nod, but I don't want to remember.

"Is there a number we can reach your parents at?"

"I already called," I lie. I don't want my mother here. Not when I'm like this. "Before 911. She's on her way."

"Okay, good. Our focus is on cleaning and closing those lacerations, but now that the shock has worn off, I wanted to ask one more time if you are experiencing any pain besides the wounds on your leg and face? Abdominal pain? Sharp pain when you inhale?"

Once he says this, I am hit with a vague recollection of answering a string of earlier questions, but recalling their specifics is like trying to remember a dream. I breathe deeply, feel nothing sharp, and confirm the injuries he's already aware of.

"That's what we thought. We're getting you ready for surgery now," he says and must see the panic on my face because he continues quickly. "You're going to be fine. Really. That wound on your leg just needs a little more attention than we can give it here. I imagine it's starting to feel better already, though, right?"

I realize it's true. In fact, my leg doesn't feel bad at all. There's a sense of pressure but the lightning bolts are gone.

"We've already given you painkillers and something to help you relax before the surgery. We're going to get that leg all cleaned up and—"

Suddenly my hand flies to my face. Someone I can't see on my left side catches my wrist and pushes it down.

"My eye?" I croak.

The person holding my wrist moves into my line of sight. Another pair of blue scrubs, this time on a motherly-looking woman. "We're taking care of that too. But I need you not to touch it," she says. "Just lie still."

She disappears again, but I can feel her doing something to my forehead. I want to sit up, I want to run, but the very thought of moving exhausts me.

"The doctor is prepping for surgery now," Aram says as if I hadn't interrupted him. It scares me that he's not acknowledging my eye. "The anesthesiologist will be in momentarily to finish getting you ready."

"I don't want drugs," I say, panic edging back in. I've never been under anesthesia before, but when Ashlyn had her appendix out the side effects made her violently ill. I have an extreme phobia about being sick. Extreme enough that it overrides all my other worries. "Please, can't you just stitch it up here? Please, I don't want you to give me any more drugs."

"I need you to lie still," the woman I can't see on my left reminds me, hands holding each side of my head.

"You don't need to be afraid," Aram says. "It's very safe. There's quite a bit of debris in the wound and the muscle needs repair. You'll be much more comfortable if you're asleep."

"I don't want to throw up," I confess, feeling like a baby. I know how stupid this is. I really do. Especially right now. But the thought of being sick is worse than the thought of someone digging into my leg while I'm awake.

"Oh, we can take care of that," he says, dark eyes crinkling with a reassuring smile. He turns to a laptop sitting on a high rolling stand and starts typing. "I'll tell the anesthesiologist to bring you an anti-nausea patch."

That makes me feel a little better, but not totally.

A sudden racket from outside stops me from thinking about it.

"You need to go back to the waiting room," a woman says firmly.

"My sister is in there and I want to see her," someone demands. Someone who is most definitely not my brother.

Finn.

I struggle to sit up, no longer caring about the people tending to me. The faction is here and that's all that matters.

"Finn!" I cry, voice raspy and desperate. I'm light-headed and the room closes in. I collapse back on the bed, fighting to keep from passing out. Whatever drugs they're giving me are no joke.

"Sir, your sister is being prepped for emergency surgery,"

the official-sounding woman says from the hall. "You can see her when she comes out."

"Please, ma'am, I understand you're busy and trying to help her," Lyssa says, voice straining as she tries to sound calm. "But can we just see her for a minute? Just one minute and then we'll go to the waiting room."

"And who are you?" she asks.

"Her cousin," Lyssa lies.

"And I'm her sister," adds Ashlyn. Another lie. And Ashlyn never lies. It's against her religion. Literally. She must remember this and amends, "We're her family."

That's not a lie.

That's the only thing that matters.

The door swings open and I get a glimpse of Ashlyn's pink hair as a short woman in pale green scrubs and a paper hair cover comes into the room with a small cart.

I turn my head to Aram, begging. "I need to see them. They can come in. I want them to come in."

He looks conflicted and I think he's going to let them in. Instead he introduces the anesthesiologist as she places a sticker behind my right ear.

"Your anti-nausea patch," she explains briskly. She plucks a syringe from her cart and fills it from a small vial of clear fluid.

"Please let me see them," I say again, to her, to Aram, to anyone who will please just listen to me.

From the hallway, I can hear the other woman explaining that this is a surgical ward and that they're welcome to sit in the waiting area, but they can't have this kind of noise in the halls.

The anesthesiologist inserts the needle into the port that's taped to my hand. Cold floods up my arm as she presses the plunger. "You're going to start to feel very sleepy," she says. "I want you to breathe deeply and not fight it."

For a moment I don't feel anything and then I'm falling through the bed. I do exactly what she warned against and fight it. I don't want to give in. Not yet. But unconsciousness overtakes me without caring what I want.

3

When I wake, perhaps for the first time, but probably not, I'm parked in a room with several other people, fading in and out of consciousness as the anesthesia works its way out of my system. Doctors are talking, issuing instructions I don't heed. Something about staying quiet and still.

I fade out.

Time is funny here.

At one point I'm aware of being curled up on my side, sobbing, not caring if the whole world hears.

I fade out.

Gentle hands are on me and I flail about, trying to dislodge them, my body still not in sync with my brain. My throat is impossibly raw.

I fade out.

My brain is clearer now and that's worse. So much worse. I want oblivion back. I close my eye, courting the blackness.

I sink.

//

My hospital room is nothing like the ones on TV. It's tiny;

only my bed, two uncomfortable-looking wooden chairs, a small square table, and a narrow, curtainless window that shows nothing but a slice of inky sky. The cinder-block walls are painted a sickly, tired yellow that looks all the worse under the dim lighting.

I'm flat on my back, and there's a contraption dangling from the ceiling that keeps my leg raised in a sling. I try to wiggle my toes and am flooded with relief when I can. That has to be good. A deep ache lurks above my knee, but whatever is being pumped into my IV is working its magic because the pain is nowhere near as bad as it was before.

Before.

Oh god.

As soon as I remember *before*, cramps spasm my gut and I feel an aching hollow collapsing my entire being. I guess the IV is good for more than just pain, though, because I don't lose it. I want to, but I don't.

One hand is still a mess of tubes and tape, and I liberate the other from beneath the stiff white blanket.

Moment of truth.

Gingerly, I explore my face. Where I expect to find ravaged flesh, I find only soft, dry bandages.

This does nothing to make me feel better.

"Oh good, you are awake," says the portly, gray-haired nurse who comes into the room. She's dragging a rolling computer stand behind her like a reluctant dog. "I thought so. How you feeling, sugar?"

I drop my hand from my face. She's as wide as she is tall, but she doesn't let that stop her from wearing scrubs covered in a rainbow of flowers, and she strikes me as the kind of old lady with a couch full of hand-stitched pillows, but funny ones, with sayings like *Friends Are Like Snowflakes. If You Pee on Them, They Disappear.*

I try to answer and start hacking instead. The nurse tuts and raises the back of the bed so I'm half-sitting and hands me a plastic cup of water. Her name tag swings forward on a lanyard bedecked with ladybug pins: Francine Baker, RN.

"Sip slowly," she warns.

I do and I think I have never felt anything as wonderful as the cool liquid soothing the fire in my throat. When I finish I hold the cup out for more.

"Sorry, baby, got to take it slow. Let's make sure that stays down, then we'll see about a refill, okay?"

I nod. There's no way I'm letting it do anything except stay down.

She's looking at the machines around my bed and types something into the computer.

"On a scale of one to ten, how is the pain in your leg right now?" she asks.

I consider.

"Six." I can barely hear myself. I cough and try again. "No, five. It's not too bad now."

"Tough cookie," she says, pushing her red glasses back up her nose before entering it into her computer.

I have so many questions that I don't know how to start.

"Is my eye gone?" I manage to squeak.

She laughs, not unkindly. "No, honey, your eye is in there. We just have it bandaged up. Now that you're awake I'll be sending a doctor in to talk to you. And your mom should be here soon."

I blanch. Not my mom. Not yet.

"Are my friends still here?" I ask, then remember their lie. "My brother and sister, I mean?"

"I'll see if I can find them," she says with a conspiratorial wink.

I want to tell her to hurry.

///

I hear the squeak of sneakers on tile and my skin prickles with overwhelming apprehension. These may be my friends, but this is no longer our normal life and I have no idea how they're going to react.

Lyssa is the first in, tall and striking and entirely too intense for this claustrophobic little room. Finn and Ashlyn tumble in after her, and Ashlyn bursts into tears the instant she sees me. My best-friend-since-preschool throws herself at me, heedless of the tubes and wires and the fact that my leg is trussed up like a Thanksgiving turkey. I hug her tightly, and it doesn't matter that my bruised ribs sing with pain.

They're here.

My family is here.

"You just hit that button if you need anything," Nurse Francine says, pointing to a blue button on the wall before she steps out, closing the door behind her.

Lyssa shoves a hand through her long black bangs and exhales a broken breath. "Oh, Seelie," is all she says and the lament in those two words threatens to unmoor everything I have so carefully dammed up.

Finn stands rooted to the floor, arms overflowing with ridiculous mounds of neon daisies. He must have bought every bouquet the hospital had. Over the top of Ashlyn's pink hair, I force a smile.

"I'm okay, really. I'm okay," I say. I'm not sure if I'm reassuring them or myself. I even laugh a little. "Hell, you should see the other guy."

I don't know why those words leave my mouth, but the moment they do reality kicks me in the chest.

I am adrift.

Tears pour down my face, soaking through the bandage on the left side. I regret saying it with my entire being, the brutal acknowledgment of my catastrophe, and I want to take it back. I want to take it all back. Ashlyn holds me tighter, as if her thin arms can keep me from coming apart. Lyssa's hands clench and unclench into fists and she looks shattered and dangerous.

"Good," she says. "Good. I hope you killed that piece of shit."

What I say next physically hurts, as if each syllable is being ripped against its will from the prison of my throat. They creep forth in a reluctant whisper, trembling, wanting to stay hidden and silent forever.

"I think I did."

4

I expect my confession to break us.

It doesn't.

Lyssa moves to the side of the bed, pries Ashlyn off me, and sends her toward Finn. "You should know Momthulu is descending," she says, pulling a chair close to my head and settling in. "We held her off as long as possible. By which I mean Finn and I ignored her calls and then Ash screwed the pooch."

"It was an accident!" Ashlyn protests. Her tears have tracked dark streaks of mascara down her cheeks. "She kept calling! What was I supposed to do?"

"Not answer," Lyssa snaps. "She knew you were the weak link."

"She was going to find out anyway," Ashlyn says, her tiny shoulders hunching forward. She's right, of course.

"Lys, don't be a dick," Finn says easily, setting his load of flowers on the low table and knocking a box of tissues to the floor. Two bouquets tumble after it. He drags the second chair closer to my feet and flops back, legs spread wide. Ashlyn perches bird-like on the foot of the bed.

I wonder if my admission has even registered. Then I wonder

if I was stupid to think it would've mattered to the faction. Something soars in my chest when I realize this is true.

"It's okay," I tell Ashlyn. I sniffle hard, igniting a small galaxy of explosions in my sinuses. "Eventually she had to be told."

"Plus the nurses kept asking us where our mother was," she says, looking pointedly at Finn. "I had to tell them something."

"It was the first thing I thought of!" he says, throwing up his hands.

"Finn, on what planet do we remotely look like siblings?" I say, smiling in spite of everything. "You and Ashlyn, maybe, to someone half-blind. But not us. Definitely not."

"Well, it was more convincing than Lyssa being your sister," he says and laughs.

"That's the truth," Lyssa concedes. Her birth parents were Japanese and French-Canadian, a combination she finds no end of amusement in. Last Halloween, she came to school dressed as a samurai-Mountie and earned the entire school an assembly on cultural sensitivity. She was very proud.

"How pissed is she?" I ask Ashlyn.

"A couple county lines past furious. She wanted to know why you could call us but not her."

I roll my uncovered eye. "Right, because she would've been such a help. All I'm gonna hear about is how I'm taking her away from work." I sound bitter even to myself. I don't care.

"She's worried about you," Finn says. "We all are."

There's a silence while that settles.

In the quiet, Lyssa reaches forward and brushes a thumb against the side of my bruised neck and my body jolts as if electrocuted, my brain turning the soft caress into a calloused hand tight around my throat. I hiss in pain as I jostle my dangling leg, but at least that pain is real, not in my head, and it chases away the phantom hand.

"Sorry," I say, too loudly. "Sorry. You startled me."

She holds her hand up in silent apology, dark eyes heavy with hurt. She asks the unthinkable then, the thing that everyone wants to know and doesn't want to know in equal measure. "What happened?"

I shake my head, mouth open for words but finding none there. I can only shake my head.

"It's okay," Ashlyn rushes to reassure me. "You don't have to talk about it."

But Lyssa has to know. Her eyes bore into mine. "Who did this?"

"Shane," I whisper.

Lyssa shoves herself up, sending her chair skittering back like a frightened animal. I flinch.

"That bastard," she growls, hands balling back into weapons.

Ashlyn and Finn leap to their feet, hands up like bunnies trying to placate a bear.

"Relax, Lys," Finn says. He's keeping his tone neutral, but a heavier trace of his southern accent has crept in, betraying his stress. He may be an inch taller than Lyssa, but we all know he's no match for her temper. "This ain't helping."

Lyssa stalks past them, raking her hands over her head. She slams both hands into the sad cinder blocks over and over, until I think they're going to crumble beneath the weight of her fury. When she tires she leans there, fingers clenched white against the cold wall, head hanging low. Her back heaves with ragged breaths.

Finn and Ashlyn stand looking at each other, clearly unsure of what to do.

This is beyond all of us.

Silent tears are coursing down my face again. Am I ever going to run out of them? I screw my eye shut to stop the flood.

I want to wake up now.

I want this to end.

It's Finn who finally goes to her. "It's all right," he says quietly, giving Lyssa's shoulders a steadying squeeze. "Come sit down."

With a final halfhearted assault on the wall, Lyssa turns and allows herself to be led back to my bedside. She falls into the chair Ashlyn has repositioned and drops her head into her hands. Her voice is thick when she breaks the heavy silence.

"This shouldn't have happened to you. Someone should've been there. I should've been there. I knew you were alone." She doesn't look up, only digs the heels of her hands deeper into her eyes. Her nails are a mess of bitten cuticles. "I'm sorry, Seelie. I am so, so sorry."

My throat is too tight for words, so I just reach out and with the barest of hesitations drop my hand to the velvety hair at the nape of her neck. I can feel the corded tension as she presses into me like a cat.

Minutes as long as days and as short as heartbeats slip by.

Ashlyn's fingers are pressed against her lips like she's pray-ing. I hope she's not. Finn has an arm around her shoulders and one hand resting on the bed, close to my foot. Not quite touching it, but near enough that I can feel it there. We are a chain of broken people trying to keep one another from drowning.

5

By the time my mother pushes her way into the room, we four have somehow cobbled together a sense of normalcy. Or if not quite normalcy, at least a bit of enthusiastic denial, which is almost as good.

"I'm serious," Finn is saying, brandishing a bouquet of neon daisies like a light saber, when the door opens. "All you need is confidence. If you act natural, no one stops you."

Ashlyn laughs. "You're a sociopath."

"You encouraged him," I say. "You held the booty!"

"I wish she held my booty," Finn corrects.

"Fine, you knowingly received stolen goods," I say, ignoring Ashlyn's flaming cheeks. I'm aware of my mother's entrance but I want to hold on to this moment. I want Finn to finish his tale of what he's officially dubbed the Crazy Daisy Caper and I want to ignore reality for one more minute. Just one.

No such luck.

"Oh god, Seelie," my mother says. "What were you thinking, not calling me?"

I feel myself closing in, can see Ashlyn curl up tighter in her chair as a pall settles over the shrinking room. For a moment

Finn stands frozen, bouquet still thrust out, before he lowers it and eyes my mother. At the same time, Lyssa stands and offers her chair with a wave of her hand. But she doesn't relinquish her position. Instead, she nudges the chair aside to make room and stands close to the head of the bed, silently claiming her right to be here. She's a year older than the rest of us, but her self-possession is a match for even most adults.

"I don't think this is something to be laughing about," my mom says, dropping her purse on the vacated chair.

I'm suddenly full-blown Hulk-smash-all-the-things furious. Of course we should be laughing. It was helping. *My friends* were helping. This screwing around with stolen flowers was the one thing keeping me from completely and utterly losing it and I hate her for taking it away.

My hands curl into fists and the IV strains against the flesh of my right hand. Good. Let it bleed.

"What happened?" she asks when her eyes finish their circuit over my body.

"Nothing," I say. "I'm fine."

"That's obviously not true," she says, crossing her arms across her narrow chest. She's all angles: sharp nose, cheekbones like knives, and you can practically see the knobs of her spine beneath the tailored chef coat she wears. There's a saying about distrusting skinny cooks that could be her biography, but her highlighted hair is in a sleek ponytail and her makeup is, as always, flawless. If it weren't for the faint smell of flour and fry oil clinging to her, it'd be easy to imagine her as a TV chef.

I might've gotten her ears, but everything else came straight from Dad, and I know she must be disgusted by how I look right now. More so than usual.

I don't look at her. I gaze straight ahead, where Finn is arranging his ridiculous klepto-ed flowers in scavenged water bottles and plastic cups. I can feel the walls going up, shutting me off not only from my mother, but from everyone.

"Seelie, you need to talk to me," Mom says.

I don't.

"Cecelia," she says in her best angry mom voice. It's a voice I know well.

"I got hurt," I snap. "Don't worry, I'll deal with it. You can go back to work."

"Don't be like that," she says, but I know she doesn't care. Not really. I know she would rather be back at her restaurant, where she practically lives and where her small staff worships her. I want her to be there too. It was so much easier with just the faction here.

My nails burrow into my palms. Lyssa reaches down to touch my hand but stops short, withdraws. Probably for the best.

"Seelie, you have to tell me what happened," my mother insists.

But I don't want to. I don't want to talk at all anymore. My leg is throbbing and there's a headache ripping holes in my brain. I drop my head back and squeeze my eyes closed. When I open them, it's Lyssa I seek out. "Hit the nurse button for me?"

"What do you need?" Mom asks.

"A nurse." And silence. And a rewind button for this day.

I'm relieved when it's Nurse Francine who opens the door. She greets my mother, then asks, "What can I do for you, hun?"

"I'm getting a headache."

"That's not surprising, given the trauma to your eye. That other one is working double-time now. Let me get these lights turned down for you," she says. She does, then fiddles with one of my IVs. "This might make you sleepy, but it'll help the pain. I'll send the doctor in while you're still awake."

"Thanks."

Moments later there's a polite knock on the open door and the tall bald man who comes in and introduces himself as Dr. Vern looks too much like a mortician for me to feel entirely comfortable being in his care.

He faces my mother when he talks. "Your daughter's injuries are serious, but not permanent. We sutured several minor cuts, plus the lacerations on her face and eyelid. The corneal abrasion should heal fine, but it is susceptible to infection and will need to be kept covered for at least a week. However, there shouldn't be any permanent vision loss. The—"

"Shouldn't be?" I interrupt. "As in, there's a chance there might be?"

"Only a very small chance," he says, barely looking at me before turning back to my mother. "The damage to her forehead and cheek was easily stitched, but the wound in her leg is a bit more serious. Several layers of muscle and nerves were damaged. The recovery time for that is going to be slower, and I won't lie, it's going to be painful. We're going to keep her here for a couple days so the wound can be properly cared for, after which she'll need to use a wheelchair or crutches, depending on her comfort. We'll set her up with a physical therapist and it'll be extremely important to follow their regimen to avoid developing a permanent limp."

I guess I should be happy, and on some level I am. I still have two eyes and I'm not permanently disabled. Those are both good things. But I don't want to be here for a few days. I don't want a wheelchair. I don't want scars. I don't want people to have more reasons to stare.

When the doctor leaves, my mother leans over the bed, forcing me to look at her. "You have to talk to me about what happened," she says. "The police are asking questions."

6

I manage to avoid talking to both my mother and the police that night, thanks to the drugs. They make me sleepy, as Nurse Francine said they would, but the sleep is anything but restful. My dreams are a punishment punctuated with flashes of gore and monsters with faces like the insides of cherries. I exhaust myself trying to run on dream legs that don't move. I wake up screaming and disoriented more than once, sure that there's someone in the room with me, only to slide against my will back into nightmares.

When morning finally comes and a new nurse comes to check on me, I feel wrecked. I refuse to accept her offer of more painkillers, preferring the hell of this sallow room to the hell of my dreams, at least for now. She allows this and returns awhile later with a tray of breakfast, which she sets on a table that rolls over my bed. Scrambled eggs that match the walls, a school-sized carton of milk, dry wheat toast, and a banana.

I can't do it.

I push the table away.

"I'll take it," a voice says to the left, scaring the hell out of me.

I crane my head around, trying to see past my decimated eye.

"Jesus Christ, Lys! What are you doing there?"

She's stretched between two chairs on the side of my bed, black hoodie draped over her like a blanket.

She shrugs and swings her legs down before reaching for my tray. "Stealing your awful hospital food."

"When did you get here?"

She doesn't answer, just piles eggs onto a piece of toast.

"Did you even leave?"

"Nope," she says around a mouthful of crumbs and something in my heart swells at that, despite everything. "Didn't seem right."

"Everyone else?"

She chugs the carton of skim milk. "Finn took Ash home after your mom left. She was going to stay and skip skating this morning, but she's got that show coming up so we convinced her to go. Told them I'd take this watch."

Ashlyn takes an hour drive into Connecticut five days a week to participate in this elite Olympic development figure-skating program. It's a big deal and I'm glad they convinced her to go. Her coach is a former gold medalist who wouldn't tolerate her absence and I don't want her messing that up on account of me.

"I'm surprised no one kicked you out."

"I don't think the overnight nurse is a huge fan of rules," she says.

"Part of why I like her. Switch sides. Why are you on my blind side anyway, you creeper?"

She drags her chair back to its original spot. "They told me to stay out of the way and since all the monitors and IV stuff are on this side, I figured I'd be better off over there."

She settles back in and we both look at each other for a long moment. My brain crashes around with worry. What are people seeing when they look at me?

"How are you doing?" she eventually asks.

It's a loaded question and she seems to know it. My face flushes. If she really was here all night, she already knows the answer. I'm beyond mortified.

"Tired," I admit. "My brain's kinda being an asshole right now."

She nods. "Kinda can't blame it, though."

"True."

Lyssa sucks in a breath and holds it with her cheeks puffed out like a well-fed hamster. Her patented *We have to talk* signal.

My heart drops.

"What is it?" I ask.

"I want to say I have good news and bad news, and offer you a choice, but the truth is I have bad news and worse news."

Great.

"Your mom is planning to spend the day today," she says. "Apparently she made arrangements to cover the restaurant so she can be supporto-Mom."

I groan. "Was that the bad or the worse?"

"Depends on your perspective, I guess. The other part is there's no way you're avoiding the cops today. You have to talk to them. That's why your mom is really coming. She wants to be here for that."

"Am I in trouble?" I ask. This is my biggest fear, the one I haven't even admitted to myself until right now.

"Of course not," Lyssa says, surprised. "Jesus, of course not. But I guess they need to talk to you anyway."

It takes a long time for me to get the next question out. "Is Shane really dead?"

"I don't know," she says, anger making her eyes hard. "But if he's not, I'll kill him myself. Fucking junkie piece of shit."

I believe her. Right now, I know she has that in her. Lyssa and I may have spent a lot of time wishing all manners of creative death on a great many people, but it was only ever talk. I never truly believed either of us had the ability to remove someone from the human race. Until now. Now I know everyone has a breaking point.

"When are they coming?" I ask.

"I think around nine. I heard them talking in the hall last night, but I don't know for sure."

"Can you do me a favor?"

"Anything."

I gather up all my nerve. "I want to see. My face, I mean. I want to see it."

Lyssa doesn't answer for a minute and this scares me. A lot.

"I need to see," I say, feeling hot and shivery all at once. "Everyone keeps looking at me and I don't know what they see. I need to know."

"We just see you. The rest doesn't matter."

"But I need to see," I insist. "I need to. Please. Before my mom gets here."

She nods. She gets up and disappears around the corner to

the bathroom, only to return a moment later, empty-handed. "No mirror," she says and fishes around in the hoodie that lies discarded over the arm of the chair. She pulls out her phone and hands it to me. Our fingers brush when I take it and I want to hold her hand while I do this, but I don't know how to ask.

I sit with the phone in my lap and for a horrifying moment I'm back in the tack room of Elaine's barn, staring into my own phone as blood pours down my face. I don't even know where my phone ended up.

I glance at Lyssa. She's watching me closely, an uneasy look on her face. I try to smile but I don't think it's convincing. I can hear my heart pounding.

I open the camera app and with shaking hands, raise the phone until I can see the damage.

And I'm surprised that there isn't much to see at all.

My forehead, left eye, and left cheek are swaddled in white gauze, which hides whatever horrors are underneath. One blue eye stares back above an angry crescent of deep purple and black, and the bridge of my nose is swollen, but still reasonably straight.

My neck is the hardest to look at.

A collar of mottled red-and-purple bruises encircle my throat. I understand now why my voice has sounded so raspy and awful. It wasn't the tubes. It was this.

I hand the phone back to Lyssa. I've seen enough.

"Thank you," I say. I mean it.

She nods.

"Bet I look like Frankenstein's monster under all these bandages."

"Maybe if Frankenstein's monster was a pirate."

I laugh. Of course I can always count on Lyssa for the in-appropriate joke.

"I should probably get a parrot."

"And teach it to swear."

"Obviously. What else are parrots good for?"

We try out different names for my hypothetical swear-y bird until a knock at the door shuts us down. My grim-faced mother enters, followed closely by the police.

7

"Good, you're up," my mother says in way of greeting as she bustles in. She pulls up short when she spots Lyssa sitting exactly where she left her last night. "Alyssa. My. What are you still doing here?"

"Keeping watch," she says, folding her arms. "Seemed like someone should."

Mom doesn't rise to the bait. I don't know if it's because she thinks she's right or if she just missed the barb. Either way, I'm relieved. I don't need a ringside seat to a Lyssa vs. Momthulu fight right now.

"We're going to need a bit of privacy, miss," the male police officer says. I recognize him as the one I spoke to at the barn. His partner is a broad-shouldered woman with her dark hair pulled straight back into a stubby, no-nonsense ponytail.

"Can she stay?" I look between the officers, unsure who to appeal to. "Please, I'd feel better if she was here."

"I'm sorry," the man says. "Protocol. We need the room."

Lyssa regards the adults for a long time without saying anything. She's good at this. While silence makes most people uncomfortable, Lyssa can live there for days.

My mom breaks first. Typical.

"You can come back when we're done," she says. "But we need to talk to Seelie alone."

"I'm gonna tell her everything anyway," I say. "Please let her stay."

I'm stalling and I know it. I don't want to talk to these people. If I can just have my friend here it might be easier. I regret not doing this last night when I had a roomful of people to buffer me.

"We can't do that," the female cop says and she looks genuinely apologetic. "Police interviews must be handled privately."

"Then I don't want her here either," I say, flicking a glance at my mother. I'm being a brat, but I don't care. If Lyssa could stay I might've been able to let her stay too, but I can't do this with just her with me. I simply can't.

"That's your choice," the woman says. "Because you're still seventeen you are permitted to have a parent present, but you can also waive that right."

"I waive it." I refuse to look at my mother. She can't help me. Not like the faction can.

Lyssa stands, shrugging into her hoodie as my mother tries and fails to convince the cops that I can't make decisions for myself.

"I'll be right outside if you need me," Lyssa says, grabbing my eyes with hers. "You're going to be okay."

I hope she's right.

When I'm left alone with the cops the tiny room feels cavernous. There's a slight tilt to the world as my brain tries to flee, not wanting to be made to relive the past twenty-four hours.

"I'm Detective Robyn Mellers and this is Detective Troy,"

the female officer says. She places a digital recorder on the rolling table that still holds my breakfast tray. "We're with the Amesford PD."

"Amesford has detectives?" I blurt out. "As in multiple?"

Mellers grins. "Yup. Even small towns have their problems," she says, sitting in the chair Lyssa vacated. Her smile fades. "As you obviously know. We need to record this conversation. Is that okay?"

I nod. What else can I do?

She states her name and badge number, then Detective Troy does the same, adding that the interview is taking place at Harrington Hospital. They make me state my full name, age, and address, though they must already know all that.

"Why don't you start by walking us through what happened?" Mellers says.

"I was at work," I say slowly. There's a rushing in my head. I don't want to do this. "I was at work . . ."

"Where's that?" Mellers asks, helping me along. "Specifically."

"143 Summers Road, Amesford. Elaine Burgess's farm. I take care of her horses. I have since I was fifteen." I breathe four hippopotamuses in, four out. I'm okay. I can do this.

"And when was this?"

"Friday. After school."

"Was anyone else there?"

My heart starts hammering. Maybe I can't do this.

"Was anyone else there, Seelie?"

"Shane," I whisper.

"He was with you?" Detective Troy asks. He doesn't sit, but

wanders back and forth along the short stretch of room. "Before the alleged attack occurred?"

"Not with me, with me. But I saw him. Before," I stammer, looking back and forth between them. What does he mean, *alleged*? Is this a trick? "He was watching me ride."

"Do you often bring him to watch you ride?" Troy asks.

I want to punch him for twisting my words. I answer only to Mellers. "I didn't want him there. He creeped me out so I left. I rode into the woods."

"Where was he watching you from?" she asks.

"The road, down near the fence. He had no right to be there." I look down at my lap where I'm picking at the fraying tape on the back of my hand. I don't want to talk about any of this. "He made me uncomfortable."

"Why did he make you uncomfortable?" Troy asks.

"Because he was there," I snap. I'm not about to recount all the things Shane has said to me at school, the comments about my size and my sexuality, and the way he got all his lemmings to do the same. He was already Mr. Basketball Star when I started ninth grade and, in a microscopic town like Amesford, that almost counted as a big deal, big enough that the teachers ignored what he did. Most of the school worshiped him because he threw the wildest parties and because they have no standards. "He's scum. Everyone knows he's scum. You're the cops, you definitely know it."

The running joke in town is that Shane single-handedly keeps the police station in business. If it weren't for his father being who he is, Shane probably would've been packed off to prison by now.

"Okay," Mellers says calmly, shooting a look I can't interpret to her partner. "How long were you in the woods for?"

I think. "Maybe an hour," I say.

"And he was gone when you came back?"

"Obviously not," I say. "But I didn't know that."

"You didn't see him?" she clarifies.

"No."

"What happened next?"

Hell.

Hell happened next.

I pick harder at the tape on my hand, feeling the needle dance under the flesh.

"Cecelia? What happened next?" Mellers asks again. She sounds very far away.

"He attacked me," I say from underwater.

"I know this is hard," she says. "But I need you to describe what occurred."

Brown smudges push in on my vision until all I can see are my hands in my lap. The rest of the room—the rest of the world, maybe—is gone. I close my eye. All gone.

"Attacked me in the hayloft," I whisper. I feel like I'm in a trance. "He was hiding . . . pushed me . . . slammed my face into the wall." I'm barely aware of touching my throat until the bruises flare with pain. "Choked me . . ." Humiliation pours from my IV into my bloodstream, flooding me as I recall what happened next. My brain can't convince my tongue to form the words, so they go unspoken. I bypass it completely, as if not saying it might make it so it never happened. "Had a knife . . . my face . . . leg . . . too much blood. All I could see was blood."

45

8

"Let me get this straight," Detective Troy says. "You're minding your own business when suddenly this kid pushes you, chokes you, then stabs you. Unprovoked."

I nod.

"We need verbal answers," he says.

"Yes," I whisper.

"There was no conversation, no interaction that led up to it?"

"No." I open my eye and glare at him. What's his problem? "It came out of nowhere."

"At what point did you start fighting back?" Detective Mellers asks.

"After he choked me." It's not a lie. Not really. It's just not the truth either.

"But before he used the knife?" Troy asks.

"After," I snap. "He had already cut my face."

"But you said he pushed you, then choked you, then stabbed you," he says.

"He cut my face first." I'm getting flustered. "Before he choked me. He stabbed my leg after I tried to get away."

"Can you describe the knife?" Mellers asks before Troy can make another comment.

"A hunting knife. Like the kind that folds up." I spread my hands apart. "About this size."

"Open and including the handle?"

"Yeah."

"Witness indicates knife to be approximately six to eight inches in length," she says to the tape recorder. Then to me asks, "Did he say anything or threaten you before he assaulted you?"

"No," I say. "He pushed me into the wall from behind and started going on about 'you can't talk' and 'you can't see,' repeating it over and over like he was possessed. He cut my face when I looked at him. I think he wanted to take my eyes out. Then he tried to strangle me."

"Can you describe how you were able to fight back?" she asks.

I shake my head. Just a tiny twitch of a motion because no, I don't want to describe that. My pulse is loud in my ears again.

"This is important," she reminds me gently. "We need to know what happened."

I shake my head no again, unable to erase the pulpy image of Shane's ruined head.

"Is he dead?" I ask.

"Just tell us what happened," Mellers says.

I don't like that she doesn't answer my question.

With a wave of clarity that nearly drowns me, I realize how very badly I want her to tell me he's dead. That's the truth of it, the thing I haven't said to Lyssa, or Ashlyn, or Finn, or my mom, or even myself. I want him to be dead. I know it's wrong, but I don't care. I want to know he's gone and that my nightmare can end. I want to have destroyed him the way he destroyed me and I am enraged by the thought that he might be okay.

"There was a mallet in the hay," I say as a tsunami of fury replaces the shame. My hands are steady now, resting on the slope of my thigh where it still hangs suspended from the ceiling. I protected myself. I was strong. I am not going to apologize for that. "I hit him with it."

"How many times?" Troy asks.

"The first time didn't do anything. Didn't even slow him down." I glare at the detective. "*That's* when he stabbed my leg. So I hit him again. I hit him until I knew he wasn't going to get up and kill me."

"You deliberately continued striking him after he was in-capacitated?" Troy asks, measuring each word out.

"Yes. I knew he would kill me if he got back up so I made sure he couldn't."

"At any point did he actually say he was going to kill you?" he asks.

"Not in those words, but I knew he would."

"How many times did you strike him?" he asks again. Mellers looks uncomfortable.

"Enough."

"A number, please. More than twice?"

"Yes."

"More than three times?"

"Yes. Probably five times. Maybe six." I look back and forth between them. I shouldn't have to do this. They should be congratulating me for getting away instead of treating me like a suspect. "Don't you understand? I had to save myself. I had to."

9

The nurse must've been waiting for the police to leave, because they're barely out of the room when she comes in with a cart loaded down with gauze and syringes, Mom and Lyssa at her heels.

"Time to change your bandages," the nurse says cheerfully, as if there was nothing unusual about my previous visitors. "I'm going to lower you down a bit."

She drops the head of my bed so I'm flat on my back. She positions her cart near my raised leg and I have to strain to see her. My mother and Lyssa are standing on the other side of the bed, watching her work.

"Okay, let's get a look at this," she says mostly to herself as she lifts the blanket away. She fusses with the bandage, prying up only the very edges. She arranges a towel under my leg and picks up a syringe. "I'm going to soak the bandage so it comes off easier. This might be a little cold."

She uses the syringe to drench my leg and works the tape free. It's not until my mother gasps and turns away that I realize there might be something worth seeing. I crane my head up, trying to see.

"Definitely Frankenstein," says Lyssa with an impressed nod.

She's right. Above my knee is a riot of iridescent bruising, but that's not what made my mother turn green. A line of staples snakes over a gnarled red gash on my freckled thigh. Instead of being disgusted, though, I'm intrigued and oddly detached. It looks nothing like my own leg. I feel like I'm looking at a stranger's limb, or a picture in a book.

"Oh, that looks good," the nurse says happily.

"I do not think that word means what you think it means," I say. Lyssa snorts. But I can see why she said it. The wound is not the open, festering thing I was imagining. There's some dried blood around it and some clear ooze, but that's it. No gore. I allow myself a sliver of hope that my face is nowhere near as bad as I fear either.

"This dressing will need to be changed twice a day for the next two days, then once a day," the nurse says as she squirts some more water over my thigh. She gently wipes at the flecks of blood. "It's extremely important to keep this clean. We have you on antibiotics to ward off infection, but when you get home it's going to be up to you to keep this looking good."

I nod, wishing she had left me sitting up. My neck is killing me from trying to watch.

"No bathing, swimming, or hot tubs until the staples are removed," she continues as she lays a strip of something cool and wet across the wound and covers it with gauze. "You'll be able to shower, but only let the water run over it, not directly into it. If showering alone is too difficult—and it might be at first—sponge baths are also an option. I'm sure Mom can help you out, right, Mom?"

"Oh, of course," my mother replies and my cheeks burn with embarrassment. Like I'd ever actually let anyone see me naked, never mind sponge me. Especially not my mother.

"What about my face?" I ask.

"That should only need to be covered for another day, and then we'll leave it to the air," she says, as if this is a good thing. "The stitches will come out in five days."

"Will I still be here in five days?"

"Oh, no, we'll be getting you out of here and back home as soon as possible," she says as she finishes taping the gauze around my leg. "I'm sure you're ready to be out of here."

She's not wrong.

"That's looking good for now," she says. "As long as you can be careful not to move it too much, I can let the sling down for a while if you like."

"That'd be good."

"And how's the pain? One to ten."

"Five. It's not that bad."

"Oh, good. We'll just keep you on the Motrin then. No need to load you full of narcotics, now is there?"

///

When I realize my mother is serious about spending the day, I regret taking only the ibuprofen.

She banished Lyssa, who left reluctantly and promised to return with reinforcements, and has taken up residence in what I have already come to consider Lyssa's spot at the side of my bed.

"I know you don't want to talk about this," she says, "but you're going to have to. I need to know what happened."

There isn't a single bit of me with the energy for this conversation.

"Why?" I ask, not turning my head from the wall. My narrow window frames a gray October sky and raindrops trickle down the pane. I imagine they're racing and try to pick the winners—anything to stop my brain from really thinking.

"Because I'm your mother," she says, as if it's the most obvious thing in the world. As if it gives her a right to my every thought and experience.

"There's nothing to tell. I'm sorry if I'm not going to give you a good story for the kitchen." I may not like people very much, but I'm usually not cruel. Not even to my mother.

It's strangely intoxicating.

She sighs. "Cecelia, really. You know very well that's not why I'm asking."

"Do I? Really? Why else do you want all the details, then? The doctor already told you what happened."

"Because I care about what happened to you," she says. "I took the day off so I could be here for you. You know how hard that is."

I snort. My mom isn't a bad mother. Not really. But her whole identity is so wrapped up in being martyr-Mom (cape and mask included) that she can never just be a mom-Mom. She relishes in telling people that not only does she devote count-less hours to running a successful restaurant, she does it while single-parenting. She says this like it's deliberate, like she's this brilliant career woman and my father abandoned us, when the

53

truth is that she works all those hours because she can't afford to hire enough staff and that the cancer took Dad from both of us. I don't think she's ever forgiven him for dying and I miss him every time I see my own reflection.

Mom gets up and sits on the edge of my bed. "You need to talk to me."

The proximity makes me bristle. It would be easier if Dad were here, instead of her. He was always better at this kind of stuff. He knew to get dinosaur Band-Aids, and that chicken and stars is the best kind of soup, and that laughter really is the best medicine.

All those things would still help, even now.

I shut my eyes and sink into the pillows. "I need you to leave."

I feel the bed shift as she gets off it and I wonder if she's actually going to go. But then I hear her sniffling and the fury rolls back over me. She has no right.

"This didn't only happen to you," she says and blows her nose.

I don't open my eyes.

I draw in a breath through my swollen nose and count ten hippopotamuses. Twenty. Then I do it again while she continues to sniffle.

"Yes, Mother, yes, it did."

10

As promised, Lyssa returns that afternoon with Finn and Ashlyn.

My mother ended up going into the restaurant after all, claiming the dinner shift couldn't run without her and, in truth, it probably couldn't. As glad as I was to see her go, the time alone helped less than I expected it would. Alone time with my brain was bad and at least my mother offered a target for my rage.

"We come bearing gifts," Finn announces at a distinctly non-hospital-approved volume. He adjusts his bulging backpack and raises a large paper bag.

"Stolen?" I ask, raising my bed to a sitting position. They've left my leg down all day and I feel more like a normal human for it.

"As if I would ever do such dreadful things," he drawls in mock horror, clutching at imaginary pearls.

"Cough, flowers, cough," Ashlyn says without an ounce of subtlety, nudging him out of the way. She levers her tiny frame up onto the narrow windowsill as Lyssa takes her seat near my head.

Finn waves his empty hand disdainfully. "Poppycock," he says, somehow stuck in character now. He pulls out two hot pink cardboard cups from the bag and holds them out. "For real, though, we thought you could use a yogurt date. Fruit or chocolate?"

"Chocolate," I say, realizing how ravenous I am. He hands me one with a long orange spoon. He gives the other one to Ashlyn, then takes the last two out and passes one to Lyssa. I try to remember the last thing I ate.

"I don't know how you guys eat that stuff," Lyssa says, popping the clear plastic lid off her cup. Hers is filled with pieces of candy, cookies, and brownies held together with caramel sauce instead of frozen yogurt.

There aren't words for how happy I am to have her back by my bed. "It's not like ice cream."

"It's better," Ashlyn says, twirling a fluorescent pink spoon into her cup.

"You're crazy," she says and turns to me. "How bad was Momthulu?"

"Bad as you'd expect," I say around a mouthful of peanut butter frozen yogurt. They loaded it up with every chocolate topping that was available and I think it's the best thing I've ever eaten.

Lyssa rolls her eyes. "Full-blown narcissist mode yet?"

"Pretty much."

"Heard she was pissed you kicked her out for the police interview," Finn says.

"Yeah, well, she gets pissed about a lot of things." I stab my yogurt with the spoon. I've spent too much of the day dwelling on the events of the morning. I don't want to go back there now. The room gets quiet, so I force a smile.

"How was skating?" I ask Ashlyn, as if nothing in the world was wrong.

Everyone allows this abrupt change of topic and I'm grateful. We finish our yogurt with meaningless chatter and it's close enough to normal that I relax.

When we're done, Finn pulls the backpack into his lap.

"And for dessert," he says, pulling out a wide-screen laptop, "we have brain candy!"

"If that's your porno laptop I want nothing to do with it," I say. Finn keeps several laptops for various purposes—school, games, illegal downloading—and I have no doubt that he has one dedicated to naked women.

"It's not the porn one," he says without bothering to deny the existence of such a thing. "It's my old school one. Thought you might want some distraction. And look, we're even going old-school since I wasn't sure if you had good Wi-Fi."

He sets the laptop on my rolling table and pulls an impressive pile of DVDs out of his backpack. He fans them out like a card dealer and familiar faces from the old space dramas I used to watch with my father stare up from their covers, as well as copies of *Back to the Future* and *The Princess Bride*. Dad was obsessed with sci-fi and after his chemo sessions we would camp out in the living room to binge-watch his shows. That was before Finn moved here, but sometimes Ashlyn and Lyssa would join us and we'd eat endless handfuls of Swedish Fish, the only food Dad could tolerate after treatment. By the end, we could all recite lines from shows that had aired before we were born and there was something very comforting about knowing what was going to happen next.

"If you want anything else, I can bootleg it for you," Finn says.

"Thought you didn't do such dreadful things."

"Oh, come on, torrents don't count."

"You have a strange code," I say and Lyssa and Ashlyn nod in agreement. "This is perfect, though. Exactly what I need."

Really, the faction is exactly what I need, but I don't say so. The gratitude is so raw and infinite that expressing it would just embarrass us all.

There's a clatter from the hall and a cheerful voice says, "Knock, knock!"

Nurse Francine comes in, carrying a dinner tray in one hand and pulling her rolling computer stand behind her with the other. Today she's wearing navy scrubs with big white polka dots, but the ladybugs still crawl around her lanyard. She surveys the empty frozen yogurt containers and laughs. "Looks like you already had dinner."

She sets the tray next to Finn's laptop anyway. Sliced meat-loaf, mashed potatoes, floppy green beans, and orange Jell-O. I'm pretty sure the hospital uses the same food as the school lunches, which is gross. Finn takes the Jell-O without asking.

She checks my blood pressure, injects something into my IV line, and types a flurry of words onto her computer. "I see you've been refusing painkillers," she says.

"I don't like how they make me feel," I tell her. "The Motrin they gave me is fine."

She nods, types again. "Okay, let's get that bandage swapped out again. You want an audience for this?"

"Doesn't matter. Lys already saw it."

Neither Finn nor Ashlyn reacts when they see my Franken-stein leg, although the uncomfortable silence is a reaction in itself.

Nurse Francine is faster than the morning nurse, but insists on hauling my leg back up into the sling for the night. I allow it, albeit unhappily.

While she's busy tidying up her cart, I sneak a glance at my friends and, emboldened by their presence and my sugar high, blurt out, "I want to see my face."

Everyone looks at me like I've gone mental, even Lyssa.

"You saw it this morning, remember, matey?" she says with a pirate lilt.

I don't laugh. I look at Nurse Francine. "Can you take the bandage off? Please. I want to see."

"Aw honey, it's better if you give it a chance to heal. The stitches make it look worse than it is," she says.

"I don't care," I insist. She hasn't said no. I turn to Ashlyn. "Get me a mirror."

She hesitates, looking at the nurse for direction.

Nurse Francine pulls a roll of gauze off her cart and I know I have her. Nervous sweat beads above my lip and I wonder if I'm making a mistake. Maybe they're right. Maybe I don't want to know.

"I guess there's no harm in changing the dressing," Francine says matter-of-factly.

No going back now.

"C'mon, Ash, I know you have one."

She slides off the windowsill and rummages through her purse until she finds her makeup pouch. Since her mother started letting her wear it the summer before seventh grade, I've never known Ashlyn to go anywhere without her makeup. She's a wizard with the stuff and is always trying to use Lyssa and me as guinea pigs. She extracts a green compact from the small zippered bag and hands it over. I hold it closed against my belly and stare straight ahead as Nurse Francine unwinds the gauze from around my head.

When she steps back I don't meet anyone's gaze, although I can feel their eyes on me. I don't want to see what's on their faces until I see what's on my own. The frozen yogurt is an iceberg in my stomach.

I raise the mirror up to my face.

It's not like my leg.

It's not like looking at a picture.

It's so, so much worse.

I bite down hard. My hands are jumping around so much it's hard to get a long look with the small mirror, but I've seen enough. It's already burned into my brain. Yet, like a rubbernecker passing a car crash, I can't stop staring.

Here's the thing about me and mirrors. We don't get along. As in ever. Even on the rare days when I don't feel like a total troll, I still don't look at my reflection if I can help it. I don't pose for pictures, don't preen in front of windows, and I never take selfies. But today, I can't tear my gaze from the wreckage that is the new me.

I don't know how long I stare at the jagged canyon transecting my freckled face. Maybe seconds, maybe days. It's hard to keep track of time now.

A rushing fills my head and I think it's the sound of silence. Lyssa hasn't even made a smart remark yet, which scares me.

The gash is longer than I thought it'd be. It starts above my eyebrow, disappears under the thick oval pad that's still taped over my eye, and skirts over my cheekbone toward my ear. I try to count the stitches but it's disorienting with the shaky mirror and only one good eye. I make it to sixteen twice before giving up.

I lower the mirror.

I've seen enough.

"'Tis but a scratch," I say in a deliberately awful British accent. I still can't look at anyone, but I feel compelled to try to joke it away.

Nurse Francine rescues me with a chuckle. "That's my girl," she says and dabs some ointment on the cut before beginning to wrap my head again.

My heart is galloping like mad. Come on, guys. Don't let me drown here. We can joke about this. It can be okay. It has to be okay.

Tears are slipping down Ashlyn's pink cheeks. Finn is fidgeting with the strap of his backpack, not meeting my eye, and Lyssa looks like she's already halfway to Hulk mode.

Perfect.

What the hell was I thinking?

11

Nurse Francine finishes her ministrations and when the damage is safely hidden by pristine gauze she leaves us.

Silence thunders in her wake.

Lyssa heaves a dramatic sigh, as if resigning herself to something. "I feel like a parrot just isn't going to cut it anymore. You're gonna need a ship and everything."

I sink against the pillows with relief. Okay. Not drowning, then.

"Looks that way," I say, but what I really mean is thank you.

"And a crew." Her words are light, but her eyes aren't.

I know I should say something. About my face or about what really happened. I should do it right now, while we're alone and so much has already been revealed.

But I can't.

"I'm in," Finn says. "I could totally rock one of those pirate man blouses."

"Ew, no." Ashlyn laughs. She plucks *The Princess Bride* out of the stack of DVDs. "I think we have to watch this. Because pirates."

She arranges the laptop where we can all see and settles onto the arm of Lyssa's chair. She stretches her legs over to Finn's chair and he drapes an arm across her feet.

I try to lose myself in the familiar story but I can't focus. Too much of me is back at the hayloft, with Shane, and I don't know how I can ever tell them about it. I don't know how I'll manage to look in the mirror every day with the constant reminder carved into my flesh. I sneak glances at Lyssa, who's leaning on the edge of the bed, and study the smooth, unmarred line of her cheek. I know that even if things were different between us, I could never ask her to choose a face like this.

When the movie ends, Ashlyn swings her legs down from Finn's chair and stands, looking uncomfortable enough that I start to worry.

"What?" I ask, not sure I want to know.

"My mom wants me home by ten." Despite her ever-changing rainbow of hair colors, Ashlyn has the strictest parents out of all of us, so this curfew doesn't surprise me.

"Aw, stay," Finn says, ever the bad influence. "You know you want to."

"I do," she says, drawing the short sentence out until it's clear there's more.

"Ash, spit it out," Lyssa says.

She looks at me, cringing. "They want to pray for you. Tomorrow. At church," she says in a rapid-fire burst.

Lyssa snorts. "To who? Satan? Krampus? The tooth fairy?"

Balls.

I sigh. "It's okay," I tell her, although I wish she hadn't said anything.

"You're gonna get struck by lightning," Lyssa warns me. "You don't need that on top of everything else."

I kind of agree with her, but I also know Ashlyn's parents mean well.

"I just felt like I should tell you," she says.

"It's cool," I say. It's not like I'm out burning Jesus statues in my spare time, but God and I aren't exactly on speaking terms anymore. Not since Dad.

"And I'm supposed to go with them," she adds. She rarely attends church these days, preferring to spend her mornings on the ice, but her parents never miss a Sunday. We don't talk about it a lot, but I think she's outgrowing the whole church thing.

"I can go with you," Finn says. "If you want."

"You realize church starts at eight in the morning, right?" she asks.

"I can do it."

"Eight o'clock real time," I say. "Not Finn Standard Time."

"I can be on time!"

We all stare at him, eyebrows raised. He pretends to be hurt.

"Now I'm definitely going," he says, folding his arms.

"Your choice," Ashlyn says, but I can tell she's happy by the way her dimples are showing even though she's trying not to smile.

Lyssa pulls her keys out of her pocket and tosses them to Finn. "Try not to crash," she says.

He catches them easily. "You want me to come get you after?"

"Nah, just bring it back tomorrow. I could stand a *Sherlock* marathon," she says with a nod at the computer. "You should get to bed anyway, Deacon Luckman. Early morning tomorrow and all that."

"We'll come by after church gets out," Ashlyn promises.

As they leave, Lyssa drags both chairs to the blind side of my bed and sets herself up as she was last night.

"You don't have to stay, you know," I say, knowing I would hate it if she left.

"Yeah, I do."

///

Lyssa is asleep halfway through the first season of *Sherlock*.

I'm grateful she stayed. Even though I can't see her and we haven't been talking much, knowing she's over there is comforting.

It's that feeling that gives me the courage to do what I'm about to do.

I minimize the media player without closing it. Like Lyssa's soft snoring, the familiar dialogue is calming and I need that right now. I adjust the zoom in the web browser and pull up the *Union News* site. Amesford is too small to have its own paper, but the *Union News* covers the whole region, so if there's a story about what happened, it will be there.

I click into the search bar and hesitate. What do I search? My name? Shane's?

It turns out I don't have to search anything at all, because on the right-hand side of the page, under the "Most Read" heading, my story tops the list.

With my heart hammering, I click the link.

1 DEAD, 1 HOSPITALIZED AFTER ALLEGED ASSAULT

Brandy Alves, *Union News*

An Amesford man was found dead in the second story of a barn on Summers Road following what appears to have been a brutal attack on a minor. Shane J. Mayfield, 20, of Brook Road, was discovered by police Friday evening when they responded to a 911 call from the farm's address.

A 17-year-old female was removed from the scene and taken to Harrington Hospital for treatment of multiple lacerations and contusions. The patient is listed in stable condition, but the family was unavailable for comment.

Records show that Mayfield has been arrested twice for driving under the influence and possession of a Class B and D substance. It is unknown whether he was under the influence of any substance at the time of his death. Amesford police are investigating the incident and an autopsy has been scheduled.

Preliminary interviews indicate that this was a case of killing in self-defense, but the deceased's brother, Trevor Mayfield, 17, believes there's more to the story. He says, "Shane was my best friend. He would never hurt anyone. Everyone loved him. He's not a criminal, he's the victim here."

This story will be updated as more information becomes available.

Goose bumps make mountains on my arms. I feel like all my blood has drained away.

I think some foolish part of me actually believed there wouldn't be a story. And as far as stories go, it's not even anything special. Hardly any information at all. But it's out there for everyone to see.

Beneath the article there's a tab to open up the comments. One hundred twenty-seven, to be exact. I click the icon and they spill down the page.

LanaM: RIP Shane!!! ♡♡

Jax11: RIP Shane—miss you man

Gobruins: how about some real reporting instead of inflammatory comments from the scumbag's relatives?

Picknotu: Shane was the man! RIP bro

Anonymous: RIP Shane

WildCatsGO: RIP!!!

SoxFan63: Prayers to the poor child who had to defend herself against such an awful attack. I can't imagine what you're going thru

Anonymous: Murder ain't called defending

SoxFan63: It's justifiable homicide if they feared for their life. Sounds like the case.

Anonymous: Shane's the real victim here

Bradf: rip shane. champs 4ever!

Queleh: 2 DUIs and possession? Why wasn't he locked up already???

RealParent: Family ties

Queleh: No excuse

413_abu: he's off the street now!

CheyCheyX: Love you shane! RiP! ♡

TMayfield: My brother is the victim of this crime. Please remember him for who he was, not who the news wants him to be

WC243: peace man. rip shane

RedRight: RIP Shane

anonymous: JuStIce WiLl B SeRvEd!!!

413_abu: Justice HAS been served

Code3: stay strong trev

Bruinsbabe: rip shane!

StarPup: Prayers to both families. This is a tragedy all around

Lemon145_0: Agreed

And on and on and on.

My stomach climbs up my throat and I swallow hard. I try to close the article but my hands are too shaky to guide the pointer and I push the entire table away instead. I look over at Lyssa and consider waking her, but what would it help?

At least they didn't print my name. That has to count for something.

I wonder if the Mayfields know who killed their son?
Do they know he is—was—a monster?
Do they care?

12

At some point I must drift off because later I slam awake, sweat pouring down my face and my heart racing like an overcaffein-ated roadrunner. Sunlight streams into my narrow window. Good morning, stupid world.

I crane my neck around, but Lyssa isn't there and my heart dips.

Nurse Not-Francine, however, is very much there.

"Morning," she chirps.

"So it is."

"I have good news for you, if you're awake enough to hear it," she says, adjusting something on the side of my bed. She's young, probably fresh out of nursing school, with a tight blond ponytail pulling at the edges of her eyes. She's my opposite in every way: skinny, tanned, unscarred, not a killer.

I want Nurse Francine back.

"I'm going to remove your catheter," she says as if this is something celebratory. "If you can handle the bathroom on your own, you'll be able to go home today. So yay, no more urine bag!"

She plunks something into a plastic tub she has on her little cart and I'm suddenly *thrilled* Lyssa is gone.

She's got my sheet raised before I can protest. It's way too early to be dealing with this. I'm not even all the way awake.

"You might feel a bit of tugging," she says, raising my hospital gown, and I do feel it.

Holy hell, do I *feel*.

Horrible flashbacks fire behind my eyes. My breathing becomes ragged gasps as she reaches between my legs and pulls out whatever it is she has to pull out.

"Did that hurt?" she asks, looking bewildered. "I'm so sorry. It usually doesn't hurt. Just feels kind of funny."

"Get out," I say through gritted teeth. "Stop touching me and get out."

She backs up, hands raised. "I'm sorry," she says, pretty eyes wide. "I didn't mean to upset you. I just have to—"

"Please leave, please leave, please leave," I chant, each plea pitched higher than the last. I'm too panicked to be embarrassed. Tearless sobs choke me and I swear the bruises on my neck tighten. "Don't touch me. Please don't touch me."

She scrambles out of the room, cart rattling behind her.

I raise my bed to full-sitting position and pull my good leg into my chest. I wrap my arms around it, dig my nails into the flesh of my upper arms, and rock as I gulp huge lungfuls of air in through my mouth.

It's like this that Lyssa finds me.

Of course it is.

"Don't," I say when she crosses the threshold. I shoot my leg out, ignoring the pain that the motion sends through its mate. Crescent moons flare on my arms where my nails were. Lyssa has the sense not to mention it.

"I had Pop bring us breakfast," she says, warily hoisting a plastic bag. I can tell she wants to ask what's going on, but I love her for not doing so. "From Cranberry Creek. Apple pancakes and hash browns."

I nod. I don't know what to say. More than half of my brain is still back in the hayloft.

Apple pancakes are my favorite food in the world. If I were on death row, I'd eat these, followed by more for dessert. But when Lyssa places the Styrofoam to-go box in front of me it's like I've forgotten how food works.

"Or we can eat later," she says. "You good?"

"No," I admit, then rush to add, "but it's fine. Really. Supposedly they're springing me today."

"That's good news."

"Yup."

"Seel, if you need to talk—"

"Not even a little bit. Really. Everything's shiny. Hey, what about those pancakes?" The words ring false even to me, but I don't want to dwell. Dwelling is bad.

After choking down a couple bites of breakfast, my brain remembers that food is good and that I need it. We eat in companionable silence.

"Want to place bets on if Finn made it to church?" Lyssa asks after we finish.

"I bet he did," I say, surprising myself by believing it.

"Yeah, but on time?"

"Less than ten minutes late. No, less than twenty."

"That's practically on time for him."

"He's still hauling that torch around for Ash," I remind her.

Finn has been wanting Ashlyn from the moment he moved here, though that hasn't stopped him from flirting with a plethora of other girls while waiting for her to see the light.

"True."

And while I know it's an awful thing to say, there's a part of me that wants Ashlyn to keep holding out forever, the way I am. The dynamic of our group is perfect as it is. No matter how much I may want it to be otherwise, a single romance could be catastrophic to our faction. It's not worth the risk, not when friendships have the potential to last forever.

Before I can voice any of these thoughts, Dr. Vern barges in with a huge black-and-silver leg brace dangling from his hands. The nurse I chased out earlier hangs back behind him, shielding herself with a wheelchair.

"Ms. Stanton," Vern says. "I hear you had quite the morning."

I don't say anything.

"We're going to take you down to the physical therapists to see about getting you outfitted with a walker," he continues. "We need to put this brace on your leg first, is that okay?"

I nod. The nurse looks worried when Dr. Vern moves the sheet. I let him Velcro the contraption around my leg, clenching my teeth and trying to focus on anything other than the fact that this man is touching me. I need to allow this if I want to go home. I can do it. I have to.

Between the doctor and Lyssa, I'm able to make it from the bed to the wheelchair. It's not a graceful transition.

Nurse Not-Francine wheels me through the hallway and I keep my eyes cast down, afraid I'll find pity and disgust on everyone's faces. Lyssa follows at my side. The nurse is all too happy to park me and scurry away.

A muscular woman with short black hair and no makeup approaches me, smiling wide with her hand outstretched. "Cecelia?"

I nod and take her hand, though I really don't want to. I doubt she's past thirty, which is way too young to be a handshaker.

"I'm Jacqui Velez," she says. She has a remarkably strong grip. "And who's with you today?"

"Lyssa," she says, taking the offered hand.

"Are you family?"

"Yes," I answer for her. I don't elaborate.

"Perfect," Jacqui says, unfazed. I like her for this. "Let's get started."

The first thing she brings me is a walker. An honest-to-balls old-lady walker. "I don't want that," I say. No way.

"Treat it like step one," she says. "You have some trauma to your leg and you've been in bed for a couple days. Your body is going to need a little help getting going."

"Step two," Lyssa corrects. "Step one was the wheelchair."

Jacqui smiles broadly, like she's found a co-conspirator. I glare at Lyssa, which is probably not as threatening as I want it to be, since she laughs.

"Argh, matey," she says, clamping an eye shut. "Just do it."

"I hate you," I say.

"No, you don't."

"No, you don't," Jacqui parrots, looking between us. She places the walker in front of me, stands to one side. Lyssa instinctively moves to the other. "Okay, let's have a go."

I hesitate, but not for the reason I'm sure they're thinking. The blue vinyl of the wheelchair is sticking to the backs of my thighs—and my very bare butt. "Um, I'm pretty sure if I stand up you're gonna get an eyeful."

Jacqui laughs and agrees. She gets me a second hospital gown to cover the open backside of the one I'm wearing. With this scrap of dignity somehow intact, I haul myself up. I lean heavily on the silver walking frame, feeling stuck. The brace keeps my leg completely straight and I'm not sure how to maneuver. After a minute I just go for it, heaving the walker forward and pulling myself along after it. Little daggers shoot through my leg and I bite down, move another couple inches. It's slow going.

"I think I'd be better off with crutches," I say.

"Dr. Vern wrote the order for a walker, but we can certainly give crutches a try," Jacqui says.

I stand there leaning on the walker because it's not remotely worth the effort to make it back to the wheelchair to sit down. If I have my way, I'm not parking my ass in that thing ever again.

Jacqui hands me the crutches and I'm convinced Vern just set up the walker as punishment for being mean to the morning nurse. I can swing myself around the room all day on these bad boys, no problem.

"I'll stick with these."

"I'd say that's a solid plan," Jacqui agrees. "After they remove the staples we're going to set you up with a PT schedule. It'll be three days a week to start, and we'll back it down as you get stronger. How's that sound?"

Like nothing I want any part of, but I agree. "How soon until I can ride horses again?"

"How about we start with walking and work our way up from there?" Jacqui says with another smile. Normally I want to punch people who are this relentlessly cheerful, but for some reason I'm not annoyed by her.

"Maybe you can keep the wheelchair and have a horse pull you around in it," Lyssa says. She's commandeered the contraption now that I'm mobile and is popping little wheelies in it. "Like chariot racing."

I laugh and to my surprise Jacqui does too.

I'm disappointed when she tells me I have to ride the dreaded chair back to my room. Something about hospital policy. But she lets Lyssa do the honors of pushing me, despite the very real chance she's going to crash me into a doorway, and we return to my room for the long wait until I get to go home.

13

Getting discharged from the hospital takes forever.

Finn and Ashlyn are waiting in my room when we get back, and to my complete disappointment, so is my mother.

Great.

"Why have you been ignoring my calls?" my mother asks before I'm all the way in the room.

"Because I don't have a phone," I snap.

"Where's your cell phone?"

"Probably where I dropped it at the barn. I don't know."

"That explains it," Ashlyn says brightly. "I texted you about Finn actually being on time this morning. I thought maybe you were still sleeping because there's no way you would ignore something that shocking."

"I was expecting praise and adulation," Finn says. "I was disappointed."

"Life is hard," I tell him. "But nicely done, sir. I'm duly impressed."

Jacqui beckons my mother into the hall, leaving the four of us alone.

"So on a scale of one to brimstone, how bad was it?" Lyssa asks. She parks my wheelchair and leans on the edge of the bed.

"It was actually kinda nice," Finn says. "But early. Way too early for that much singing."

"Did they make a spectacle?" I ask. Not being a spectacle is the guiding principle by which I live my life.

"They mentioned you in a list of other people," Ashlyn says. "No personal business."

"Good."

"Hey, if your phone is really missing, I can give you one of my old ones to use," Finn says. He changes phones more than anyone I've ever met and often carries two at once, claiming he likes the way certain apps perform on different operating systems. I mostly think he's a tech hoarder. But I'm more than happy to benefit from his collection of castoffs.

"Yeah, that'd be good. I must've dropped mine at the barn." Something else occurs to me. "Hey, did anyone get Wedgie?"

Everyone shakes their head.

"Shit, sorry, didn't even think of it," Lyssa says.

"We can go today," Finn adds.

Wedgie is my vintage convertible VW Beetle. Along with my taste in sci-fi, the car was a gift from Dad. When he was first diagnosed, Dad painstakingly restored the fifty-year-old jelly bean to a thing of beauty, with gleaming dark green paint and white hood stripes that match the roof and side mirrors, as a very early sixteenth-birthday present. I love that car as much as anyone can love an inanimate object, but not as much as the letter that he hid in the glove compartment for me to find after his funeral.

"Thanks," I say. "The keys should be in the barn."

"Or I could hot-wire it," Finn offers and we all laugh and tell him no.

When my mom and Jacqui come back in, trailed by Nurse Still-Not-Francine, my room starts to feel uncomfortably like a sardine tin.

"Okay, Seelie," Jacqui says, making her way to me. "We have to get you back up onto the bed so Tricia can change your bandage, then you're welcome to change into the clothes your mom brought. Dr. Vern will be by shortly and then we can get you out of here."

Shortly doesn't mean the same thing in hospitals that it means in real life. Three hours later I'm still sitting on the bed, wearing a hoodie and sushi-print pajama pants, waiting for Mortician Vern to make his appearance. Lyssa is gone with Finn and Ashlyn to retrieve my car, Ashlyn being the only one among the trio who truly enjoys driving the tiny vehicle. Lyssa prefers her massive black Jeep and Finn manages to afford a brand-new red Mazda despite his extremely part-time job at Dunkin' Donuts. Ashlyn is the only one without a car and I guess anything beats driving the family minivan.

The plan is to meet up at my house later, and I'm ready for later to be now.

"Your physical therapist seems nice," my mother says into the silence that's settled around us.

"She is."

"I think it will be good for you to be able to focus on your fitness. Maybe she can help develop a meal plan to go with your exercises."

I roll my uncovered eye. "Physical therapy is so I can walk, not so I can lose weight."

"I don't see why it can't be about both."

It doesn't occur to her that this isn't helpful. I grab the laptop, desperate for a distraction.

Before I can get a show on, she starts up again. "We're going to have to figure something out about school."

"I'm not going to school like this." I'm horrified that she would even consider it an option.

"You're going to have to go back at some point. Not this week, maybe, but eventually."

"I'm not going. I can just homeschool."

"No, you can't. I would have to homeschool you, and I simply don't have the time. Not with the restaurant."

I snort. "Right. Of course not."

"Seelie, I understand this is hard for you. I talked to Dr. Vern and he's recommended a psychologist, but I think the important thing is getting back on the horse. You know, get back to normal."

"Normal?" I can't believe I'm hearing this. "Normal? You haven't even seen my face yet, so don't talk to me about normal. Normal doesn't exist anymore."

"Watch your tone. I'm doing the best I can here," my mother says, her voice breaking. I hope she doesn't cry again.

I turn back to the computer, angry and uncomfortable.

It feels like an eternity before Vern comes in with a sheaf of papers.

"These are care instructions, the physical therapy schedule, plus a prescription for Percocet, just in case," he says, giving the papers to my mother.

"I don't need Percocet," I say.

"Just in case," he repeats. "You've been getting a steady dosage of ibuprofen, which I encourage you to continue with, but if the pain peaks, you'll want to have something stronger on hand. You shouldn't have to worry about it for more than a few days, though. Now all we have to do is remove your head bandage and you can be on your way. I do have an eye patch I would like you to wear until we take the stitches out."

I shake my head. I don't want my mom looking at my face. Not yet. "Nurse Francine changed the bandage last night," I say. "Can't I just leave it on?"

Dr. Vern checks my chart and decides it's not worth the fight. "Okay, then, leave it on for now. I'll send the eye patch home with you. Tomorrow you'll want to take the gauze off, let it get some air, but keep the pad over your eye."

I nod.

"Tricia will wheel you down to the front desk to be discharged. They'll make appointments to remove the stitches and staples then," Dr. Vern says. "Jacqui said you were doing well with the crutches, so we won't send you home with the walker."

"Thank you," I say.

"Good luck, Cecelia."

I'm going to need it.

14

I ride home sideways in the backseat with my leg stretched out in front of me. With my back against the door, I have to crane my head to see out the window. Familiar streets and landmarks seem utterly foreign, as if the world has reoriented itself while I was gone. I peer at the quiet houses like they're some exotic museum exhibit. The sun is already fading and warm light pools behind curtains, illuminating glimpses of normal lives as we pass by. At a stop sign I can see straight into someone's dining room, where a woman is setting a table, and I know in my bones that she's never killed anyone. The same way I know I will never have her kind of life. Not anymore.

We stop to pick up the prescription I continue to insist I don't want and the pizza that I do, and it's clear from the silence that my mother wants to be in this car about as much as I do. When we turn down our street I'm relieved to see Lyssa's Jeep, Wedgie dwarfed in front of it, parked in front of our duplex.

Lyssa, Ashlyn, and Finn are sitting on the deck and they all come down when we park. Getting from the car to the house is a production, but at least Mr. and Mrs. Markham don't come out of their side to see what the fuss is about. While they're nice-enough people who always pay their rent on time, I don't like them. At all. Mrs. Markham likes to keep her baby strapped to her like a fashion accessory and seems incapable of talking about anything except little Steven's cloth diapers, which are always fluttering off a clothesline on her side of the yard. One of my goals in life is to never get that boring.

We immediately head for my room upstairs, but stairs are easier said than done with crutches, and in the end I resort to sitting on my butt with my leg held out straight and bumping my way up one step at a time while the others carry pizza, plates, and drinks. Oh dignity, how I miss you.

"Well, that sucked." My leg throbs from so much movement and I ease myself onto my bed. My room, like the streets on the drive home, has a surreal quality to it now. The blue walls and white curtains should've been a welcome sight, but I feel like I'm surveying a stranger's room. The books that overflow the white shelves were read by someone else. A different girl won the horse-show ribbons that flutter on a wire strung over the simple white headboard. The dinosaur figures marching across the desk are relics from another's childhood.

Ashlyn leaps into the ugly-but-comfy bowl chair and curls up like a kitten. Lyssa waits until I'm settled on the bed before sprawling down next me. Her leg is close enough to mine that a slight shift would bring us into contact.

"So my mom's already trying to send me back to school," I tell them, easing my leg a fraction of an inch away from temptation. "Can you believe that?"

"What are you going to do?" Finn asks from the floor as he dishes out pizza.

I shrug. "I want to homeschool but she said no. Was trying to be all inspirational with this little 'you have to get back on the horse' speech."

"That blows," Lyssa says. She reaches for one of my furry pillows and rolls and tucks it between her back and the wall. The movement closes the gap and her bent knee is against the flannel of my sushi pants and it's no longer the wounded leg I'm most aware of.

"I'll get your work for you," Ashlyn offers. "At least you won't fall behind."

Like everything else right now, the thought of school is alien. How can I ever walk through the halls with my mutilated face and the knowledge that I killed the brother of a kid I have English with? As much as I hate the thought of returning, it's weird knowing that they'll all be going to school without me tomorrow.

But with them here, I finally feel like I'm home. This is our normal life—stuffing our faces and talking about nonsense. Finn remembered to bring one of his old phones and he transfers my number to it while we eat so I'll at least be able to text them after my mother unceremoniously evicts them at nine.

The room echoes in their absence.

I hobble to the bathroom down the hall and brush my teeth without looking in the mirror. I swallow a couple Advil, ignoring the amber Percocet bottle my mother put in the cabinet, and manage to pee without further injuring myself. When I return to my room I find my mother parked on my bed and I have to fight the urge to just go sleep in the bathroom.

"I'll be leaving early tomorrow," she says. "The inventory

hasn't been done and I need to get an order in to the suppliers before we open. Are you going to be okay alone here?"

"Yes. Obviously. I'm hurt, not stupid."

She sighs. "Seelie, I'm sorry this happened to you. You're going to get better, though."

"Yup," I say, just to get her out of there. "Everything's shiny."

She shakes her head, gets up, and says, "I do love you, Seelie."

I don't say anything, just wait until she's gone so I can lock the door. I lock both the windows and then I check that the door is really locked. Then I check the windows again. And the door, one more time. I swing myself back and forth across the room with the crutches, touching locks and pulling on windows for over ten minutes. I can't help it. When I finally convince myself that everything is really, truly locked, I climb into bed without turning the light off.

I grab Finn's iPhone from the desk. **Thank you**, I type into a new group text. Tears blur the screen as I try to figure out how to explain what I want to say. I don't know how. **For everything. There are no words for what it means to have you guys.**

The replies are instantaneous:

ASH: **Love you too** ♡
FINN: **The faction sticks togethr**
LYS: **You don't have to thank family idiot**

15

I wake to my mother pounding on my locked door, announcing her departure.

I'm nowhere near rested. I lay awake for hours last night after everyone left as my brain obsessively rehashed everything that had happened in the past few days. It was impossible to turn the thoughts off. I tried reading, but focusing on the words with only one functioning eye is hard and my mind kept straying. What sleep I got was punctuated by nightmares and several times I woke with an uncontrollable need to check the locks. Needless to say, I'm not pleased by my mother's early morning drum solo.

I try and fail to get back to sleep.

I'm still wearing the sushi pants and hoodie I left the hospital in and I desperately need a shower. I force myself out of bed.

I lock myself in the bathroom and start with removing the leg brace. The easy stuff. I peel the gauze away from the cut and find the staples still don't gross me out. If anything, the wound is less angry looking today.

Unwrapping my face is the hard part. I give myself a one-eyed stare down, waiting for the black eyes and choker of bruises to become less shocking before I unwind the gauze. This time

I'm prepared for what I'm going to see, but that doesn't stop me from wanting to smash the mirror when I do.

I run the shower as hot as I can stand—just shy of lava—and use the towel bar to help get myself in. I know I'm not supposed to take the eye pad off, but I don't know if I'm allowed to get it wet so I keep my back to the spray. I stand with the bulk of my weight on my good leg, letting the water course down my body before I lather up my purple loofah and start scrubbing. I'm careful to avoid my cuts, but I want to scour the top layer of skin right off, shed it like a snake would. I don't want the skin that Shane touched to be my skin anymore. I scrub and scrub until my skin is raw. I still don't feel clean.

I wonder if I'll ever feel clean or whole or normal ever again and I doubt it. How can I?

I wash my hair in the rapidly cooling water, being careful not to let the suds run into my eyes. When I turn the water off, mango-scented steam hangs so thick in the air I can barely see my towels. I wrap one around my dripping hair and one around my body, more than a little concerned I'm going to slip and die getting out of the wet tub.

I successfully avoid killing myself and even crutch my way back to my room without losing my towel. Score. I tape gauze over the staples on my leg and put the brace back on over penguin-patterned pajama pants and pull on a *Doctor Who* hoodie. I twist my wet curls into a messy bun and don't bother slapping mascara—the single bit of makeup I can actually handle—on my one exposed eye, since it's not like I'm planning to see anyone today. This fact also stops me from immediately rewrapping my face. Besides, I don't think winding gauze around wet hair is super sanitary anyway.

I slide my crutches down the stairs and bump down behind them like a little kid.

I check the locks on the front door and the slider that leads to the deck, then forage around for breakfast. Cold pizza fits the bill. I eat leaning against the counter, because sitting in chairs is more trouble than it's worth with the brace on. Feeling brave—or stupid—I let my foot settle on the floor and shift a fraction of my weight onto it. It hurts, but it's bearable. I'm not dumb enough to try to walk on it, but the fact that I can almost stand cheers me.

My mom's laptop is on the counter and I use it to check my email. There's one from Elaine and my stomach tightens with anxiety.

Seelie,

I am so so sorry for what happened to you. My god, I should never have left you alone. I blame myself. Please let me know if there is ANYTHING I can do to help you. I don't know how you're feeling but please know you are welcome to come by any time, day or night. Sometimes pony snuggles are the best medicine.

Thinking of you,

Elaine

I exhale a sigh of relief. She doesn't hate me. I was worried that she would, and I couldn't blame her. There's blood that will never come out of the wooden floorboards or out of the memory of that place now.

A sudden knocking at the door startles me so much I drop

my pizza and my crutches topple to the floor. "Shit," I curse, gathering the crutches. Who the hell could possibly be here? I bet my mother asked Mrs. Markham to check on me. Double shit.

The knocking starts again, louder.

"Coming," I snap, swinging myself through the living room. I open the door.

It's not Mrs. Markham.

Detectives Troy and Mellers are on my doorstep. Mellers stands slightly back, eyes hard and jaw muscles twitching.

This can't be good.

"Cecelia Stanton," Troy says. "You are under arrest for the murder of Shane Mayfield."

16

They don't cuff me.

Mrs. Markham has appeared on her porch with her spawn strapped to her chest, just in time to see me being guided to the back of the police car. She's frantic, yelling that she'll call my mother. I'm barely aware of her.

Troy opens the rear door and it gapes like the mouth of an alien cave. I balk, unable to go in. All instincts scream that this is an inhospitable environment for human life. Danger, do not enter.

A slash of silver duct tape is peeling at the edge of the scuffed vinyl seat. Troy puts a hand on my shoulder, nearly dislodging my crutch, and pushes me forward. I flail away from his touch, feeling the spot where each finger was like a burn.

"Don't touch me," I say, before I can think better of it.

"Get in or I'll put you in," he says.

"Troy," Mellers says in a low voice and I turn to her, hoping she's my way out.

"This isn't right," I tell her. Panic is making me light-headed. "You don't understand. Shane attacked me. He's the bad guy! I didn't do anything wrong."

"You killed a young man in the prime of his life," Troy says before his partner can answer, and for a moment I think he must have me—or Shane—confused with someone else. "I think the state will agree you most certainly have done something wrong. Get in the car."

Mellers nods and I know I have no choice. I won't let Troy put his hands on me again though, so I prop the crutches on the trunk of the car and obediently fold myself into the backseat. The car reeks of stale coffee, sweat, and vomit, and I don't know how anyone can stand to drive in it all day.

It takes no time at all to get to the police station. On the way we pass the high school and tears sear my eyes at the thought of the faction in class without me. Just a normal boring Monday for everyone else. How did everything get this complicated?

Amesford is too small to have a real downtown, even though that's what we call it. It's more like a town square. The red-brick police station, town hall, post office, and fire station ring a large grassy common. The towering, gothic-looking stone library sits on a small hill, and at the far end of the common is the church Ashlyn's family goes to, its white steeple piercing the cloudless sky.

It's all so picturesque it hurts. It may look like a postcard, but it's a lie. This is not a good place.

It takes me awhile to get out of the car and I'm afraid Troy is going to drag me out by my bad leg. As it is, he practically throws my crutches at me.

"Let's go," he says.

The officer manning the front desk is Maria Morales, Julie's mom. Julie and I were always in the same class in elementary school and Maria would sometimes come in and give safety assemblies. I've been to her house, back when birthday parties meant inviting the whole grade over. Something about seeing her familiar face rocks me. The news might not have printed my name, but now Maria knows it. She'll tell Julie she saw me. She'll tell her why. And Julie will tell Amelia, who will tell Ryan, who will tell Matt, who will tell everyone.

I wonder if maybe it would've been easier if Shane had killed me.

I'm brought to a cluttered office crowded by two desks. Troy directs me to a wooden chair near the more-battered of the pair. I have to perch on the edge of it to keep my brace from cutting off my circulation. He takes a seat at the desk and Mellers leans against the doorjamb with her arms crossed.

Troy takes his time keying something into the computer in front him.

"You're being charged with the murder of Shane Mayfield," he says, as if I might've forgotten why I was there. "As you were already informed, you have the right to remain silent and the right to an attorney. Anything you say may be used against you in a court of law and if you can't afford an attorney, one can be appointed to you free of charge. Please confirm that you understand these rights."

"I do." My mind is racing. There's no way in hell I can afford a lawyer, but I shouldn't even need a lawyer. I'm the one who got attacked. Why am I even sitting here?

"Please state your name, address, and birth date," he drones, fingers poised over the keys.

I do and he enters the information.

"Are you currently on any drugs?"

"No." I turn to Mellers. "Shouldn't my mother be here?" It's not that I really want her there, but I think she's supposed to be. Nothing about this seems right.

"You'll get a phone call after you're processed," she says.

"This isn't right," I say, because it's true. None of this makes sense.

Troy pulls an ink pad and a card out of his desk. "We need to print you," he says, taking my hand.

I pull back hard. "Don't touch me. I can do it myself."

"This is how it's done," he says, reaching for me. "Don't make it harder than it needs to be."

I snatch my hand back. The bruises around my neck feel tight and I turn to Mellers. "I don't want him touching me." I know I sound close to crazy; I don't want to explain why. She doesn't make me.

"I'll do it," she says. She presses each of my fingers into the ink and rolls them across the card, then my whole palm. She is brisk without being rough, like she just wants this over with too.

They don't give me anything to clean the black smudges from my fingertips, so I wipe them on my flannel pants. The ink clings to my fingers.

When I think this can't get any worse, Troy orders me to stand against the blank wall to be photographed.

The images that flash up on his computer screen are repulsive. My face is a riot of rainbow bruises and freckles and horror. I don't have cute freckles. I have the kind that look like someone threw a handful of cinnamon at me, the kind that make people stare. Under the fluorescent lighting I look like an extra for *The Walking Dead*.

"Okay," Troy says to Mellers. "Lock her up."

"What?" My stomach nosedives.

"You don't just get to go home," he says. "Not when you've been arrested for murder."

"Come on," Mellers says to me, nodding once. Stunned to the core, I follow her out of the room. We take an elevator down one floor. Four small cells comprise the room we step out into. All are empty.

Mellers stops at the first one, opens it. In a daze, I go in. She closes the barred door behind me with a devastating clang.

"Why is this happening?" I ask her. "He attacked me. I was only defending myself. I don't deserve this."

She meets my gaze and sighs. "I know. All I can say is trust the system. We're going to investigate this very thoroughly."

I don't believe her. When she leaves, the silence of the cell is so complete that I can hear the blood rushing through my veins. The cell is barren, with only a narrow cot attached to the wall and a stainless-steel toilet with no seat at the end of it like a footboard. I pray I don't have to pee. Or worse.

I drop onto the cot, trying to quell the panic filling my chest. I close my eyes, willing myself away from this place. Any minute Mellers will be back to let me go, to apologize, to tell me I'm not the guilty one in this. I just have to stay calm until then.

When the door clunks open at the end of the room I'm so caught up in my fantasy that it takes me a minute to realize that it's not Mellers coming toward me, but Maria Morales. She smiles tightly and glances around the cramped room before approaching my cell.

"I heard what happened and I'm so sorry," she says. I stand awkwardly, not sure how to respond. She pulls a business card from her front pocket, hands it to me through the bars. "You'll get a phone call soon. Make it this. She's expecting you and is ready to take the case. Pro bono. Seelie, they're charging you as an adult."

17

My fingers tremble as I dial the lawyer's number. Cara Dewitt. A defense attorney. I'm calling a defense attorney. My head swims.

I want to call Lyssa or Ashlyn, or even my mother. Not this stranger. But I call her anyway.

"Cecelia?" the voice on the other end asks before the first ring finishes. She sounds breathless.

"Yes." I'm afraid I'm going to cry. I don't know what I'm supposed to tell her but she doesn't give me a chance to say anything.

"Stop talking to the police. That's the first thing," she orders. She has more than a hint of a Boston accent. "Including Maria. She's good people, but we're past that now. She works for the force and this has to be by the book. She filled me in on your situation and I want to help. I'm already on my way. I'll be there in less than an hour if this damn traffic ever clears. Once we get off the phone I'm going to start arranging bail. We'll get you out of there, don't you worry. I'm going to need your mother's number."

Her words are a rockslide and for a moment they just bury me.

"Seelie? Are you still there?"

I nod dumbly, then say, "Yes. Sorry. How is this happening? I didn't do anything wrong."

"Just stay calm," she says. "This is politics. Maria said the boy was a judge's son? That's how this is happening."

"But you can help me?"

"I'm going to do my best."

Cara Dewitt is not at all what I was expecting. On the phone, the lawyer sounded assured and confident and definitely older than the girl Mellers is leading to my cell. There's no way she can be more than twenty-five, and she looks more like a model than a lawyer. Even a TV lawyer. She has dark skin and a short afro that doesn't draw attention away from her ax-blade cheekbones and precisely lined cat eyes. She has on a high-waisted, navy-blue pencil skirt and white blouse with a pink belt and matching heels.

Really.

Pink heels.

I'm so screwed.

I'm also distinctly aware of my marred face and the penguin pants that conceal a belly I could never put into such a form-fitting skirt.

"Is there an interview room we can use?" Cara asks Mellers, gazing around the cell-lined room. "This is uncivilized."

"Unfortunately there's not," Mellers says, keeping her voice neutral. "Troy has it occupied."

"Of course he does," Cara scoffs. "Unlock the door, then. I'm not going to sit outside her cell like she's Hannibal Lector."

I almost smile at that.

Mellers opens the cell and Cara walks in, extending a French-manicured hand. "Cara Dewitt," she says.

I shake her hand and she sits at the other end of the cot, crossing one leg over the other.

"I'll be outside," Mellers says. "Knock when you're done."

Cara thanks her, waiting for the door to close before she begins speaking.

"How are you doing?" she asks.

"How do you think?" It comes out snarkier than I meant. She's here to help.

She's not fazed. "I think you're scared, confused, and probably somewhat bored by now."

"Pretty much all of that."

"The good news is bail is being set and we'll have you out in time to have dinner at home."

"The bad news?"

"This isn't going away," she says, looking straight at me. "What do you know about the Mayfields?"

"Rich, entitled assholes," I answer without hesitating. Fury wells in my chest.

"Go on."

"What do you want to know? There are two boys. Were two," I correct, feeling my face flush, but I continue. "Shane and Trevor. Trevor is in my grade. He's a dick. Worships his scum-sucking brother."

Worshipp*ed*, I amend in my head.

"Do you have a history with either boy?"

"A history?" Right. "They've made my life hell for the better part of high school."

"In what way?"

The thought of explaining the particulars to a woman who looks like she could be a Victoria's Secret model is too mortifying to contemplate. "They made comments. Posted shit online."

"Prior to the attack, had Shane ever put his hands on you?"

"Not really," I say, because I don't think pinching my muffin top is what she's talking about. "It didn't matter anyway. He was untouchable."

Cara's eyes narrow. "Because his father is a judge?"

I nod. "That's how he got away with all the DUIs and drug stuff," I say. "The only reason he lost his license the last time was because he drove through a Dunkin' Donuts. Literally. Like through the front door, not the drive-thru. There was no way to hide it."

"You're right. Michael Mayfield may be a housing-court judge, but he's still very well connected in the criminal court system. That's our biggest problem. He's hell bent on seeing you prosecuted and he's going to use every last one of those connections to see that it happens."

"Can he do that?"

She sighs. "He's going to try. If it was anybody less connected I would say no, but he's got an army of influential friends to call on. I want you to know, though, that this isn't like TV. You're not going to prison next week. You're not going at all if I have anything to say about it, but this is still going to be a process. A fairly long, tedious process."

The thought of prison sends a wave of fear through me. If I can't even tolerate this little cell in this empty room, there's no way I'll survive actual prison. I see the toilet just beyond Cara and have to fight down another rush of panic. Is that how they are in prison? Out in the open?

I force my eyes back to Cara's face. "How can they even charge me with murder when he's the one who attacked me?" I ask. "Aren't there laws about self-defense? This shouldn't even be happening."

"I know, and there are laws, but it's complicated. They're most likely going to argue that you used excessive force and intentionally planned to kill him."

"I had to kill him," I say, punching down at the cot. I accidentally knock the crutches that are leaning on the bed and the crash echoes like an exclamation point. "Why can't anyone see that? He was going to kill me if I didn't save myself!"

Her sharp eyes turn on me. "I know that, but you absolutely need to stop saying it like that. I'm getting transcripts of your interviews, but Mellers already told me that you made similar statements at the hospital. I understand that it's true, and there is no part of me that faults you for what you did—hell, girl, I applaud you—but saying it that way is going to hurt your case. That's a fact. This isn't about truth anymore. It's about perception and the interpretation of facts," she says. "I understand this is overwhelming—"

I snort, not looking at her. "You understand nothing."

She doesn't say anything for a long time.

"Do you know why I'm here?" she finally asks. "Did Maria explain why she called me and why I volunteered?"

I shake my head.

"My sister was killed by her husband when I was your age. He was a cop. He got away with it," she says, steel behind each word.

"So now you defend killers?" I can't imagine why.

"No," she says. "I'm not a defense lawyer. I'm a human rights lawyer. But after my sister's murder I saw firsthand how the justice system can work in favor of those who are politically connected. You are the victim in this case, and I won't let you get railroaded for doing something I only wish my sister had been able to do."

I'm speechless.

"Maria isn't from here," Cara continues. "She's from Somerville. She was friends with my sister. That's why she called me. This kind of case is why I went into law."

18

True to her word, Cara has me out in time for dinner. She drops me at the door with instructions to get some rest. My arraignment is at eight thirty the next morning and we need to be early.

I'm surprised to find my mother sitting at the table with the laptop open and a nearly empty glass of white wine beside it. There are two black plastic to-go containers from the restaurant on the counter and I wonder why she even bothered leaving early.

"Do you have any idea what you've put me through today?" she asks, closing the laptop harder than necessary.

I almost want to call Cara to take me back to jail. "What about what I've been through?"

"I had to put the house up for collateral just to get you out," she continues as if I hadn't spoken. She sounds as tired as I feel, which doesn't seem fair. "We could lose the house over this. I could lose the restaurant."

"Well, we wouldn't want to risk the precious restaurant," I say, but I didn't know that was even a possibility. The sudden pressure of feeling responsible for our impending homelessness is more than I can take. "It's not like I got arrested on purpose."

"It doesn't change the fact, though." She heaves a sigh and

drains the rest of her wine. "Did you really have to fight with that boy? Couldn't you have just, I don't know, run?"

I don't feel attached to my own body. "You have no idea what you're talking about." I'm not yelling and somehow that unnerves me. "I got arrested for saving my life today. I didn't see you at all. Not once. A lawyer had to drive me home. Not once have you asked me how I'm doing. Not once. I get that there was bail and that sucks, but you know what, Mom? This sucks so much more for me than it does for you. So much more. You have no fucking idea."

"Well, I might if you told me anything," she says, but she knows we don't have that kind of relationship. She's not Dad.

I shake my head and scan the kitchen for my phone. It's still on the counter where I left it a lifetime ago before the cops showed up to rip my life apart. I shove it into the pocket of my hoodie.

"Don't even think about inviting anyone over," she says as I turn to go.

I stop, glare at her. "You leave me to rot in a goddamn jail cell and now you want to stop me from seeing the few people who actually care about me? How is that fair, Mom?"

"Cecelia, I have had enough to deal with today without having a house full of teenagers right now," she says. "And I still have to figure out coverage for the restaurant so I can deal with the court tomorrow. It's not like I have a lot of people who can fill in."

"Well, I'm sorry for being such an inconvenience to you." If I stay in this kitchen for one more minute I'm going to take my crutches and smash everything. She doesn't try to stop me from going upstairs.

Locked in my room I see my phone is flooded with texts and missed calls from the faction. I don't bother reading them and open a new group text. There's no subtle way to break this news.

ME: **Got arrested. Spent the day in jail. For real. How was you guys' day?**

FINN: **WTF?????**

LYS: **Coming over right now**

ASH: **OMG R U OK???**

ASH: **Coming over 2**

ME: **Mom says no company**

LYS: **My house then**

ASH: **K**

FINN: **Seel ill pick you up**

I hesitate.

Barely.

ME: **K.**

Finn lives only a few minutes away, so instead of wrapping my head I just put on the eye patch that Dr. Vern sent home with me. I can hear Mom moving around in the bathroom and I bump down the stairs without having to see her and am outside before she notices.

Finn already has the door open and I drop into the backseat of his low-slung car.

"I can't wait till I can ride in a car like a normal person," I say as I arrange the crutches on the floor.

"Dude, I can't believe you were the first one to get arrested!

Lyssa owes me ten bucks," Finn says triumphantly. "She bet I'd be the first."

"You guys are idiots," I say, but I'm glad we can joke around about it.

Ashlyn lives one street over from Lyssa and is already waiting on the porch with her when we get there. They both come over to help me out, and by help I mean watch uselessly while I extricate myself.

"The eye patch is a good look," Lyssa says as we make our way slowly toward the house. "Really gotta get on that parrot thing, though."

I show her an unladylike finger.

Lyssa's fathers are standing in the doorway, watching our odd procession. They both hug me when I come in and I'm surprised by how okay I am with it. Not for the first time I wish they were my parents too. They adopted Lyssa just before her thirteenth birthday, after she had bounced around foster homes for much of her life, and I'm grateful beyond words to them for bringing her to Amesford and into my life. It's not something she talks about a lot, but I know she chose them as much as they chose her and it shows in the love that permeates their house.

"Seelie, if there's anything we can do, you let us know," Peter Arroyo—Pop, to Lyssa—says after he lets me go.

"Thanks," I say, relaxing. Standing here in Lyssa's living room with her parents and the faction feels more like home than anything I just left.

"Lyssa told us you got arrested today," Rick Dante—Dad—says. Concern fills his handsome face.

I nod, feeling my ears burn. I don't want them to see me as Lyssa's friend who got arrested. I like it here too much.

"That's a travesty," he says, shaking his head. "After all you've been through. Do you need a lawyer? I can talk to the law school for some recommendations if you want."

Lyssa's dads are both college professors—engineering and history. This is not the land of stupid people.

"That's okay," I say. "I have one. She seems good."

The adults nod. From the kitchen, a kettle whistles.

"Tea? Cocoa?" Peter offers, moving to silence it.

I nod, glad to be swept up in the normal domesticity of Lyssa's house. She might make fun of her parents for being such happy homemakers, but I secretly love it, and I know she does too. We pile into the kitchen and start pulling out mugs and cocoa packets and marshmallows. Finn rifles through the overflowing pantry and emerges with a box of oatmeal-cream pies and peanut butter Oreos. Armed with ample sugary sustenance, we retreat to Lyssa's room.

I weave my way around piles of discarded clothes and comic books to the futon that's tucked beneath Lyssa's towering loft bed. The place is a disaster, as always. The squat dresser is littered with more hair products than I can name, mostly left over from last year's questionable foray into multicolored Mohawk spikes.

The drafting table in the corner is the only island of order in the room. Pens and markers stand at attention in wire-mesh cups, and various-sized pads of paper are neatly lined up on shelves below. A single pad lies centered on the table, closed, but bookmarked with a pencil. Tacked to the wall are completed drawings and graphic-novel panels, including one where the four of us star as a band of renegade space pirates.

"What the hell happened?" Lyssa asks as she shuts the door. The mirror on the back of the door is plastered with so many band stickers you can barely see yourself. My kind of mirror.

I settle onto the black futon and haul Shoebox, Lyssa's sleepy white dog, to my side. He lays his big Shepherd head on my uninjured thigh and I rest my mug on his wide skull. I love Shooby because he looks like a mistake: big-dog body, little-bitty Corgi legs.

"I don't even know," I say.

"What were you arrested for?" Ashlyn asks tentatively.

"Murder."

Finn chokes on his Oreo.

"Are you fucking serious?" Lyssa explodes.

"Yup," I say, too tired to muster the same outrage.

"How is that legal?" Finn sputters, spewing Oreo crumbs everywhere. "It was self-defense."

"It's complicated. So says my lawyer anyway."

"But you're not going to jail?" Ashlyn asks.

"Bailed out. My mom's being a massive bitch about it too."

"She needs to get over herself," Lyssa says, full lips curling in disgust.

"It's fine," I say. "It's how she is. I can deal."

"Yeah, but you shouldn't have to," she says. "It's like she's trying to make it harder."

"I know. I have to be arraigned tomorrow. Don't even know if she's going."

"What happens there?" Ashlyn asks.

"I don't really know, other than I get formally charged. They want to charge me as an adult."

Her eyes widen in shock. "They can't do that!"

"They actually can," Finn says. "Depends on the crime and the prosecutors. They've tried kids younger than us as adults before."

"He's right," I say. "The lawyer said they might try to put me back in jail until the trial, but she said she won't let that happen."

"You believe her?" Lyssa asks.

"I think so. She seems to know what she's doing."

"You can afford her?" Finn asks.

"Pro bono. I guess I'm kind of her cause."

"Probably just doing it for the publicity," Lyssa says bitterly.

"Maybe. But it doesn't matter. Finn's right. It's not like we have the money to pick someone different and I really do think she's going to help."

As I say it, I realize how much I hope I'm right.

19

I scan the lower parking lot, searching for Cara's silver car or the blue umbrella she said she'd be carrying. There's no way I'm walking into that courthouse without her, especially not with the news trucks I saw parked out front.

The bottom lot is nearly empty and was chosen as a meeting point precisely for that reason. It's obscured from the front of the courthouse by a hill and a long flight of steps. Cara said that would give us a chance to gather ourselves before going in, but I'm dreading the long walk on crutches. In the driver's seat, Peter sips coffee from a Styrofoam Dunkin' Donuts cup and scrolls through his phone. The wipers chase the drizzle dripping down the windshield.

"We're all here, you know," Lyssa says, twisting around to face me from the front seat. "Ash and her mom are coming and so is Finn. You can do this."

I don't say anything. My stomach is folding itself into a complex origami of fear.

My mom didn't feel the need to bring me herself. She needed to go into the restaurant early to make sure all the prep lists were right or something. At least that's what she told Peter when they spoke last night. I know it's for the best.

I fell asleep on Lyssa's futon the night before and no one bothered to move me. I'm grateful for that. With Shoebox's long body pressed against my side and Lyssa snoring above me, I made it through the night without having to do a million lock checks. Despite the nightmares, it was the most rest I've had since the attack.

When I woke I had a long text from Cara detailing what to wear and where to meet. Her style choices aren't making me feel any better about my situation.

Cara asked for a skirt and I hate skirts with a fiery passion. I have blindingly white legs and knees that look like fat alien faces. No one needs to see that. Besides, the only skirt I own is the one I wore to Dad's funeral and I don't like the implication of that. My leg brace screams for attention below the lace hem.

But the hardest part isn't the skirt. It's my face. Cara insisted that I keep my hair back and make no attempt to hide my injuries. The green-and-purple ghosts of bruises still linger under my eye and around my throat. (**No turtlenecks**, Cara's text said. **Let them see what he did.**) My hair is scraped up into a high bun and the eye patch is giving the leg brace a run for its money in the "Who's More Conspicuous" contest.

"That's her," I say, spotting Cara walking beneath a blue-and-white umbrella toward the courthouse. She has on a chocolate-brown pantsuit with a blue blouse, and yup, blue heels.

Lyssa flings her door open and gets out, calling her over. I try very hard to get out of the backseat without flashing anyone.

Peter holds an umbrella out as I right myself and, before I can think, I wrap my arms around him.

"Thank you for doing this," I say, letting go quickly. My face flushes. "It means a lot."

"Seelie, you know we love you like our own," Peter says. "Rick wanted to be here too, but he's hosting a guest speaker and the dean would have his head if he wasn't there. We're with you every step of the way through this."

"Anything for a day off from school," Lyssa says with a grin as she hands me my crutches.

"Good morning," Cara says as she joins us. "Where's your mother?"

"She'll be along," Peter answers and introduces himself.

Cara nods and looks me over. "You look good. Maybe less black next time, but good."

I'm about to protest that the black cardigan is over a very not-black gray top, but she doesn't give me time.

"Let's walk and talk," she says, setting a pace I have to work to match on the crutches. "Seelie, I know this is overwhelming, but the good news for you today is you don't actually have to say anything. In fact, I'm ordering you not to say anything. Not in court and especially not to the media."

The thought of being on the news makes my stomach roil.

"I'll be frank," Cara says, as if she's ever anything but. "You're a middle-class white girl being charged with murder as an adult. The media is going to be all over this, and all over you. I need you to ignore them. No matter what. After yesterday's story everyone will want to score an interview."

"What story yesterday?" I ask.

Lyssa scowls. "Nothing," she says, practically biting the word in half. "Don't worry about it."

"This is already a sensational case," Cara says, slowing so I can make my way up the steps leading from the parking lot to the front entrance. I'm getting pretty good at stairs but Lyssa and Peter still hover behind me like they're going to save us all if I tumble into them. "We're going to try to use that to our advantage, but right now they're all looking for an angle."

As we climb, the courthouse looms into view and with it comes the sight of the journalists crowded near the entrance. As we top the final step, the dozens of cameras turn almost as one, flashes bursting like lightning in the gray morning. Reporters with microphones and pocket recorders swarm us, shouting questions. Panic blooms in my throat as they close in.

"Back the fuck off!" Lyssa shouts, throwing her arms out and pushing through the crowd. Her long black coat billows out behind her, and combined with her supermodel height and recovering goth hair, she's dramatic enough to get their attention off me for a moment. Cara and Peter hustle me through the distracted crowd.

Once inside the vestibule, Cara considers Lyssa while she and Peter fold up their umbrellas.

"That was decidedly not the media angle I was going for," she says sternly. "But it is what it is."

Lyssa ignores her, her hands grabbing angry clawfuls of air by her sides. "Are you okay?" she asks me.

I nod, but I'm shaking. I wasn't expecting that. At all.

Compared to the scene outside, the inside of the courthouse is almost comforting in its hush. We wait in line to pass through the metal detector. I have to go around the scanner and the bored-looking guard waves a wand over me while my crutches go through the X-ray machine alone, like they might be covert ninja weapons.

Cara leads us to a small conference room with no windows where she walks me through what's going to happen. Peter texts my mother but gets no reply.

"Finn and Ash are here," Lyssa says when her phone chirps. She rolls her eyes. "Finn set off the metal detector three times."

"Of course he did," I say, but I'm just relieved that they got here on time. A clock, identical to the ones at school, ticks ominously from high on the wall.

When the hands mark eight thirty we hear a deep voice announce, "First call!" and the rustling of bodies moving.

"That's our signal," Cara says.

I'm liquefied by fear.

"I don't want to do this," I say.

"I know, but you have to," Cara says gently.

"It's okay," Lyssa says. "Just keep breathing."

Peter squeezes my shoulders and opens the door.

We file out, Cara, Lyssa, then me. Peter follows, letting the door close with a soft hydraulic whoosh. I nearly collide with Lyssa, who's slammed to a sudden stop.

Then I see why.

We're face-to-face with Trevor Mayfield.

20

"You bitch," Trevor growls.

Lyssa plants herself in front of me. "Get away from her," she says, voice barely audible beneath the weight of threat.

He leans around her. "You killed my brother," he says, stabbing a finger at me. He's in an impeccable navy suit, hair carefully combed to look like it's not, but his eyes are bloodshot and haggard. "You fucking bitch, you killed my brother!"

Lyssa shoves him away and the procession into the courtroom slows as people turn to look at us. Whispered comments don't quite make it to my brain, but I can't miss someone's excited, "Ooh, they gonna fight!"

The two security guards leave their posts at the metal detector, shouting, "That's enough! You want to be banned from the courtroom?"

They get between Lyssa and Trevor, but Trevor tries to push through them, still shouting at me. "You're going to fry for this! You fucking bitch!"

"Okay, you're done," one guard says as they both grab Trevor by the arms. "Let's go."

They haul him away as he continues to scream at me. I stare

at the floor, cheeks burning. If it weren't for my crutches there's no way my legs would have kept me upright. Peter is saying something to Lyssa and Cara is saying something to me but none of it penetrates. My world is the black-and-white speckled tile beneath my feet. Something I never expected to feel washes over me.

Guilt.

"Cecelia, listen to me," Cara says close to my ear. "Listen to me. This is important. Don't shut down. We have to go in there and you have to hold your head high and remember that you've done nothing wrong. People are watching you. Keep it together."

I nod, but I can't look up. I follow them in, my eyes on the back of their calves. I don't want to see anyone.

We slide into a bench near the back, Cara at the edge. Lyssa nudges me and gestures. Finn, Ashlyn, and Mrs. Anders are sitting across the aisle. They all smile and give little waves. I raise my fingers back but can't manage the smile. They don't seem to know what just happened. I drop my eyes back to my lap.

"All rise for the Honorable Judge Ballard," a booming voice commands. A wave of people rises around us and I pull myself up along with them, using the back of the bench in front of me. I still can't bring myself to look up but am aware of a robed figure making his way across the courtroom.

"Be seated," the voice says, and we are.

A woman announces that they will begin with arraignments and starts reading quickly through an alphabetical list of names. When she says mine my whole body jerks involuntarily.

"Present with counsel," Cara says, half-standing.

There are only two names after mine and then the proceedings begin. I know I should look up, should pay attention so I know what to do when it's my turn, but I can't. I feel like the entire room has shrunk to the size of my lap, where my hands are clenched together. I can't stop raking my nails into the back of my bottom hand. It's oddly soothing, although Lyssa must find the scratching sound annoying because she silently offers me her own hand instead. I clutch it gratefully. She uses her thumb to trace soothing circles over the red welts I made and I relax a fraction.

In less time than it takes to blink, it's my turn.

"Now calling docket number 74351J, Cecelia Stanton," the clerk announces.

Lyssa gives my hand a tight squeeze and I rise like a zombie to follow Cara to the front of the courtroom. Only now am I aware of sad wood-paneled walls and the sea of people teeming in the church-like benches, all watching as I make my way down the center aisle. My palms are sweaty against the grips of my crutches. Two tables are in front of the judge's bench. Cara and I stand behind the unoccupied one.

"Cecelia Stanton, you are accompanied by counsel, Cara Dewitt, acting on your behalf, is that correct?" the judge asks. His lined face is captured in one of the many painted portraits that hang in heavy gilt frames on the wall behind him.

"Yes, sir," I say. My voice trembles and I'm glad I don't have to look across the crowded room to speak.

"Ms. Stanton, you are being charged by the state of Massachusetts with the crime of murder. It is alleged that you willfully, unlawfully, and intentionally, with malice and forethought, murdered Shane Mayfield on the evening of October twenty-first. How do you plead in the matter?"

"Not guilty," Cara says for me.

"I am entering a plea of not guilty in this matter. I understand the state would like to revisit the issue of bail?"

A man in a black suit stands from the table across from us, saying, "Yes, Your Honor. Given the extreme violence of this crime, the state wishes to remand the defendant into the care of a corrections facility until the time of trial."

I go rigid beside Cara. Not jail. I can't go back to jail.

"Objection," Cara says. "Cecelia is not guilty of the charges being brought against her, as will be shown. She has no criminal record. She is a good student and has ties to the community. She is neither a flight risk nor a danger to herself or others. As you can plainly see, she is in need of medical care that is best received from the doctors already familiar with the extensive injuries she suffered at the hands of Shane Mayfield. She has already experienced enough trauma. There is no need to compound it by locking her up."

I hold my breath as the judge mulls this over.

"I understand this is not a straightforward case and we will leave the matter of guilt or innocence for another day. However, I'm inclined to agree on the other points," he says, then looks at me. "Bail will stand as set, on the condition that you submit to GPS monitoring and return to school as soon as medically feasible."

I nod, relieved. As much as I dread the idea of returning to school, the thought of going back to jail is worse.

"Thank you, Your Honor," Cara says.

"Thank you," I echo.

"Then we will schedule a pretrial conference," the judge says, consulting his calendar. "Is December sixth agreeable to both sides?"

Both lawyers accept the date and Cara takes me up to probation to be fitted with an ELMO monitor. The officer who straps the boxy cuff around my ankle explains that I'm not under house arrest, but that any attempt to remove the device will trigger an immediate police response.

The tracker weighs less than a pound, but it feels like an iron shackle.

21

"I thought that went really well," my mother says with entirely too much enthusiasm. She had slipped into the courtroom after we were seated and completely missed the showdown with Trevor.

I snort. Our attempt to meet in the diner across from the courthouse was thwarted by more reporters, so Cara ended up following us home. I wanted to ride with her, to talk in private, but Mom wouldn't allow it, so instead we drove home in stony silence.

"It went largely as expected," Cara says evenly. I'm glad she doesn't mention Trevor. "Like I told Seelie in the beginning, this is a process. And not a particularly quick one, either."

"What now?" I ask her. I'm tracing the wood grain on the kitchen table and don't look up when I ask. I feel wrong talking about this with my mother here. Like it's not her business.

"Now the state is going to begin gathering their evidence, as will we. It's the state's job to prove that you're guilty beyond any doubt. It's our job to give them that doubt."

"But I'm not guilty," I protest, looking up at her. I'm painfully aware that every single defense client probably says the same thing. "It was self-defense. You're allowed to kill in self-defense!"

"You are, with certain caveats," she agrees. "Which is what we will bring up during the pretrial hearing. There's a chance we can get the charges fully dismissed there and be done with this completely."

"How much of a chance?" I ask. The GPS monitoring bracelet feels heavy around my ankle.

She hesitates. "In a perfect world, that's exactly what would happen. Given the particulars of the people involved, though, I don't want you thinking it's guaranteed."

I nod and go back to tracing patterns on the table. That's what I expected.

"What do we need to do?" Mom asks.

"For now, don't talk to the media. At all. Seelie, I would really encourage you to not even look at what the media reports about this," she says. "But if you must, do not respond. Under any circumstances. You will not win this case on the Internet."

I wonder what's out there that has everyone so worked up.

"The other thing," Cara says, and from her tone I know I'm not going to like this thing. "You need to get back to school. Sooner rather than later."

"That's what I told her," my mother says, smug with vindication.

I don't say anything and this apparently says everything.

"Trials are won and lost on image," Cara says gently. "We need to show the court that you're trying to pick up the pieces of your life after being attacked. That you're not giving up. We have a better chance of getting the charges dismissed if we show that you're just a normal girl, doing normal-girl things."

"I want to talk to Cara alone," I say after a long silence, not raising my eyes from the table.

"Anything you have to tell her you can say in front of me," Mom says.

"Alone," I repeat.

"Ms. Stanton, perhaps it may be best—" Cara starts, but Mom cuts her off.

"Call me Rebecca. And really, there's no reason she should be shutting me out," Mom says.

I push back from the table. "Whatever. It doesn't matter. I'll call you," I tell Cara as I get up.

"Seelie, you did good today," she says, touching my hand as I go by.

Then why do I feel so awful?

//

In my room, I open my laptop and pull up the news. Might as well make this day even worse.

Once again, I top the "Most Read" section of links, but this time my mug shot is there at the top of the website for everyone to see. My whole body starts shaking. Maybe I don't want to see this.

Maybe I have to.

I force myself to click the link.

AMESFORD TEEN CHARGED IN DEATH OF SHANE MAYFIELD

Brandy Alves, *Union News*

This story contains updated information

Seventeen-year-old Cecelia Stanton of Ranier Street, Amesford, has been charged with murder following the death of former high-school star athlete Shane Mayfield, 20. Mayfield was killed on October 21. An autopsy revealed that Mayfield died as a result of blunt-force trauma to the head. Toxicology reports indicate that Mayfield, who has a history of substance-abuse problems, was under the influence of marijuana and PCP at the time of his death.

Mayfield's death was originally believed to have been a result of self-defense as Stanton suffered multiple serious injuries the night the incident occurred. She was treated and released from Harrington Hospital prior to her arrest. A source who wishes to remain anonymous attests that Stanton did indeed kill Mayfield only after being brutally attacked and is being "railroaded" by the prosecution.

Despite the seriousness of the charges, Stanton is free on bail, a decision that is not popular with Mayfield's family. Mayfield's mother, Brenda Mayfield, 46, told reporters "[Stanton] is a monster. She killed my son and should be locked up. My boy is gone; she has no right to be free."

Cara Dewitt, attorney for Stanton, released a statement saying she "understand[s] that this is a difficult time for the Mayfields, but it is also a difficult time for my client. Cecelia Stanton was the victim of a violent crime. She should be focused on healing, not fighting for her freedom."

Stanton is due back in court in December.

Below the article are 351 comments. I feel sick.

RealParent: Praying for both of these families

elemental: ahahaha sexy mugshot!! Ugly cow

Venomly: so becuz he was high it was ok to kill him?

413_abu: Way to go MA. Real criminals walk free but we're charging this poor girl with murder?? Srsly??

> **Code3:** She killed someone. Which makes her a MURDERER!

> **413_abu:** Clear case of self defense

> **Code3:** Were u there? U have proof?

> **413_abu:** Look at her injuries!

> **Code3:** so he fought back, good for him

Bannigon: The 90s called—they want their drug back lol

SoxFan63: That poor child. Look at her face. There is more to this story than we know

AnonyMouse: I hope they don't let her off just because she's a chick

Neolantic: What an animal

TMayfield: She's a murderer. She killed my brother then took selfies before she called the cops. She staged her injuries. It's all fake. You can see it here.

> **AnonyMouse:** WHAT!!! That's messed up!!

> **WildCatsGO:** Wtf

> **Bradf:** who does that??

elemental: surprised she didn't break the camera with that face!

Picknotu: I think she looks good in red

My stomach knots when I see the next comments are from Lyssa. The thought of her reading this makes me hot with shame.

Lyssanthrope: Take it down. You have no idea what you're talking about.

TMayfield: Screw you. People deserve to see what an animal she is.

Lyssanthrope: You're despicable. To everyone reading this and supporting this freak of nature, know this: Seelie Stanton is innocent. She is not a murderer. Shane messed with the wrong person when he went after her. He got what he deserved.

TMayfield: That bitch is going to prison for the rest of her life over this. Bitch deserves the death penalty. She should be there now. She's going to wish she was when I get through with her.

[comment deleted by moderator]

Goose bumps break out over all of my body. I click the link in Trevor's comment. It's a photo, as promised. The angle is weird, too low and tilted sharply. Most of the picture is of the tack room, saddle racks and bridles, but on the left-hand side is half my face, awash with blood. Panic makes a hornet's nest around my heart. I must have snapped a picture when I was using the camera as a mirror.

But how does Trevor have it?

22

Thirty-four days.

That's how long I manage to avoid school before the planets of Momthulu, Cara, and Jacqui, my dreadfully optimistic physical therapist, all align to usher in the end of days.

I've been surprisingly good about completing the epic piles of work Ashlyn brings home for me because really, there's not much else to do. I can binge-watch Netflix with the best of them, but there's still been enough time for homework. Anything that keeps my brain too busy to remember is good, even math. I think I convinced myself that if I kept doing the work that was delivered to me then I would never have to go back.

But no.

If I'm honest, the timing could've been worse. With Thanksgiving break already done, I have only a couple weeks to get through until Christmas vacation, but that's a small consolation as I stand before my closet, my stomach tying itself into a hangman's noose.

It doesn't matter what I wear. I know that. The only thing anyone is going to be able to see is the mess of my face and the blood on my hands.

I pull a *Supernatural* T-shirt on over a black thermal and dark jeans. I can wear jeans now that I don't have the leg brace to contend with. Little victories.

I slide my feet into the galaxy-print Converse Lyssa painted for me as a Christmas gift last year, happy that at least she'll be here soon with Ashlyn and Finn. We're all riding together today, like a cavalry going into battle.

I don't know what to do about my face. With no eye patch to break it up anymore, the scar looks miles long. I'm regretting not taking Ashlyn up on her offer for makeup lessons. I try brushing my disobedient curls over the bad side of my face, but I can't get them to cover the scar without looking stupid.

In the end, I just run out of time. My phone dings with a text from Ashlyn. **Two min**, it says. I give myself one last glare in the mirror and grab my cane. Jacqui insisted it was a necessary last step between crutches and freedom, but it makes me feel as awkward as the walker did in the hospital.

I'm putting on my coat when I hear the blast of Lyssa's horn. I swing my backpack over my shoulder and go out to meet them, exceedingly glad my mother has already left for the restaurant and isn't here to see me off. Mrs. Markham watches me from her porch, the ever-present baby sling wrapped around her like a boa constrictor. I ignore her.

Ashlyn and Finn are in the back and the passenger door stands open for me. I throw my backpack and cane in and use the oh-shit handle to haul myself up.

"Ready?" Lyssa asks as I pull the door shut.

"Not even a little bit."

"It won't be that bad," Ashlyn says, passing me a muffin

wrapped in a paper towel. "Here. My mom made them. They're really good."

There's no way I could possibly eat it. Not when my belly is already so full of nerves. I put it in the cup holder and Finn immediately reaches forward to grab it.

"I'll take it," he says.

"You already had two," Ashlyn says.

"They're good!"

The drive to school is short. Too short. I don't have enough time to steel myself.

"Drive around," I say as Lyssa's about to turn into the seniors' parking lot. Being a grade above the rest of us, she gets to park in the lot closest to school. My palms are sweating. "I'm not ready."

She nods and drives by the lot. Everyone is quiet. Buses disgorge their swarming passengers near the front of the building and I don't know if I can walk among them.

We follow the long road leading to the junior parking lot and then off school property.

"I can't do it," I say.

"So we'll keep driving," Lyssa says with a shrug. "Fuck it."

"You can totally do this," Ashlyn says, ignoring Lyssa. "It'll be okay, really."

"Plus you need to do it for the lawyer," Finn reminds me, like I need reminding. Like I don't know exactly why I'm doing this.

I punch the dashboard. Twice. Then I drop my ruined face into my hands with a growl.

"Your call," Lyssa says softly, only to me.

"Just go back," I say, not raising my head. "I don't think I have a choice."

She drives slowly back to the school and by the time we park, the buses are gone. At least there's that.

Finn comes around to help me down, help I embarrassingly need, and we make our way to the building. Every step is harder than the last and it has nothing to do with the ache in my thigh. Lyssa holds the door for us and crossing that threshold is one of the hardest things I've ever had to do.

The front hall is a teeming mess of people.

My heartbeat thunders in my ears and I know my cheeks are scarlet. I look down, paralyzed.

"C'mon," Lyssa says, breaking the spell and tugging me forward. Finn and Ashlyn flank us as whispers erupt behind cupped hands all across the hall.

"Hey there, Scarface!" someone shouts and people snicker. "Say hello to my leetle friend!"

Lyssa whirls, zeroing in on the voice. I reach for her sleeve to stop her, but it's like I'm moving through quicksand. She already has Ryan Leland, a lanky varsity hockey player in an orange Wildcats jacket, shoved up against the locker, Finn at her heels.

"If you ever so much as look at her again, I will give you a matching one," Lyssa snarls, pushing Ryan higher up the locker. The boy's toes are barely on the ground. Laughter and catcalls tear through the crowd as students form a loose semi-circle around them, phones out in hope of catching a boy get his ass handed to him by a girl.

Mr. Baker, the vice principal, comes barreling through the crowd, barking in his best drill-sergeant voice to clear out. Lyssa drops Ryan and backs off with her hands up. Her glare keeps Ryan pinned to the lockers.

"Leland, what are you starting this early in the morning?" Mr. Baker demands, getting as close to Ryan as Lyssa was a second before. He's ex-Army, but still has the attitude. He points at Lyssa. "And I expect better from you. Get to class."

As Ryan sputters about his innocence, the shrill peal of the warning bell hurries us along.

"Don't get in trouble for me," I say. "It's not worth it."

"It's the very definition of worth it," Lyssa says, still seething.

"Bunch of fucking animals," Finn mutters, shaking his head. The strange thing is, before the world went to hell, Finn actually liked Ryan. They were lab partners and, in true Finn form, got along swimmingly. Finn has always gotten on swimmingly with everyone.

"What did you expect to happen?" I ask them, caustic tears burning my eyes. "That I'd be welcomed back with open arms? On what fucking planet? These people didn't like me before this happened, they're certainly not going to like me any better now."

No one says anything to this. They can't, because it's too true.

23

There are more stares and whispers as we make our way to our lockers and I know with devastating certainty that I should've lobbied harder for homeschooling, or online classes, or anything other than this gauntlet.

My eyes are on the ground, watching where I'm placing my cane so it's the puddle I notice first, not the word.

"What the fuck," Lyssa curses, and I know she's seen it too. That everyone has.

Scrawled down the dull-orange door of my locker, in dripping scarlet letters, is the word *MURDERER*. I touch the *M* as the first-period bell shrieks and my finger comes away red. It's fresh. The hall empties around us, but all I can do is stare at the paint pooled like blood at my feet.

An explosion of sound makes me jump, and I almost drop my cane. The echo of clanging metal doesn't completely fade before detonating again. Lyssa drives her fist into some kid's locker over and over until the metal buckles under the force and her blood leaves red splotches on that locker too.

"I'm going to kill whoever did this," she says and I know in that moment she means it.

"Hey, the rage-monster routine isn't helping," Finn says, but his voice is tight.

Ashlyn fishes her phone out of her pocket and snaps a couple photos of my locker.

"It's evidence," she says. "Of harassment. You need to show it to your lawyer."

"Forget the lawyer. We're going to find out who did this," Lyssa promises, chest heaving. "And they're going to pay."

"It doesn't matter," I snap. "Nothing matters. This is my life now."

"It matters! This—" Lyssa stabs a bleeding finger at my locker "—is not okay."

"What are you going to do?" I ask. My lips twist in a rictus of rage, and tears are making her blurry. I don't know why I'm suddenly so furious at her. "Beat up the entire school? Punch more lockers? For what? You can't fix this!"

Lyssa's eyes harden and she nods, just once, her face an unreadable mask. Before she can say anything, Mr. Baker comes storming down the corridor.

"Ms. Dante-Arroyo, what's the problem now?" he says, bearing down on Lyssa.

"Someone vandalized Seelie's locker," Ashlyn says, stepping forward and pointing.

Mr. Baker actually looks startled when he sees the locker. He runs a hand over his gleaming head. He looks at me for a long time and then sighs.

"Get to class," he says. "All of you. Now. We'll get this cleaned up."

"What about the person who did it?" Finn asks.

"Go to class," Baker repeats.

"That's not right, though!" Finn says.

"Administration will look into it," Baker says, tone hardening. "Get to class."

"C'mon, let's just go," Ashlyn says, trying to keep some peace. She touches my arm and I flinch involuntarily. I'm still too keyed up. "You can share my book."

We all have English first period: Finn, Ashlyn, and I together, Lyssa one hall over with the senior teacher. Lyssa walks with us to our room, then peels off without a word.

Mrs. Givens is a big fan of group learning and has the desks arranged in pods of four. Luckily she also believes in letting you choose your own group, so the three of us are at a pod with Lynette, a quiet, gawky girl who is completely smitten with Finn. I cast a look around at the other pods and almost collapse with relief. There's an empty seat at the pod in the back corner and I make it all the way to the end of morning announcements thankful for this small reprieve.

The feeling lasts only until Mrs. Givens finishes taking roll, when the door swings opens and Trevor Mayfield walks in to claim the vacant desk.

"What is she doing here?" he demands, slinging his backpack onto his desk from halfway across the room.

"Trevor, take your seat and be quiet," Mrs. Givens orders, giving him the hairy eyeball. She has one of the best mean teacher looks in the building, despite not actually being all that mean. She's just serious. Plus she gets badass points for being the only teacher with a visible tattoo—an open book, high on her arm, with the words *There are other worlds than these* flying from the pages.

"I'm not sharing a room with a murderer," Trevor says.

I stare at my desk, eyes tracing years' worth of names and curses on its surface. My cheeks burn. Everything about this day is a mistake.

"Trevor, you're welcome to go discuss this with Guidance," Mrs. Givens says firmly, moving to stand in front of him. "But we're about to begin class. I have no time for your histrionics."

"This is bullshit," he spits. "She's—"

"A student of this class as much as you are and has a right to an education as much as you do," Mrs. Givens says. "I will not have you interfering with my class."

"Fuck this," he says, snatching his bag off the desk. "I don't need this shit."

"There will be a write-up for the language, Mr. Mayfield," Mrs. Givens says coolly as he stalks out of the room.

He doesn't need this?

He doesn't?

Molten fury radiates through me but I don't look up. Mrs. Givens starts in on a lecture about dramatic irony that I barely hear as I stew on Trevor's words. He doesn't need this? He should be apologizing to me for what a monster his brother was, not painting filth on my locker. And now that I've seen him I have no doubt that his hand was behind that nastiness. No doubt at all. Maybe he thought I wouldn't show up to a class I knew he was in.

Maybe I shouldn't have.

"Keeping in mind the definition of dramatic irony," Mrs.

Givens goes on, "I would like you all to turn to page 238. Avery, would you like to read?"

Avery is a theater kid and amazing at doing different voices. She does the most reading out loud in class. "'Lamb to the Slaughter,'" she begins. "By Roald Dahl."

What she reads is evidence that I am dreaming.

I must be.

There's no way Mrs. Givens is this sadistic.

The story is about a devoted, pregnant housewife, who, upon hearing that her detective husband is leaving her, bludgeons him to death with the frozen leg of lamb she was planning to make for dinner. Instead of confessing, she cooks the lamb and feeds it to the investigating police, who never suspect a thing.

An awkward silence cloaks the room as Avery reads the last line. I can feel eyes on me, although I don't look up. I want to die.

"That's awesome," a kid in the pod across from us blurts out. "That would be, like, a perfect murder."

"It's usually the most popular short story in the unit," Mrs. Givens says and she either doesn't notice the tension filling the rest of the room or she doesn't care.

Or maybe it's only at my pod.

She begins handing out charts. "I would like each member of your group to come up with a different example of dramatic irony that Dahl uses in the story and explain its significance to your group. Each group needs at least four examples, even if they're missing group members."

As groups start discussing the assignment, Finn shoots a look at me across the desk. "Well, that was fucked up."

"No kidding," Ashlyn says, eyes wide. "I can't believe she picked that story."

Poor Lynette sits there without comment, filling out the first spot on her irony chart and probably wishing she had picked a different pod back in September.

"This is not my best day ever," I say. Understatement doesn't begin to cover it.

As we wrap up our charts, Mrs. Givens announces she wants a one-page reading response for homework. Several people groan.

"It's one page of your own thoughts. If you don't have a single page of thoughts, then you have a problem with your brain being missing," she says. There's laughter. "We'll be continuing with this story for the rest of the week, so make sure you have your books with you in class."

Students begin gathering their stuff in anticipation of the bell that rings moments later.

"Seelie, a word, please?" Mrs. Givens requests as people file out of the room.

Finn and Ashlyn hesitate. I'm not in art with them next period and I don't want to make them late. "Just go," I say. "It's fine."

They do, but I can see their reluctance and it makes me feel oddly cared for.

This must be Mrs. Givens's prep period because no students come in from the hall.

"I just wanted to let you know how happy I am to have you back in class, and to check in with how you were doing," Mrs. Givens says, sitting on the desk across from where I'm standing.

"Uh, fine," I say awkwardly. I'm not sure what she wants from me.

"Was the story too much for you?"

I shrug. "Kind of a weird choice, I guess."

"I considered taking it off the syllabus," she admits. "But to be honest, I thought you could handle it. Too often we teach stories that have no connection to real life, especially for high schoolers. But literature is supposed to make us feel something, even something unpleasant. It's a sign of life."

It mostly made me feel sick and sort of surreal, but I don't say that.

"If you find this week's assignments are too emotional for you, please let me know. We can find you alternatives, but I hope you stick it out."

I can't tell if she's completely crazy or completely sincere. The scary part is I think it's the latter. Or maybe they're the same thing.

"One more thing," she says, handing me a slip of paper from her neat desk. "Mr. Banville would like you to stop by today to discuss how things are going."

I glance at the sheet without really reading it. Mr. Banville is the school psychologist and has the indubitable honor of being the only person I've ever seen with more hair in his nose than on his head. There's no way I'm telling him anything. "That's okay," I say. "I'm already seeing someone."

She regards me for a minute and I feel the heat of the lie spread up my neck.

"It's important to talk through these sorts of things," she says.

She doesn't even know what sorts of things she's referring to.

"I know. I am." It's not a total lie. I have the faction and that counts.

"You should stop by his office anyway. It might be worth discussing a schedule change so you don't have to worry about a repeat of this morning's outburst," she says. "And my door is always open. I'm happy to listen any time you want to talk. I know coming back must be tough on you."

She has no idea.

She writes me a late pass and I hobble through empty halls toward psychology. I'm almost ten minutes late by the time I get there, late enough that I almost don't go in. But Mr. Lynch catches my eye through the narrow rectangle of glass in the door and I don't have a choice.

Psychology is a junior/senior elective taught in a biology room and instead of desks we have high lab benches. Everyone, mostly seniors, stares in silence as I hand Lynch my pass and head to one of the back tables.

The table I share with Lyssa.

Lynch goes back to discussing Maslow and when I sit down Lyssa doesn't look at me, just keeps sketching on the edge of her notebook.

My heart clenches like a fist.

Lyssa's knuckles are swollen and still crusted with remnants of dried blood. The middle one juts out above the others like a wretched bruising mountain, but her pen moves in sharp, stabbing strokes across the page. It must ache.

The tall stools are viciously uncomfortable and I have to

prop my leg on the support bar running across the front of the table. I pull my notebook out and flip to a blank page.

I'm sorry I yelled at you, I write.

She's not looking. Maybe she thinks I'm taking notes.

I put my pen down and reach across for her hand. I can't help it. She stops drawing as I carefully touch her broken skin. She doesn't look at me, but stills her fingers and opens her hand flat, letting me see. I brush my fingertips across the scraped flesh and my heart contracts again. I have to resist an overwhelming urge to bring her battered knuckles to my lips. Instead, I pick up her pen and write on her notebook the same thing she didn't see on my own: *I'm sorry I yelled at you.*

She takes the pen, writes *I'm sorry*, and freezes, pen poised for words that don't come. She puts an emphatic period at the end of the two words, piercing the page. Then she starts again, in a barely legible rush. *I'm sorry I couldn't protect you.* She scribbles it out. *I'm sorry I CAN'T protect you.* She scribbles that out too. *I'm sorry EVERYTHING is so FUCKED UP.*

I take the pen back before she can cross that out.

Not everything, I write. *Not us.*

24

It takes every ounce of willpower I have ever possessed in my entire stupid life to get myself out the door for school again.

This time it's only Lyssa waiting in the driveway and even though I knew she was coming, I'm still relieved to see her. She's also taking me to physical therapy after school while Ashlyn goes to skate practice and Finn gets into whatever trouble he has planned for the day. I see Mrs. Markham on her porch, wearing her wrinkled kid against her chest, and I abandon my half-formed plan of just telling Lyssa to come in and forget school. Fucking nosy neighbor. I know my mom put her up to this. Secondhand parenting at its finest.

The passenger door swings open as I approach and I lever myself in.

"I hate everything," I announce before I'm even buckled up.

"Understandable," Lyssa says, nonplussed. She nods at a steaming travel mug in the console. "Peanut butter cocoa. Heavy on the peanut butter."

My stomach feels like it's eating holes in itself, but I pick up the cocoa anyway. "Okay, maybe I don't hate cocoa."

"Or me," she says, grinning as she backs out of the driveway.

"Or you."

Finn and Ashlyn are waiting for us at the seniors' parking lot when we pull in, breath fogging in the cold air. Ashlyn bounces on her toes like a manic rainbow sprite, hands tucked into the mittens dangling from a furry, fox-eared hat.

As we approach the main entrance, my stomach heaves and I'm afraid I'm going to lose the cocoa. Sweat prickles the back of my neck and I swallow hard. Fuck. Fuck.

I stop, breathing hard through my nose. I will not be sick, I will not be sick, I will not be sick.

The others realize I'm not with them anymore and turn back.

"Are you okay?" Lyssa asks, looking concerned.

I am.

I will be.

Right?

I nod. The stress is wreaking havoc on my period and I have cramps all the time now, some days worse than others. This is a worse day.

"I just hate this place," I say as the awful feeling recedes.

"Oh, let me count the ways," Lyssa agrees.

Finn holds the door and we go in.

///

Today it almost seems like I'm old news, right up until history.

It happens near the end of the period. Mr. Wilkins never lectures to the bell, because he's more concerned with being friends with his students than actually teaching us anything. This makes the last twenty minutes of class a special brand of hell for me since the demographic of this class skews painfully toward the upper echelons of Amesford's social hierarchy. A group of field hockey and basketball players, the school royalty, make up a solid two-thirds of the class, clustered toward the front of the room, Wilkins's biggest fans. Aside from them, there's a pair of band kids who keep to themselves, and a smattering of semipopular miscreants.

Jason Francone, definitely a miscreant, is Trevor's best friend. More often than not, he sits at the desk next to me and continues what Shane started years ago with whispered comments about how I'm into bestiality because I ride horses and animal cruelty because I'm big when I do it. I hate him with a fiery passion. So when I see him walking over I grit my teeth, prepared for more of the usual. I have my book and headphones and all I have to do is make it to the bell, when I can escape to lunch with Ashlyn and Lyssa.

Today is not the usual, though, because instead of sitting down, Jason smoothly reaches out and swipes my cane. He sticks it between his legs and starts skipping around the room, waving an imaginary lasso over his head. He leaps over a desk, calling, "Ride 'em, cowboy!" and everyone cracks up. Even Wilkins smiles and rolls his eyes at the shenanigans.

I don't acknowledge it. I never do. I glue my eyes to my book, but I'm not reading anymore. From the corner of my eye I can see the band kids looking at me, sympathy thick on their faces, but I ignore them too.

"Jase, you're such an idiot," someone says and I can hear the cruel smile behind the words. That voice belongs to none other than Madison Tierney.

Perfect.

Madison is at the very top of the royal-bitch pyramid, ranking even higher than the senior cool girls. If anyone rules the kingdom of Amesford royalty, it's her. Graced with brains as well as the kind of looks celebrities pay big money for, she's captain of the field hockey team and poised to be valedictorian.

She occupies an impressively high spot on the list of people I despise.

"Jase, you know that's not how you ride a horse," Madison coos and turns to me. "You really have to put your hips into it, right, Seelie?"

More laughter spreads out from the front of the room as Madison does a sexy wiggle.

I'm done.

I put the phone back in my bag and stand up. The room grows quiet.

I know this is going to hurt.

I don't care.

I walk to the front of the room, my limp more pronounced than it is when I have the cane. Every step shoots a deep ache up my thigh but I cling to the pain and it keeps me going.

"That's enough, now," Wilkins says, entirely too late and without anywhere near enough authority.

I stop in front of Jason, who smirks at me, twirling the cane in lazy arcs. "What?" he says, flipping his blond hair out of his eyes with a spastic jerk of his head.

Hulk-like rage courses through me. I want to grab that stupid hair and rip his head clean off. Instead I wrench the cane out of his hand before he can stop me and walk out of the room to a chorus of "Oooohs." I slam the door.

I don't care that there's still six minutes until the bell.

In the empty hall, a sharp sob shreds my throat and echoes down the corridor. No tears come, though, and I'm glad. Adrenaline has left me shaking. Finn is in math at the end of this hall, and I lean against the wall near the door to wait for him. He surprises me by coming around the corner just seconds before the bell.

"Hey," he says, looking flustered. "I was in the library. How was history?"

"Fine," I lie. "Walk me to lunch?"

"Of course."

Finn doesn't have first lunch with us this year because of gym, but half the time he winds up sneaking in for a few minutes to hang out anyway. I know he won't mind if I make him late. He has Ms. Belgrave for gym, a first-year teacher who is defenseless against his southern charm.

The cafeteria is its usual eruption of chaos. Lockers clang and students jockey for position in line, like being the first to get sloppy joes is something worth fighting for.

I have no intention of joining that throng and tell Finn so. He leads the way to our normal table and then stops.

"Wait a sec," he says, holding an arm out to block me.

"What is it?" I ask. Something in his tone has my hackles up.

"Just wait," he repeats, craning his head to scan the crowd. He tries to turn me away, but I slip around him.

And instantly wish I hadn't.

Our table is a mess. Someone printed out copies of my mug

shot and the photo Trevor posted online and papered the round table with them. Long streaks of ketchup shoot across the whole mess.

No, not streaks.

A word.

Killer.

I swallow hard.

"Help me," I say, lunging forward and gathering the soggy pictures into a heap. "Please, Finn, help me get rid of it."

He does. He takes the stack of pictures from me, returning with a damp cloth from the dish lady that he uses to wipe down the table. Knots of muscle vibrate along his jaw.

"Don't tell Lyssa," I beg. "Or Ash. Please. Just let it go."

"This isn't right," he says. He's scanning the room again, most likely looking for someone to blame, or maybe just for our friends.

"Please don't tell them," I say again. I think I'm going to cry and I don't want that. Not now.

He looks at me for a long moment. "Fine," he says. "I guess we don't need Lyssa getting suspended on your second day back."

He chucks the dirty rag into the garbage can and sits down with me.

Lyssa and Ashlyn arrive a few minutes later with an array of food. Ashlyn holds out two bagels on little paper plates. "Cinnamon or everything?"

"Cinnamon," I say, because it's easier than explaining my lack of appetite. She hands me a tiny tub of cream cheese.

Lyssa has a tray heaped with radioactive-looking nachos

and three cans of soda. She slides the Sprite to me and a Diet Coke to Ashlyn. "You staying?" she asks Finn. "You can share my nachos."

Finn hesitates and a chunk of bagel lodges in my throat as I think he's going to tell them what we found.

"Nah," he says finally. "Should probably make an appearance in gym. Just didn't want to leave Seelie alone."

25

"I might've done something stupid," I tell Jacqui when she asks how I've been doing. Today she has me walking on an inclined treadmill, my weight supported on the handrails, while she watches my gait.

"You? Stupid? No way," Lyssa says. She's straddling a huge inflatable blue yoga ball and managing to make it look comfortable.

I take a hand off the handle of the treadmill and flip her off, which just earns me a grin from her.

"What did you do?" Jacqui asks, adjusting the incline again.

I take the other hand off the grip. "This."

There's a dull pain in my thigh and I try not to lean into the limp. After my caneless foray across the history room, I spent the rest of the day sneaking real steps in, raising my cane for a few feet here and there when it wouldn't be noticed. Walking with my full weight hurts, but it's manageable.

Lyssa straightens on the ball. "Dude, you can walk! Why didn't you tell me?"

"Well then," Jacqui says with a smile.

I grab the handrails again, trying to be smooth about it and probably failing. Smooth is not something I excel at. My left leg is tired already, thanks to the incline, but I don't want to say so.

"When did you start trying this?" Jacqui asks.

"Today," I admit. "But it's good, right?"

"It's a start," she agrees. She lowers the incline until it's flat and slows the speed. "Here's the thing, though. You need to be careful about taking pain medication and walking. Pain has a purpose, it keeps you from overdoing it. If you turn off those pain receptors and try to power through, you could be doing more damage and setting yourself back."

"What?" I say, stepping up onto the sides of the treadmill so I can look at her. I have no idea what she's talking about. "That's not what I'm doing."

"How has your pain been?" she asks, like she's getting at something. She kills the power on the treadmill.

"Fine," I say, bewildered. "I mean, it hurts sometimes, sure, but less than before and not unbearable. I don't even take Advil every day anymore, and when I do it's usually just at night. Most days I just suck it up."

Something passes across Jacqui's face, something I can't identify. It makes me nervous.

"Look, it's not like I'm OD-ing on Advil so I can get rid of the cane," I say, trying to laugh.

She gestures me off the treadmill. I step down carefully, deliberately not reaching for the cane. I'm proving a point now.

"You've had no increase in pain lately?" she asks, concerned eyes locked on mine.

"No," I insist. What the hell?

"Your mom called me this morning," she says and I almost

fall over from shock. "She said she was worried about your pain levels and wondered if we needed to adjust your routine."

"What? My mom barely knows what's going on with me!"

"It's true," Lyssa says, bouncing her ball closer to join the conversation.

"And to be honest, even if I was in more pain than usual, it's not like I'd ever tell her." It wouldn't be her business and she'd probably just tell me to lose weight. "Seriously, I don't know why she'd say that."

"She said she noticed you started taking the Percocet," Jacqui says, seeming to realize that we're not all on the same page. Or even in the same book. "And are almost out."

"That's a lie!" I explode. What the hell is my mother playing at? I inhale deeply, trying to calm down. It's not fair to flip out on Jacqui. "I'm not taking the Percocet. Honestly. I didn't take it in the hospital either. I don't like the side effects. My pain is manageable. All I want to do is get back to normal."

She considers me for a moment, then says, "I believe you. Maybe your mother was confused about how many pills were in the prescription. But if you do experience any increase in pain, I need you to let me know. It's my duty to tell you that prescription painkillers are highly addictive and there are other options we can look at."

I flush. She thinks I'm the kind of person who would take pain pills for fun?

"So," she says, clapping her hands together, "now that we've had our extremely awkward conversation of the day, shall we finish up?"

It's dark when we get back to my house. My mother's car is in the driveway and lights are on in both sides of the duplex. Guess this happens now.

"Want me to come in?" Lyssa asks as she helps me out of the Jeep.

"Nope," I say, shouldering my backpack. "This is my fight."

She nods and for a moment we both stand there, breath fogging in the glow of the headlights.

"Hell of a day," she says after a while, tucking her bangs behind her ear where they refuse to stay.

My fingers itch to know what brushing them back would feel like. "No kidding."

"Call me if you need anything," she says. "Actually, call me even if you don't. I want to know what happens."

"I will," I promise.

Lyssa watches me until I get to the door. A magnetic pull in my belly keeps me rooted to the spot for a minute, that same gravity that made me want to kiss her hand in psychology. It would be so much easier to just get back in the Jeep and drive around than to face the scene inside, but this has to happen. I give her a little wave and let myself in.

My mother is on the couch, a notebook on her knee and dog-eared cookbooks open around her.

"We need to talk," I say, slamming the door. She looks up sharply, but before she can say anything, I continue. "On what planet would you lie to my physical therapist about drugs? More importantly, on what planet do you think you have a right to speak to her at all? She's my doctor, not yours, and you have no say in what we do."

"Watch your tone," Mom snaps. "I don't know what you're raving about, but you are my child whether you like it or not and I have every right to speak to your doctors."

"You made her think I was a fucking drug addict!"

"I did no such thing," my mother says, setting her notebook and pen on the coffee table. "I am legitimately concerned that you're hurting and not telling me. You keep shutting me out."

"Boo hoo," I say, waving my arm. "You don't care. You were just looking for attention and I'm the one who had to suffer for it. Do you have any idea how embarrassed I was?"

"I'm not fighting with you about this," she says. "The fact that you're suddenly needing to take narcotics shows something is wrong and needs to be addressed. You should be getting better, not worse."

"Oh my fucking god, I'm not taking narcotics!" This must be what going crazy feels like.

She studies me for minute and I hate every second of it. "Seelie, I think you need to reconsider seeing the psychologist. You clearly have a lot of misdirected anger," she says.

"It's not misdirected! It's directed at you, because you're the one who's hell-bent on making my life harder!"

"I don't think that's fair."

"I don't care." I wave at the books she has spread out. "Look, you obviously have enough to worry about with the restaurant, so worry about that, not me."

I storm out of the room, taking the stairs like a normal person even though it hurts like hell.

I dump my coat and backpack in my room and go down the hall to the bathroom. I open the medicine cabinet and rifle around for the Percocet bottle, realizing I haven't seen it since the night she got the prescription filled. I find it tucked behind a box of Benadryl and pop the lid.

At the bottom of the amber bottle sits one lone little blue pill.

26

As usual, none of us are in a hurry to get inside. We stay in the warmth of the Jeep, where there are munchkins and cocoa, watching buses unload students until the first warning bell sounds. Maybe it's cowardice, but it also gives us enough privacy to rehash the insanity that was yesterday. The part I still can't figure out, that none of us can, is why nineteen pills are missing.

"What's that thing Lynch was telling us about, where parents make their kids sick for attention? Maybe it's like that," Lyssa says.

"Munchausen by proxy," Finn says and manages to look smug as he pops a donut hole in his mouth. We all gape at him. "What? I can know things!"

"Did you see that on TV?" Ashlyn asks, grinning.

"*Criminal Minds*," he admits sheepishly. "But it's still a thing."

"I don't know," I say, wrapping my fingers around my travel mug. "It's just friggin' weird."

"Where do you think the pills went?" Ashlyn asks.

I shrug. "No clue."

"Maybe your mom sold them. Drugs are big in restaurants,"

Finn says, then turns to Ashlyn, changing the subject. "So, what are we supposed to wear to this Nuts on Ice thing? Do I need a suit? I look good in a suit."

"Nut*cracker* on Ice," Ashlyn corrects. We're all going to see her skate the lead part this weekend. "And no, you don't need a suit. You mostly need a coat. It'll be cold."

The second warning bell rings out over the parking lot.

"Ugh, it's cold now," I groan. The cold makes my scar turn a deep blue, which is absolutely no better than the angry pink it usually is. "I don't want to get out."

But we do. Lyssa walks us to English, but before I can go in, she catches my hand. My entire body jolts at her touch, but I try not to let it show as Finn and Ashlyn duck around us into class, oblivious to the current coursing from her fingers to mine. With a grin, she presses a rolled-up tube of paper into my palm and disappears down the hall.

In class, Trevor's desk is empty and I'm glad. Maybe he's not coming back. He wasn't in chemistry yesterday either. I take my seat and unfurl the paper like a scroll and have to stifle a laugh when I see what I'm holding. It's a drawing, a chibi pirate girl with an adorable green parrot on her shoulder, a speech bubble full of asterisks and exclamation points spilling from its beak. A blue Post-it is stuck to the corner, the words *Still think you'd be a badass pirate* scrawled across it.

"Okay, class," Mrs. Givens says, as I hold the drawing up so Finn and Ashlyn can see it, unable to stop smiling. "How many of you have seen the show *Law & Order*?"

"*SVU*?" someone asks.

"Any of them," she says. Hands shoot up around the room.

I carefully roll the drawing back up and slide it into the front pocket of my bag where it will be safe.

"Today you're going to pretend you're on *Law & Order*. Within your pods you're going to put Mary Maloney on trial for the murder of her husband. Your job is to craft the closing statements the lawyers would present at the end of the case. Make sure you use evidence from the text, which means properly cited quotes, people. This half of the room," she says, sweeping her arm to the row of pods across from us, "will write as if they were prosecutors, or the people trying to get her sent to jail. The rest of you will write as her defense. You have the entire class to work on this."

The warm glow of happiness the drawing sparked cools as the meaning of the assignment sinks in.

Finn stares at me, eyebrows climbing up his forehead. "Does she hate you?"

I drop my head to my desk. "She must."

Lynette has the decency to pretend she doesn't know what we're talking about.

"Do you want to see if we can do something else?" Ashlyn asks, eyes sympathetic beneath pink bangs.

"It's fine," I say. "No big deal."

But it is.

My stomach is doing backflips as I scan the story again, taking in the details of how she killed him with a single blow to the head, how he swayed drunkenly before crashing to the ground, and her shock. All I can picture is Shane, not swaying, not falling after that first strike. How I had to hit, and hit, and hit. And I was nothing like Mary Maloney, so calm and cool in the aftermath, setting up a perfect alibi.

I feel like too much time has passed and I wonder if everyone can see what's going on inside my head. I have to fake it. If I can pretend it's okay, that's almost as good as making it okay.

"It wasn't premeditated," I say to get things going, but for a surreal moment I don't know if I'm defending Mary or myself.

"The other side will argue it was," Lynette counters, playing devil's advocate, but she writes my words down anyway.

"But it wasn't," I say. "She didn't know she was going to do it."

"Crime of passion?" Ashlyn suggests. Lynette makes another note.

"I think we should call it temporary insanity," Finn says.

"That could work," Lynette agrees. She'd agree with anything Finn said.

"She wasn't crazy, though," I say, louder than I mean to. "She had to—"

I clamp my mouth shut.

Fuck.

Am I talking about me or Mary?

The three of them look at me and my ears burn. The GPS bracelet seems to tighten like a python around my ankle.

"Let's go with temporary insanity," Ashlyn says slowly. "Supported by the fact that it wasn't premeditated."

"What about what happened next?" Lynette asks. "That was too rational to be crazy. She went to that store specifically to set up an alibi. She even rehearsed it."

"No one has to know that," Ashlyn says. "I don't think. We

can just say when she came out of it she realized her child was in danger and was trying to protect it. We could say she was driven mad by the need to protect the baby and that's why she set up the alibi. She even says she doesn't care what happens to her as long as the baby isn't punished."

"That's like she admits it, though," Finn says. "How can we defend her if she said she did it?"

"No one knows she said it," Ashlyn insists. "She just thought it. That doesn't have to count."

Does it?

Is this what it's going to be like when it's my turn? Is this what Cara is doing, trying to find an angle that makes me look crazy? Because didn't I do the same thing as Mary Malone? Didn't I admit it?

The enormity of my mistake swirls around me like a cyclone.

I killed Shane Mayfield because I had to. That wasn't the mistake, no matter what anyone says. It was him or me, and after what he did to me, he deserved to die.

My mistake was saying it out loud.

27

Finn wears a suit.

I didn't even know he actually owned such a thing.

"Dude, it's ice-skating, not prom," Lyssa says. In her usual uniform of dark jeans, combat boots, and long coat, Lyssa looks like she could be security in a particularly violent anime.

"Yes, but see, I'm hoping to parlay this into prom. And Winter Gala, and a lifetime of wedded bliss," Finn says with the air of someone hatching a master plan. He gestures grandly at his outfit. "Preview of coming attractions."

"You're ridiculous," I say, but I have to admit, he looks good. Beneath the charcoal suit coat he has on an eggplant-colored shirt that makes his eyes flare like emeralds. He's even wearing a tie. And cuff links.

If nothing else, Finnegan Luckman has style.

When I slide into the backseat of his little Mazda, I see that he also has a gargantuan bouquet of pink and purple roses. I hold them up as Finn and Lyssa get settled in the front.

"Did you steal these?" I demand.

"Of course not!" Finn says as he starts the car. "I would nev—"

Pop music erupts out of the speakers at max volume, drowning out the rest of his proclamation of innocence. He scrambles to turn it down before our ears start bleeding. Lyssa quickly changes it to a rock station.

"Shotgun picks the music," she says, before Finn can object. "Driver shuts his cakehole because he has no taste."

It's true. Finn's musical affinities run the gamut from Bob Marley to Justin Bieber. Leaving him in control of the radio is like musical Russian Roulette.

"You were saying?" I say, waving the flowers in the rear-view mirror.

"Not stolen," he says proudly. "I ordered them from the florist. Bought and paid for."

A bouquet that size must have cost a fortune. I'm impressed, but don't say so. "So you only steal hospital flowers?"

"Something like that," he says, backing out of Lyssa's driveway. When he meets my eyes in the mirror a tiny flush colors his cheeks. "I wanted ones that matched her hair."

"They're letting her perform with fairy hair?" Lyssa asks and I'm inordinately proud of her for not busting Finn's balls about the bouquet.

"Yup," I say. I asked Ashlyn the very same thing as I watched her run the colored chalk through her hair the night before. "She did it to match one of her costumes. The director was fine with it."

"Cool."

"You think she'll like them?" Finn asks, still on the subject of his not-stolen flowers.

"Yes, Finn," I say, acting more exasperated than I am. It's cute. A little weird, but cute. "She'll love them."

Somehow we make it to Hartford without hitting much traffic, which is good, considering we have to do eighty the whole way there. None of us took Finn's extra primping into account when planning the Finn Standard Time buffer.

"Why don't I drop y'all here, then park?" Finn asks, shooting me a glance in the mirror.

"I'm not an invalid," I say, rolling my eyes.

"Just trying to be helpful," he says evenly. "Parking is gonna suck. It could be a hike."

"I'll manage."

The truth is, the crush of bodies I see waiting in line outside the XL Center's door worries me more than the walk. I knew this show was a big deal for Ashlyn, but I didn't quite realize what a big deal it was for everyone else. The line stretches to the corner of the building, families with children and couples huddled close together against the cold.

"I could stand not walking," Lyssa says. "Let us off here, we'll meet you inside."

Finn's phone chirps with an incoming message, but he ignores it while he signals and double-parks.

"I can manage," I repeat.

"No shit, but you don't have to," Lyssa says.

I bristle. "Seriously, I don't need to be babied."

"I get that." She's already out and opening my door. "Look, I don't want to wait alone. I'm asking you to wait with me while Finn drives around like an idiot looking for a parking place."

"Hey! I resent that," Finn says. He ignores an incoming call and turns in his seat to face me. "No one's coddling you. The fact is I can get parked and run back here faster if I'm alone."

"Fine," I relent and get out of the car. I reach to get my cane off the floor, then stop. I'm not going far. I don't need it.

Lyssa is hanging up her phone when I join her on the sidewalk.

"C'mon," she says, and surprises me by not getting in line. I follow her anyway. Away from the crowd is always a good choice in my book.

We move slowly, neither of us commenting on the lack of my cane. I watch the ground carefully, aware that any patch of ice could be disastrous.

"You don't have to prove stuff with us, you know," Lyssa says. She loops her arm through mine and for the barest of seconds I let myself pretend this is more than just a friendly faction outing to see Ashlyn perform. "And there's nothing wrong with letting us help you."

I nod. "I know." I don't say how hard it is, though. I don't have to.

She takes us around the edge of the building to an unmarked door. She presses a buzzer and the door is pushed open from the inside by a pudgy blond man in an XL Center sweater. "Hi, welcome," he says. The words *ADA Services* are embroidered above his heart.

My cheeks burn. Lyssa brought me to the handicapped entrance. I duck my head, hoping my hair will cover both my flaming face and my scar.

The man offers to escort us to our seats, but Lyssa says it isn't necessary and he moves off.

"*That* wasn't necessary," I hiss, dropping her arm to stab a finger toward the door we just came through. "Didn't I just get done saying I'm not a bloody invalid?"

Lyssa stops. "Skipping the line is a problem? Really? I know you, Seelie. You might not like that, but I know you. On your very best day you wouldn't want to be stuck outside in that crowd of morons, never mind now. Don't get pissy at me for being aware of that."

I shut up.

She's right.

Our seats are down close to the ice and there are quite a few stairs between us and them. They're not steep, but when Lyssa offers her arm again I take it without protest. I'm mortified by the line piling up behind our slow descent, but if Lyssa notices it she doesn't let on.

The lights are dimming when Finn comes crashing into his seat beside me, flustered and breathing hard. He sets the flowers on the floor.

"Damn things," he huffs, toeing the bouquet under his seat. "Got halfway here and realized they were still in the backseat."

The lady in front of us turns around to investigate the commotion, then does a double take. She turns quickly and whispers something to the man with her. He turns around.

They're looking right at me.

My hands clench and I stare past them at the ice.

They rise, gathering the two little girls with them, and make their way to the stairs. Finn props a foot on one of their empty chairs like nothing is wrong.

My gaze is glued straight ahead. The familiar sting of angry tears bites my eyes as the spotlights come up over the ice and music swells around us. I feel the warm press of Lyssa's shoulder against mine and I lean into her, just a little, and decide right there that I'm not going to let strangers ruin this night, this small break from the chaos of everything back in Amesford.

Ashlyn glides across the ice like she was born with blades instead of feet. I try to lose myself in the performance, but the heat of Lyssa's arm against mine is like a beacon and I want nothing more than to burrow in. Again, I find myself pretending we are more than just friends, pretending that such a thing wouldn't irrevocably alter our group, and Monday's court date is the furthest thing from my mind. I pretend this is my normal life and that my biggest problem is whether or not I should just take Lyssa's hand and say to hell with the consequences. The frosty air and swirling music make it seem almost possible.

When the cast assembles for their final bow, Finn bellies up to the edge of the rink, cotton candy roses held aloft. The skaters bow together, then Ashlyn and the male lead slip ahead to greet the audience on their own. Everyone around us gets to their feet, applause thundering. Finally, Ashlyn skates forward alone, launching into a blistering spin that ends in an elegant bow, and the audience completely loses it, whistling and stomping their feet. Flowers rain onto the ice and Finn, not to be outdone, leaps over the railing and hand-delivers his extravagant bouquet on bended knee to a shocked and laughing Ashlyn. Lyssa and I cheer as he clambers back over the railing just ahead of security and I am overcome with such a staggering rush of love for these three people that I almost cry.

28

I couldn't ask for a worse day to be back in court.

Not only did the universe see fit to dump seven inches of snow on us last night, granting Amesford High a snow day I can't even enjoy, but my mother has insisted on being part of the proceedings.

Joy of joys.

When I come downstairs Cara is already waiting, drinking coffee at the kitchen table with Mom.

"Do you think that's likely?" Mom asks.

"It's best-case scenario," Cara says.

It bothers me that they're talking without me.

"Seelie, Ms. Dewitt thinks she can get your case thrown out today!" Mom says with the manic enthusiasm of a game show host.

Cara looks aghast. "No, Seelie, I said we were going to try to get your case dismissed," she says, shooting my mom a harried look. "But it's not guaranteed."

"I know," I say. "We already talked about it. I also know better than to think I'll get that lucky."

"You should eat some breakfast," my mom says. "How about a yogurt?"

I ignore her. Juice is about all I can handle right now. My stomach is already churning, compounding my anxiety. All this stress is keeping my guts in a near-constant state of upheaval.

"Court is still running on schedule despite the snow," Cara says, "which means we'll need to be leaving soon."

She looks me over as I sip my juice. In my funeral skirt and green—not black—cowl-neck sweater, I feel like a lab specimen about to be dissected.

"Pull your hair up," Cara says.

I sigh. I knew that was coming and I use the elastic I'm wearing on my wrist to bundle my hair into a puffy knot. I don't bother checking a mirror; there's no way it's going to look good with the canyon spidering down my face, but Cara nods in approval.

I ride with Cara so we can go over everything one more time while Mom follows in her car. My phone chimes with texts from Lyssa, Ashlyn, and Finn, all assuring me that they're on their way despite the snow. Classes at the college are canceled too and I'm glad both of Lyssa's dads will be there this time.

But it turns out *everyone* is here this time.

The parking lots are overflowing and I recognize too many of the lifted pickups that would normally be parked at school on any other Monday.

"This is bad," I tell Cara. Sweat dampens my hairline. "Really bad."

"What is?"

"All these trucks . . . they're from school."

She doesn't answer, just keeps looking for an empty spot.

I group-text the faction: **Whole school is here. Fuck fuck fuck**

ASH: **I saw :(**

LYS: **Row J in bottom lot. All parkd together. Saving a spot.**

"Go to Row J," I say. "My friends are there. They're saving us a spot."

In Row J, Finn is standing in an empty space between Lyssa's Jeep and Mrs. Anders's minivan. He steps aside as we pull in.

Cara greets Lyssa and Peter and gets introductions to everyone else. She points at Lyssa. "You, missy, are not to make the news again," she says.

Lyssa raises her hands. "No promises."

"Can I make the news?" Finn asks hopefully and Ashlyn swats his arm.

We're a small army advancing on the courthouse. I have no clue where Mom parked but feel better without her anyway.

The stairs are poorly shoveled and treacherous, making the ascent painfully slow even with my cane. I wanted to leave it behind, but I knew Cara wouldn't stand for it. The mob of reporters I expect to swarm us when we reach the top doesn't.

They can't, because they're too busy interviewing my classmates.

I stop, wanting more than anything to turn tail and flee.

"Ignore it," Lyssa says through gritted teeth.

Private earthquakes threaten to take my legs out, but I'm pulled along with the others.

Trevor, surrounded by acolytes, is holding court with a stunning brunette reporter, and I spot Madison Tierney making sad-puppy eyes at a reporter old enough to be her father. Several other students are being interviewed, and it seems like all the Wildcat royalty and miscreants are in attendance.

A sharp whistle pierces the air and as one, the assembled students turn to us, conversations dying until the only sound left is the murmur of interviews.

The air turns electric.

It starts with one voice, soft, but spreads like a plague.

"Mur-der-er!"

Chanted.

Three distinct syllables.

"Mur-der-er! Mur-der-er!"

I can feel the earth spinning beneath my feet.

"Keep moving but don't react," Cara says and I can scarcely hear her over the rising din. She steps in front of me, her bearing incongruously regal as she leads our charge to the door. Lyssa rides point with her, fists balled like clubs. Ashlyn clutches my hand and Finn slots in on my cane side. Behind us, Peter and Rick guard the rear while Mrs. Anders mutters prayers. A well-oiled machine. How did we get so good at this?

A reporter breaks away from his interview, running over to thrust a microphone at our group.

"Cecelia, what is your response to this?" he shouts, keeping pace with us.

"Leave her alone," Lyssa orders. She keeps her fists down, but everything about her body screams war.

My response to this?

I'm falling down the rabbit hole.

The chant grows louder and faster and never once do Trevor or Madison or the others stop their interviews, even as cameras

166

turn to capture the chaos. They make it the background, where everyone will see. No matter whose interview gets aired, this will be the soundtrack.

29

I expect to see the same judge as last time, but it's not. When the courtroom rises at the command of the bailiff, a stern-faced woman strides out to the bench.

"Your Honor, I would like to file a motion to dismiss," Cara announces when we stand before her. To our right is the same black-suited lawyer who represented the state at the arraignment, only this time he shares his table with Trevor and his parents.

Behind us, half of Amesford High is packed into the pews, giving the gallery the look of a school assembly. Extra security lines the walls.

"On what grounds?" Judge Frances Crowley asks, arching a penciled-on eyebrow.

"Your Honor, there is irrefutable proof that evidence in the case against my client has been grievously mishandled. I have no doubt that Michael Mayfield has used his standing as a member of this court to gain access to elements of the investigation that he has no legal right to possess."

"Objection!" the black-suited lawyer interrupts.

"I'll allow it," the judge says. To Cara she asks, "You have proof of this allegation?"

"Yes, Your Honor. Trevor Mayfield, brother of the deceased, has been found in possession of crime-scene evidence, namely Ms. Stanton's cell phone. Further, he has posted details of the case, including photographs, on multiple online sources, thus completely violating my client's right to a fair trial. The Mayfields are using their considerable political influence to turn this case into a witch hunt."

"Mr. Blakely?" the judge asks, looking to the black-suited lawyer.

"A moment, Your Honor," he says, barely looking away from the heated whispered discussion he's having with a scowling Trevor. Judge Mayfield's face has taken on the hue of an eggplant.

"Mr. Blakely, I take it there is some element of truth to this?" she asks impatiently.

Blakely stands and leaves Trevor fuming, arms crossed tightly across his chest like a sulking child.

"Your Honor," the lawyer says, a barely perceptible twitch in his jaw, "it is unclear how young Mr. Mayfield came to be in possession of Ms. Stanton's cell phone, but it is irrelevant. The phone is not evidence. It was merely an artifact recovered at the scene. It was not used in the commission of the crime. Further, I can assure you that Judge Mayfield had no hand in it. It's simply an unfortunate case of teenage shenanigans and will have no bearing on this case. The state wishes to proceed as planned."

The judge steeples her skeletal fingers and surveys the room. I steal a glance at Cara, wondering if the hope I feel is reflected on her face, but her expression is carefully neutral. I want to look back at my friends to see if they're with me. I mean, this is good, right? The judge is really thinking about it. Maybe she gets it. Maybe this ends now.

"Counsel," she says, eyeballing Cara and Blakely with equal disdain, "this is not high school. I understand there are teenagers involved but I expect better from you both than this nonsense. Ms. Dewitt, I know Judge Mayfield quite well and I don't for a second believe that he is engaging in evidence tampering. You are skating very close to slander by making such comments."

A murmur swells behind me as any hope I had dissolves. How could I have been so stupid?

"And Mr. Blakely," Judge Crowley continues, "you have put your entire case in serious jeopardy with your ignorance. I am dismissing you both until second call. It seems you're not quite ready to proceed this morning."

///

Our small army is stuffed into a cramped conference room. I'm sure that somewhere in a similar one, Trevor Mayfield is being reamed out by Blakely. This thought should cheer me, but I'm numb. I still can't believe I let myself hope this would all be over so easily, but I did.

I really did.

"Isn't it a conflict of interest?" Rick asks Cara. "If the judge is friends with Mayfield?"

"To an extent, all judges know each other. Especially in small states," Cara says. Her plum-colored heels clack like machine guns as she paces the cramped room. "It would only be a conflict of interest if Judge Mayfield himself were up there."

"What now?" Lyssa asks. She's leaning against the door with her arms folded. Finn mirrors the pose on the other side as if they're sentries expecting an invasion.

"We wait," Cara says. "We see what the prosecution does."

Waiting sucks.

When a dull knock sounds on the heavy door nearly an hour later, Lyssa and Finn stand at attention. Lyssa pulls it open to reveal Blakely, and the lawyer looks slightly taken aback at the number of people in the small room, like maybe he's in the wrong place. When his eyes finally settle on Cara, he asks, "A word?"

She nods and joins him in the hall.

When she returns, Blakely isn't with her.

"We need the room," she says gently. She catches my eye but I can't read her look. My stomach tightens anyway.

"What happened?" Lyssa asks.

"I need to talk to Seelie privately first," Cara says, raising a placating hand. "Legally."

"I'm going to tell them anyway," I say. I don't want to be left alone with whatever news is coming.

"I know," she says. "But first this is between you and I."

"We'll wait outside," Peter says, gesturing everyone toward the door.

Lyssa, Finn, and Ashlyn linger. My mother doesn't move from her chair by the window and I hate her for staying. Cara's expression stops me from making an issue out of it, though.

"You too, guys," Cara tells my friends. She doesn't look happy about it.

I nod at them and they leave. I know they're not going far.

The room seems to grow in the emptiness. Cara sits on the table near me.

"The prosecution would like to discuss plea deals."

///

"I trust you're ready to proceed now?" Judge Crowley asks when we return.

"Yes, Your Honor," Blakely says.

In our absence, the courtroom has nearly emptied of Amesford students. Apparently blowing an entire snow day on court wasn't as much fun without the cameras around.

"And?"

"The prosecution is prepared to offer Ms. Stanton a plea deal. In order to save everyone the time and cost of going to trial, we are prepared to accept a guilty plea for a reduced charge of voluntary manslaughter, accompanied by the shortest recommended prison sentence of eight years."

Judge Crowley turns to us.

"And how does the defense respond?"

"We reject the deal," Cara says.

The judge straightens a bit in her chair. "Are you sure, Counsel? I would strongly advise your client to reconsider. Murder comes with a life sentence. Eight might be an offer worth taking."

"My client is not a fool, Your Honor. Once again I must remind the court that Cecelia Stanton is the victim of this crime. She is guilty of nothing more than defending herself against a deranged and dangerous attacker. She will not plead guilty to any charge because she has not committed a crime."

Have I?

"Then we continue to trial," the judge says.

As the lawyers discuss dates and details, my mind swims with the possibility that maybe I am guilty of something. Not murder, surely not that, but something else.

Lying.

If I had told the truth, the whole truth, that first day in the hospital, would I still be standing here?

30

I skip school Tuesday.

I just don't have it in me.

We're halfway there when I tell Lyssa, my self-appointed chauffeur these days, that I can't do it. She doesn't hesitate and drives right by the school, beeping a merry honk as we pass.

I lean my head back on the seat. "I'm weak, huh?"

She glances at me. It's a funny look. "Uh, no. Not even a little bit."

I sigh and close my eyes. I don't know how I even got up this morning. My lock fixation went into hyperdrive after court yesterday and I spent the vast majority of the night hobbling back and forth between my door and windows, double-checking. Making sure.

At least the paranoia kept my brain too busy to dwell on the other thing.

"My house?" Lyssa asks. "Or drive around?"

"Drive away?" I ask hopefully.

"Wherever you want to go," she says.

I wonder where I could go that would be far enough away.

"Shit," I say suddenly, pulling my phone out and starting a

text. "I should tell Ash and Finn that we're bailing. Or I'm bailing. You can go back, if you want. Just drop me home."

"Don't be stupid."

We drive for a long time without talking. Yesterday's snow has been reduced to dirty gray piles that blur along the roadside. Finn and Ashlyn both text back that we should've made it a skipping party, but I don't reply. I'm too busy trying to convince my mouth to say the words in my brain.

"I want to go to the barn," I announce in the silence between two songs.

"Now?" Lyssa asks, turning the radio down.

"Now."

It wasn't planned. I don't know why I said it, but I know it's what I need to do. Now that I'm thinking about it, I can't believe it's taken me this long.

She knows the way and when we pull up the long, curving driveway, I'm relieved to see that Elaine's battered blue Explorer isn't parked at the top. I received several emails from her over the past few weeks and I've responded, but I'm not ready for a face-to-face yet. I don't know if I'll ever be. I can't help feeling like I've somehow sullied her peaceful farm and I don't know how to act with her.

Lyssa pulls up close to the barn but leaves the Jeep running.

"You want me to come?"

I shake my head. "No."

"Okay. I'll be right here if you need me, though."

It takes me a minute to gather the courage to leave the Jeep, but she doesn't rush me.

The barn is quiet when I slide the heavy front door open

and step inside. The horses must be out back. To my right is the tack room and I can hear the hum of the heater through the closed door. My heart is galloping, but I force myself to go in. It's almost tropically warm compared to the frigid air outside. The room has been rearranged and it takes me only a second to realize why.

The large grain bins are now centered on the back wall, instead of pushed to the side as they used to be. It's almost, but not quite, enough to cover the dark stain soaked into the wooden floor. Now that I'm aware of it, I notice several other areas where blood penetrated the untreated wood floorboards.

My stomach tries to crawl up my throat at the sight.

I grab a handful of horse treats to stuff into my pocket and let myself out. The rush of cold air hits my lungs like a sledge-hammer and I force myself to breathe slower. It's okay. It's broad daylight. Lyssa is right outside. There's nothing here to get me.

I move slowly down the aisle. The stalls are clean and empty. I wonder if Elaine is doing the barn work or if she hired someone else. I couldn't blame her if she did.

I slide the back door open and a shrill whinny cuts through the air.

Tears spring unbidden to my eyes and I'm smiling, really smiling, like my face might crack, as Tulsa comes cantering across the snowy paddock. He pulls up just shy of the fence and snorts, thrusting his fuzzy head over the top rail to nudge my shoulder.

"Hey, old man," I say, giving him a few of the treats. I rub the side of his freckled face, enjoying the tickle of his whiskers against my bare hand.

When the other three realize there are treats to be had, they abandon their hay piles and trot over. I lean my cane against the fence and duck under the bottom, which hurts but isn't impossible, and stand among the little herd. The woolly white pony is trying to turn my coat pocket inside out in the pursuit of more snacks. Their breath makes a frosty cloud around us and in that moment I think maybe I can be okay again.

Bolstered by this feeling, I give each horse a final pet or kiss on the nose and go back inside.

I stand at the base of the hayloft stairs for a long, long time. I flip the light switch and a warm amber glow bathes the stairs. My throat is tight, like the memory might strangle me.

I text Lyssa: **Come in**

She's there before I have the phone back in my pocket.

"Don't say anything," I say before she has a chance to. "Just come with me, okay?"

The stairs are the steepest I've tried since the attack, and even with the cane, it's tough. But maybe it's not the stairs. Maybe it's what's at the top that makes it so hard.

The loft is packed floor to ceiling with rectangular hay bales, enough for winter, but I barely see them. Standing at the top of the stairs I see the hayloft how it was that day, half-empty of hay and full of disaster. I see the wall where he slammed my face. I see the precise spot where I landed right before he tried to cut out my eye. I see the spot I found the mallet while he . . . while he . . . while he . . .

It's too much. Too much. I'm seeing it all now, feeling it all, all of it, and this was a mistake, I shouldn't have come back here, because all I can see is him and all I can hear is the awful wet sound of heads opening like dropped pumpkins, and the light isn't enough to chase it away and did I really think it would be, and oh god, what have I done?

"Hey," Lyssa says softly, carefully, like she's trying to calm a frightened horse. She looks as worried as I've ever seen her.

I can't answer, because I can't get enough air into my tattered lungs to form words. My chest is making the black noise it made that day. It has to be what panic sounds like. It has to be what's making Lyssa look at me like I'm dangerous.

"It's okay," she whispers. Her hand is out like she's going to touch me, but she doesn't. Maybe she knows better, or maybe she's just making sure I don't tumble back down the stairs.

"It's not," I manage to say, and it isn't, because I can still see it, I can still smell the putrid stink of him, the penny reek of all that blood, and it's so real I think Lyssa must sense it too.

"Talk to me," she says and it's close enough to a plea to physically hurt.

My chest splits apart but I can't find the words.

The world is tipping, and I think maybe that's for the best. My cane clatters to the ground. Falling.

Then Lyssa is folding me into her arms, and I'm letting her. This isn't a conversation for words. I collapse against her and she's safe and solid and holding me together. Her lips press against my hair in a not-quite kiss and we stay like that for a very long time, until today comes back and there's hay to the ceiling and the lights are on and I'm here and not there.

31

I'm pretty sure Mr. Ricketti, the school librarian, emerged from the womb clad in elbow-patched tweed and glasses. He's been here for as long as the school has been standing. He insists on checking books out by hand, stamping the inside cards with due dates because he doesn't trust the computer to remember for him. He is the keeper of my sanctuary and he smiles and nods at me when I push through the swinging doors, despite the fact that I have no pass and no business being out during third period.

Every day since I've been back to school I've spent my gym period here, supposedly writing reports on various athletes. Mostly, though, I just read. After the spectacle at court on Monday, I decided I will also be spending history here for the foreseeable future. Trevor has been moved out of English, but it's not like they can take all his friends out of my other classes. At least Mr. Ricketti doesn't seem to mind my hiding.

The library is new and painfully modern, all steel and glass. There is no book smell anywhere. In fact, on the first floor, the computer bank takes up more room than the books. I'm sure Mr. Ricketti lost his mind when they did the remodel. Part of me always wishes it were more like a TV library, with dark wood and musty books and mysterious English librarians.

Near the checkout desk, I swipe my elevator card and wait for the gleaming doors to glide open. I could handle the stairs, but Mr. Ricketti is convinced I'm going to fall and break my neck, so he insists I take the elevator.

Fine by me.

I ride to the second level, which isn't a complete floor, but a balcony that rings the perimeter of the library, lined with a scattering of study carrels. It's the quietest, most forgotten spot in the whole school and I head to my usual spot at the very end of the row. From this corner I can see the entire library below, including the door to the hall and all the tall bookcases standing in the center of the room. Aside from a teacher feeding paper into a copier, there's no one else here.

Exactly the way I like it.

I pull out my English homework—still the goddamn lamb story—and try to focus. Mrs. Givens is rapidly sliding down my favorite-teacher list.

The urge to put my head down and sleep is overwhelming. I'm exhausted all the time lately. But when Jason Francone flings open the doors like a Wild West gunslinger, I snap awake. Fucking hell. My first day skipping history and Wilkins is sending the class to the library? You've got to be kidding me.

But no, it's only Jason. He slaps a piece of a pink pass paper on the checkout desk and marches into the stacks. Wilkins must've sent him on a mission for something.

He glances at his phone, then starts running his finger along the spines, mouth moving silently like he's trying to remember a title. He plucks a hardcover from the shelf, but instead of taking it to Mr. Ricketti, he pulls something from his pocket, tucks it under the inside cover flap, and puts the book back. He leaves the library empty handed.

What the hell?

I barely have time to consider the strange scene when Trevor Mayfield walks in. I pull back in my seat, but he doesn't so much as glance up at the balcony as he heads for the same row Jason visited. He finds the book he's looking for much more quickly because unlike Jason, Trevor, for all his faults, can probably read more than the labels of beer cans. He flips through the pages like he's considering checking it out, but I watch him casually slip something into the cover flap, the same way Jason did. On his way out, he takes a random book from a different row and checks out without bothering to glance at the title.

Weird.

Ten minutes pass before the door opens for the third time, but rather than a lone student from the ranks I despise, a mass of jostling freshmen spill into the library amid whisper-yelled orders to hush and get to work. They pile onto the computers as the teacher reminds them that they're here for research and not memes.

I watch them, amazed that I've never really noticed how little they are and I wonder if we used to look so young too. I guess we must've, even if we didn't feel it. They're scrolling through social media and entertainment sites, switching browser windows when they sense their teacher is near. Some of them reach over and drag their fingers across their friends' keyboards, messing up their essays like it's a truly bad thing to do. I feel a pang of nostalgia too strong for such a small age gap, but suddenly I would give anything to be back in ninth grade, back before being bad meant killing your classmate's brother and lying to your friends about everything that matters.

I'm surprised when Finn comes in near the end of the period. I was planning to leave a few minutes early to meet him outside of math as usual, so he wouldn't know I'm skipping history. I don't want to admit, even to my friends, that I'm too scared to sit alone among all those people who were at court that day, chanting that ugly word.

I'm about to text him when I see he's beelining straight for the row Jason and Trevor were in. I get up and watch over the railing as he takes a book down and fishes beneath the flap, extricating whatever was hidden there.

It's money.

What the ever-loving hell?

He counts it quickly and sticks it into the unzipped pocket of his messenger bag. He returns the book, pulls another down, and repeats the process. He glances around, sees Mr. Ricketti hovering with the freshman teacher near the computers, and takes a book from the second shelf. His hand darts into the back pocket of his jeans, but I can't see what he pulls out, only that he slides it behind the battered checkout card on the inside of the book. He pops it back on the shelf, takes another look around, and does the whole thing again with a second book.

I don't text him or call down, although I'm desperate to know what's going on. He, like the other boys, departs without ever looking up. The balcony carrels might as well be invisible.

My spidey sense is in overdrive.

This is wrong.

I shove my untouched English work into my backpack and take the elevator down. The freshmen are gathering their things and I ignore their stares as I pass, intent on my destination.

My legs are shaking enough that I'm grateful for the cane as I stand in the row Jason, Trevor, and Finn were in. It's the fiction section, authors A–K. I stand where the boys were and look at the books. From the second floor I couldn't see the titles they chose and I don't know what I hope to find.

The bell rings and as the freshmen pour out into the hall, a tidal wave of sound spills in as they hold the doors open, but then I'm left in silence save for the roar of blood in my ears.

There are only so many books on the second shelf and I start taking them down at random, skipping the paperbacks, feeling under the flaps for the truth. I'm halfway through the row when I find what I'm looking for in Charles Dickens's *A Tale of Two Cities* and Dostoyevsky's *Crime and Punishment.*

Five small orange pills, and three tiny blue ones, nestled in miniature ziplock bags.

32

I obviously don't meet Finn outside his math class.

I storm into the lunchroom, the ziplock bags fire in my pocket.

"Jeep, now," I say when I get to our table. I'm relieved to see Finn isn't visiting today.

"We'll get caught," Ashlyn says, but Lyssa is already getting up. "We're right near the teacher's lot."

"Now," I repeat in a voice that sounds exactly like the earthquake I keep swallowing.

"What happened?" Lyssa asks. She motions at Ashlyn with her keys without taking her eyes from mine. "Senior privileges. C'mon, get up."

"That only counts for you," Ashlyn says, but gets to her feet. Her eyes flick between me and Lyssa like she's at a tennis match. "Should I text Finn?"

"Absolutely not," I say, stalking toward the door. Each step is an opportunity to stab the ground with my horrible cane, and I do. Hard.

Lyssa cranks the heater up once we're in the Jeep, but I'm seething enough to barely feel the cold.

Ashlyn leans through from the backseat so she can be part of the conversation she knows she doesn't want to have.

"So?" Lyssa asks.

I pull the traitorous bags from my pocket and slam them on the console. Ashlyn jerks back as if I hit her instead of the car.

Everyone looks at the pills.

I can't speak with the rage clogging my throat.

"Explain," Lyssa says when I don't, but there's a furrow forming between her inkwell eyes that tells me she's figuring it out.

My hands shake like freezing birds in my lap, but not from fear this time. From betrayal. Which is worse.

So I tell them, watching as fury and disbelief come to war in Lyssa's features and Ashlyn sits back, hands to her mouth, gray eyes wide and stunned. She shakes her head slowly.

"This doesn't make sense," she says through lilac-painted fingernails.

"It makes perfect fucking sense," Lyssa says. She whips around to face Ashlyn, who shrinks back. "Use your head! You really think he makes enough at Dunkin's to afford that car, or the endless fucking wardrobe, or those ridiculous flowers? Think about it! Why does he carry two phones all the time? I knew it. I fucking knew something was off about him when he first moved here."

"Don't yell at her," I say, though I'm so numb it's like someone else is speaking.

The thing is, she's right.

There was something off about Finnegan Luckman when he came to live with his grandparents two years ago.

He spoke little of his Kentucky home or the parents he left behind. He was charmingly charismatic and could've easily become Amesford royalty, but he chose us instead. From day one he seemed genuinely besotted by Ashlyn, shunning the advances of cheerleaders looking to claim the cute new boy with the accent. He worried me at first, the way he tried to insinuate himself into our group. He could've picked anyone. But once I realized he wasn't setting us up for mockery, I found his easygoing sense of humor provided a much-needed balance for my seething dislike of any humans who weren't my two best friends. He even managed to win Lyssa over, albeit slowly, with his encyclopedic knowledge of comic books and love of questionable snack food.

And so the three of us became the four of us. It happened so easily that none of us really worried that we knew nothing of Finn's past. We had the Finn in front of us and that was enough.

Now I wonder if we know him at all.

Lyssa picks up the blue pills. "Were these yours?"

"I don't know," I say, but it's a lie. The memory of the sole blue pill in the Percocet bottle has been impossible to ignore. "Fuck. Yes. I think so."

Lyssa flings the bag back onto the console, where it skitters off into the crack between the seats. Ashlyn fishes it out, holding the little ziplock like it's a bomb. She stares at the pills like they might reveal the secrets of the universe.

"What are these?" Lyssa asks, indicating the orange ones.

"Adderall," I say. "I googled it before I left the library."

"Where'd he get them?"

"No idea."

"He takes them," Ashlyn says softly from the backseat. "For ADD. He sees a shrink."

I turn to look at her. She looks terribly small and alone. "What?"

"He told me," she says, still gazing at the bag of pills. "I wasn't supposed to tell anyone. He was embarrassed."

"He's probably scamming the doctor so he can sell them," Lyssa says, a contemptuous sneer making her pretty face ugly and hard.

"I don't know," Ashlyn whispers at the pills she's holding.

"And why Trevor?" Lyssa spits the name out like poison.

Tears—stupid, weak, idiotic tears—fill my eyes. "That's what I want to know. I could deal with it, I think, if it was just drug dealing, you know?" My words are halting and that phrase is foreign in my mouth, not something that should be attached to one of my best friends. "But not with Trevor. Not after everything that's happened."

"I could kill him," Lyssa says and I don't know if she means Finn or Trevor. Probably both.

Over the sound of the Jeep's heater, the bell rings to signal the end of lunch, but none of us makes a move to go back.

I feel as lost now as I ever have. When I lay in the hospital with my leg tied to the ceiling, I thought it couldn't get any worse; then I landed in a jail cell and I realized I was wrong. But sitting here in the cocoon of Lyssa's car, my heart rending into a million broken shards, I long for the lows of those days. It would be better than this. Those blows came at the hands of people I hated, or had come to hate. That this strike came from someone I care about, love, even, if I were brave enough to use such words, makes the pain all the harder to bear.

I don't want to hate Finn.

I don't know how not to right now.

"I don't know what to do," I confess. I'm wrung out, the rage ceding to bitter exhaustion. I drop my head into my hands. My scar throbs with a life of its own beneath my fingers. "I can't believe this. I can't believe he's dealing with Trevor-fucking-Mayfield after everything that family has done to me."

"We have to confront him," Lyssa says. "We have to deal with this. Not here, though. Tonight."

"Together," Ashlyn adds. "And there might be an explanation. You don't know."

It's what I don't know that scares me.

Finn sold drugs to Trevor.

What if he was selling them to Shane too?

33

Lyssa and I are silent on the way to physical therapy.

I have zero desire to go today, but skipping a session isn't worth the risk of having Jacqui call my mother and having to deal with that on top of everything else. In fact, the thought of talking to Mom at all today is so overwhelming that I text her to say I'm spending the night at Ashlyn's to work on a project for class. I don't feel at all guilty for the lie.

We tried to get Ashlyn to come with us to the hospital, but she said she wanted some time alone before seeing Finn. I know Lyssa's worried she's going to tip him off before we all meet up later on, and to be honest, I am too.

Jacqui seems to sense something is off when we arrive and we get to work without our usual joking around. Lyssa plops onto her yoga ball and broods while I climb the never-ending hill of the treadmill without using the handrails. Jacqui is pleased with how I do, but my mind is elsewhere.

After fifteen minutes of climbing, Jacqui switches me to the leg-press machine, adjusting the resistance several times as I push the plate away. With each push I ask myself why. Why Trevor? Why my pills? Why is this my life now?

"Well, I have some news that might cheer you up," Jacqui says when she signals that I'm finished.

I doubt it, but ask her anyway. "What's that?"

"You officially have permission to begin driving again," she says. "Now, I wouldn't go planning any major road trips quite yet, but you should be able to handle short drives without a problem."

"That is good news," I concede.

Lyssa looks up and flashes me a smile. "Nice."

"You're making great progress, Seelie. You should be very proud."

I wish it were that simple.

In the parking lot, Lyssa tosses me her keys. "Want to do the honors?"

I shake my head and lob them back. "You drive."

I'm so used to my little jelly bean car that the Jeep feels like a tank to me. Throw in my fraying emotions and it's probably safer for everyone if I'm not behind the wheel.

"Bet you're happy you won't have to chauffeur me around anymore," I say after I pull myself into the passenger seat.

Lyssa starts the Jeep and we sit for a minute while it warms up. "I like doing it," she says, not looking at me, but out the windshield at people going in and out of the hospital. Her words are simple and matter-of-fact, but they spread a pleasing warmth through my belly.

"Me too," I say, smiling despite everything.

I know it's probably the last smile I'm going to get today.

I shower at Lyssa's before Ashlyn arrives. Shoebox comes in the bathroom with me like the weirdo dog he is and keeps nosing the blue shower curtain aside so he can make sure I haven't disappeared. I don't let him rush me and soon the bathroom smells like Lyssa's minty shampoo.

I turn the water off reluctantly and step over Shoebox, who has commandeered the bath mat as his kingdom, and towel off. I have yoga pants and a T-shirt here from the last time I came over after physical therapy and am not surprised that they've been washed and folded. The only way that would happen at my house is if I do it myself.

I bundle my PT clothes and school clothes into my wet towels and dump them in the washer. I didn't want to risk running into Momthulu by going home for clean clothes, so these will need to do for tomorrow. I start the machine and go to Lyssa's room, Shoebox padding behind me on his stubby legs.

Lyssa's not there, but I rummage around the top of her dresser until I find a comb and start picking apart the tangles of my wet hair. Voices float in from the kitchen and I can hear the clanging of pots being moved around. I wonder what Lyssa's telling her fathers about tonight. It occurs to me that she's probably just telling the truth, or at least some of it, and I feel an irrational stab of jealousy. I would love to have parents like hers.

As I brush out my hair I wander over to the drafting table. A large piece of heavy drawing paper is poking out from beneath a sketchbook and I slide the book aside to see what she's working on.

It's so beyond the realm of what I'm expecting that I drop the comb in shock.

It's a comic book cover, but huge. At least two feet wide. Lyssa hardly ever works at this size. *The Mighty Cicatrix* is splashed across the top in blood-red letters. Beneath the title is a curvy woman clad in skirted leather armor and knee-high boots, standing atop a pair of galloping white horses with blue fire in their manes. Identical flames lick the face of this warrior woman, who wields a broadsword with both hands. Screaming in behind her, green wings spread wide, is a demonic parrot, with a vicious hook of a beak and talons like blades.

She would be enviably badass if not for one detail.

She is ruined by a thick black slash that splits her face from forehead to ear. Her eye patch does nothing to detract from the horror.

She's a classic villain.

And she is me.

God, is this what Lyssa sees when she looks at me? Is it what they all see?

I jump when I hear footsteps in the hall and barely have time to get the picture covered back up before Lyssa comes in with Ashlyn. I bend to get the comb off the floor and I know my cheeks are as red as the letters she drew. I rake the comb through the rest of my tangles, not caring that the knots are pulling right out of my scalp.

"Good news," Lyssa says, although her face is tense. "The parents agreed to an impromptu dinner date so we can have some privacy."

"And the bad news?" I ask, trying to force the ghastly drawing from my mind.

"Finn's here."

34

"Dude, I feel like I haven't seen you guys all day," Finn says, barging into the room. "Your dads let me in as they were leaving. They're all dressed up. Hot date tonight?"

He pulls up short so suddenly it's almost comic.

"Oh god, what happened?" he asks, taking in our grim expressions. The genuine concern in his face is like the twist of a knife.

"Sit," Lyssa orders, pointing to the chair she's pulled away from the drafting table. She's leaning against the edge of the dresser with her arms folded, radiating rage. Ashlyn and I sit on the futon, Shoebox nestled between us. Ashlyn's legs are folded up and she's completely curled in on herself, taking up even less space than normal.

"Uh," Finn says, reluctantly sitting down. "What's going on?"

"You tell us," Lyssa says.

"Tell you what?" Finn asks, looking truly bewildered. "What happened?"

Lyssa pushes off from the dresser and whips the bags of

pills at Finn, who has to jump sideways to avoid taking them in the face.

"What the fuck!" he cries, falling out of the chair.

I'm shivering hard and I don't know if it's from cold or nerves. I tuck my hands beneath my legs as Lyssa towers over Finn. She grabs him by the shirt and hauls him to his feet, scooping the bags of pills up with her free hand. She shoves Finn back into the chair, making it rock dangerously, and waves the tiny pill bags in his face.

"Explain this!" She shakes Finn violently by the shirt, the chair barely staying upright. Beside me Ashlyn rocks back and forth, quaking shudders like a tree in a storm. Shoebox whines low in his throat.

Recognition blooms in Finn's green eyes.

"Talk. Now," Lyssa demands, releasing her grip and hurling the pills into Finn's lap.

Finn fingers the clear plastic but doesn't speak.

The silence stretches to eternity.

Ashlyn has gone still at the end of the futon. I don't think she's looked up since Finn came in, but I can't take my eyes off him.

"We're waiting," Lyssa says quietly and it's somehow more ominous than when she shouted. She steps back, like maybe Finn needs physical space to talk, but still the silence stretches. She flicks a glance at Ashlyn and me, double-takes, and turns her back on Finn to disappear into her closet. She comes out with a black hoodie that she hands me wordlessly. I pull it on over my T-shirt, abstractly grateful for the warmth, but all I can focus on is Finn and his awful silence.

When I think I can speak without chattering teeth, I say his name. Just his name.

He looks at me, then back down at the pills. He inhales like he's about to say something, at last, but he only shakes his head.

"Finn," I say again, holding a hand out to stop Lyssa from moving in again. Finn's gaze lifts to me.

"Where did you get these?" he asks. He looks at each of us in turn, me, then Lyssa, then Ashlyn. I swear I can see his heart break when she doesn't look up.

"That's all you have to say?" Lyssa asks.

"Where did you get them?"

"The library," I say and as I picture the scene all the hurt and fury of the morning comes flooding back. I sit on my hands again, not to warm them this time, but to stop them from being fists. I hold Finn's face with my eyes, waiting for the truth.

"Did you buy them?" he asks slowly, as if he's trying on each word for the first time. He watches me intently.

"Did I—? Did I—? What?" I'm on my feet now. "Finn, just talk to us!"

"Did you buy them?" he repeats, defiant now. "Seriously. That's the only way you would know they were in the library. So did you buy them?"

"She saw you, you fucking moron," Lyssa says.

That shuts him up.

"I saw you. Third period. Finn, god, why are you doing this?" My voice breaks and as much as I want to, I can't stop the tears from spilling down my cheeks. "And why are you doing it for Trevor Mayfield?"

Finn is on his feet in an instant, looking panicked. I feel broken, standing there in a useless mess of silent tears.

"Sit," Lyssa orders him. "We're not done."

Finn ignores her. He puts his hands on my shoulders, eyes pleading. "You have to believe me. Please. I didn't know it was for Trevor. I would never, if I'd known . . ."

"You sold him drugs, Finn! How did you not know it was him?" I drop back onto the futon and look up at him, shaking my head. "Trevor, Finn. After everything. Trevor."

"It's anonymous," Finn says, looking back and forth between me and Lyssa. He runs a frantic hand over his face and pulls two phones out of his pocket. One is the iPhone we always see him with, the other a small, no-frills Android. "Look."

Ashlyn still hasn't made herself part of the conversation, but her eyes lift.

Finn opens the messages in the iPhone and hands it to me. The contact names are all familiar: us, his grandmother, a couple kids from school.

"Normal, right?"

I nod and hand it to Lyssa.

"This is different," he says, opening the message app on the Android. There are no contact names, only numbers. "I don't know who any of these people are. They don't know who I am. That's how it works. Look."

I take the phone from him and open the first conversation in the list. Lyssa reads over my shoulder.

"What is this?" I ask. I scroll through several cryptic conversations, all referencing random book titles.

"The system. To keep it anonymous. Nothing is face-to-face

so no one can snitch. No one has my name, just a number I change on a regular basis, and I don't know who they are either. Anyone who gives me a name gets blocked." Finn talks fast, like the words are desperate to escape. "All the transactions are done through random books. It's never face-to-face. I didn't know it was Trevor."

I believe him. I look at Lyssa and see she might too.

But not enough.

"Doesn't change the fact that you stole pills from Seelie," Lyssa says.

Shame rearranges Finn's handsome face into something impossible to look at. He collapses back into the chair, head hanging like a terrible weight.

"Well?" Lyssa prods.

When Finn looks up his eyes shine with tears and he shuts them tightly. "I fucked up," he says, pressing his thumbs to his eyes. "Okay? I fucked up. I saw them there, I knew she wasn't going to use them, and I left one just in case, but she sounded so certain. You heard her. She didn't want them. So I took them."

"And gave them to Trevor!" Lyssa explodes, slamming a fist into the mess on her dresser.

"Or Jason," I say stupidly.

Finn doesn't react.

Ashlyn's question is shockingly gentle when it comes. "Why do you sell drugs?"

Finn's shoulders shake and I don't know if it's because of the question or the person who asked it.

Ashlyn unfolds herself from the futon and kneels in front

of Finn's chair. She puts her hands on his knees. "Make us understand, Finn. Please," she says.

"My grandparents are on a fixed income," he says haltingly. "This lets me contribute to the house and still have money for myself."

"Then why not get more hours at work like a normal person?" Lyssa asks. Ashlyn glares at her.

"This is what I do," Finn says, and though his eyes are still closed, there's no question that he's talking to Ashlyn right now. "It's easy and it's good money. Great money. I'm lucky if I get fifteen hours a week at Dunkin's. That's barely enough to buy myself lunch."

"Why do you live with them?" Her voice is soothing and soft, like it's just the two of them talking. "Your grandparents."

"My dad's in jail. In Kentucky. It was here or foster care. It's not something I like to advertise."

"What did he do?"

"Drug trafficking."

None of us knows what to say to that.

"Do you take any of it?" Ashlyn asks.

He shakes his head. "That's not how it works. It's just business. Using is what got my father caught."

Ashlyn is visibly relieved by that. "It has to stop," she says. "No more dealing."

Finn drops his hands so they cover Ashlyn's tiny ones. He opens his eyes and when he looks into hers I feel like I'm intruding on something very intimate.

"Okay," he says at last.

Afraid to break the spell Ashlyn has cast, I force myself to ask a question I'm not sure I want an answer to. "Do you sell PCP?"

He looks up at me, shaking his head. He doesn't have to ask why. "No. Prescription stuff. Some pot, sometimes, but mostly pills," he says. "PCP isn't that popular anymore."

So he didn't get Shane the drugs he was on that night.

At least there's that.

Right?

35

For the first time ever, Wedgie feels too big. Too empty.

I wanted to pick everyone up, to cram the green jelly bean full of my friends, but I felt stupid admitting that. I should be able to drive seven minutes by myself, right?

In the silence of the warming car I realize how cocooned I've been since the attack. I'm either in my (constantly quadruple-checked) locked room or I'm with at least one of the faction. Safety in paranoia and friendship.

I put on my seat belt and try to ignore how nervous I am. My stomach lurches as I back out of my driveway.

I'm alone.

Isolated.

And I know it's stupid; I'm in my car, no one can get me. Still, I keep the radio off, knuckles white on ten and two, and spend the entire drive fighting an irrational urge to check the backseat for someone hiding there.

This is what getting back to normal looks like.

Out of habit, I almost turn into the seniors' lot, but catch myself. Someone honks at me and in the rearview mirror I see the imposing grill of Lyssa's Jeep. She follows me up the winding road to the juniors' lot.

I spot Finn's red Mazda and pull into the closest empty space and wonder how he's going to afford that car if he stops selling drugs.

I know Lyssa doesn't believe he's going to stop. She said so last night, her voice floating down from the loft bed as sleep evaded us both. I desperately hope she's wrong, but Finn did leave with the drugs. He argued that he needed to settle these last two deals since he already had their money, but then it was over. He looked so earnest when he said it, but I can't help wondering why it wouldn't have been easier to put the money back instead.

Lyssa lets the Jeep idle behind my car. Finn and Ashlyn are on their way over.

"Look at you, driving like a normal person!" Finn says as I get out.

"Something like that," I say, finally letting myself peek into the backseat. No psychopaths.

The passenger door of the Jeep swings open. "Shuttle service to the building?" Lyssa offers.

I grab my backpack and leave my cane in the footwell of the car. If I'm not walking the quarter mile from the juniors' lot, I shouldn't need it.

Getting back to normal.

In the Jeep, two steaming travel mugs sit in the console.

"Guess it's a habit now," Lyssa says, shrugging when she catches me noticing.

I have to take a long sip to hide the smile stretching across my face.

///

I manage to hold onto the feeling of nearly normal until lunch.

I leave the library early to avoid the crush of bodies that will fill the hall when the bell rings and walk slowly to the lockers. There's a dull throb in my thigh, but I feel free walking without the cane.

The orange door still bears the scars where the red paint was scoured off. I wish they'd paint over the specter of those words already.

When I open the locker, I see there's a piece of pink-lined paper, folded several times, caught on the back of my coat. Someone must have shoved it through the vents.

I just stare at it warily. I want it to be another of Lyssa's drawings, but the paper's wrong for that. A note, then, but the faction texts. Anything written and shoved into my locker is bound to be bad.

The bell is about to ring, but I unfold the note anyway. It's either from one of the faction or it's not. Schrödinger's note. The specific nature of the *not* option is the thing I don't want to consider.

Instead of Ashlyn's half-cursive hybrid or Lyssa's spidery capitals, centered on the page are three lines of stereotypical popular-girl handwriting: bubbly purple letters, complete with cheerful circles topping the *i*'s like cherries on a sundae.

You're not the first girl he hurt

I think you did the right thing

Thank You

It's not signed.

Of course it's not.

I carry the note to our table and wait for Lyssa and Ashlyn, rereading it like the sixteen words contain a code, like I must be misunderstanding them.

Who could've written this? Is it a joke?

It can't be.

Finn is the first one to sit down. Apparently he's skipping gym today. "Whatcha got?" he asks.

I shake my head. "I don't know."

When the others join us, I lay the short missive in the middle of the table. I offer no explanation because I have yet to come up with one.

"Whoa," Finn says, which pretty much sums it up.

"Who do you think wrote it?" Ashlyn asks.

"No clue." I'm tearing the bagel Ashlyn brought me into a pile of tiny pieces. With each rip I consider a new name, but none stick. It could be anyone.

"You should show Cara," Lyssa says, gesturing at the note with a french fry. "She might be able to use it."

I take a photo of the note and text it to Cara with the message: **This was in my locker. No idea who wrote it.**

Ashlyn is looking at my scar, lost in thought. The scrutiny is almost unbearable. "If he attacked someone at school, wouldn't we have noticed?"

"Not necessarily." Maybe someone followed his crazy directions. Maybe they didn't look and they didn't move and they got away with only inside scars. I can't help scanning the lunchroom, wondering if the author is here.

Wondering who else Shane hurt.

My phone buzzes with a reply from Cara: **Don't lose it. Find out who wrote it.**

How the hell am I supposed to do that?

I spend the rest of the day sneaking glances at people's papers, searching for a match. I want to demand handwriting samples from the whole school. In each period I get a bathroom pass so I have an excuse to walk by more desks and peek at open notebooks, but it's no use. That cheerful purple scrawl is missing from every page I see.

On the short drive to my car, Lyssa admits she's been doing the same thing. Finn and Ashlyn too, probably.

Maybe they've had better luck.

The parking lot is chaos. Bursts of music shoot out as doors are opened and slammed. Shouting students dart between parked and moving cars, heedless of the fact that it's a Friday and some of us actually want to go home.

"Ten points if I hit someone?" Lyssa asks.

"Twenty if it's someone we hate."

When Lyssa finally pulls in beside Wedgie, I'm still so distracted by the mysterious note that I can't quite process what I'm seeing.

36

The parking lot is nowhere near empty, but the cacophony fades to a dull roar at the sight of my beloved Bug.

"No, no, no," I moan, opening the Jeep's door and making the long jump to the pavement before Lyssa can shift into park.

They got to Wedgie.

The windshield and gleaming green paint are almost completely obscured by sickly peach-colored circles. I can't figure out what they are. Stickers, maybe, or paint. The side mirrors dangle on barely attached metal cables, prismatic shards littering the ground beneath them. One front wheel rests on a bed of flattened rubber, a gaping puncture wound flapping where the tire was stabbed.

Behind me a horn blares, long and impossible to ignore. A harbinger.

The silence that follows is deafening.

Everyone is looking in Wedgie's direction now.

In my direction.

Lyssa's voice rings out above me. "You're all fucking cowards!" She's standing on the Jeep's running board, one hand on the roof and the other braced against the open door. With her own height and that of the vehicle, there is no one in the parking lot who can't see her. Everyone has gone motionless. "All of you!"

In the pause, the pounding of feet can be heard. Finn and Ashlyn are sprinting toward us, matching looks of worry painting their faces. No one else moves. Currents of rage connect the crowd to Lyssa like manacles.

"She has done nothing to any of you. Nothing! She saved her fucking life. That's it. That makes her a fucking hero!" She hits the roof of the Jeep and the impact reverberates like a gunshot. When she continues her voice is so thick with emotion that goose bumps cascade down my arms. "She is the bravest person any of you will ever meet; she deserves a fucking medal. She does not deserve this. You should all be ashamed."

Tension crackles across the lot. Several people have phones out, recording the unhinged girl towering over them.

"If you hurt her, if any of you hurt her in any way, I will destroy you." Lyssa glares at her rapt audience, contempt contorting her beautiful features. "Now get the fuck out of here!"

She stays up there as the parking lot empties around us.

I'm overcome with a rush of affection for this fierce girl but the moment is gone the second I touch one of the round spots on the car. I recoil, disgusted. It's slick and slimy and definitely not a sticker.

"Bologna," Finn says, grimacing. "It's supposed to kill the paint."

I peel a slice of the offending lunch meat off. No question, it's bologna. It leaves behind a damp circle on the hood of the car, but no paint comes away with it. It must not have had enough time to work its evil meat magic.

Holding this slice of compressed meat scraps triggers a tidal wave of fury. I whirl and kick Wedgie's broken wheel with all my might. I kick again and again, wordless screams punctuating each blow. I kick the poor Beetle, which has already been so abused, until I'm weak with exhaustion.

No one stops me.

Lyssa has dropped from her pulpit and stands with Finn and Ashlyn, watching me.

"What?" I snap, when I see them all staring at me.

"I don't think that's good for your leg," Ashlyn says carefully.

"I don't care." I kick the car one more time for emphasis. I sag against the car only to have to jump back up when I realize I'm leaning on bologna. "Fuck!"

"Go sit in the Jeep," Lyssa says, eyes stormy. "We'll take care of this."

But I can't. Wedgie is mine and I have to help.

Pulling bologna off the Bug is a uniquely degrading experience. Each slice is a reminder that someone hates me enough to have done this in the first place. As the pile grows bigger, the final insult begins to reveal itself on the hood of the car. I peel the meat off faster, insides tied in a hangman's knot.

Murderer.

That single word keyed into the hood, straight through the green paint and all the way down to the gray primer Dad applied. For the first time in my life, I'm glad he's gone, glad he can't see what's become of his creation.

Or of me.

I sink to the freezing asphalt.

There's a gaping cavern where my feelings should be.

Lyssa comes around to the front of the car. I stare at her beat-up Doc Martens.

"Get up," she says from very far away.

But I can't do it anymore. I can't keep trying to prove I'm normal, no matter what Cara wants.

"C'mon." She squats down next to me. "You can't sit there. It's cold."

When I don't respond, she stands, grabs my hands, and hauls me to my feet.

My bad leg buckles and I stagger, shocked out of my self-pity by the burst of pain. "Shit!"

I crash unceremoniously into Lyssa, who loops an arm around my waist, and I have to fight the urge to turn into her and bury my face against the soft wool of her coat. She held me together once before, maybe she would do it again. Instead I let her lead me to the Jeep, which is still running and warm.

"Give me your keys," she says and I do.

She gets Wedgie's spare tire while Finn gathers tools from the Mazda's trunk. Any animosity Lyssa might've been harboring over the drug issue seems forgotten as the two work on the car. Ashlyn paces back and forth, talking into her phone.

She should be halfway to practice by now.

Another thing I've messed up.

The sun is dipping low behind naked trees and casting long shadows across the pavement. The three of them confer in the empty parking lot, frosty clouds of air pooling around their heads like thought bubbles as they speak. Lyssa's thumbs dart across her phone as they talk. She reaches into the Beetle and extracts my cane, then holds the door open while Ashlyn settles herself behind the wheel. Finn is already driving off when Lyssa swings herself into the Jeep.

"We're going to my house."

"I still have physical therapy."

"Not tonight."

//

Lyssa's house smells blissfully of spaghetti sauce and baking bread.

Like a home.

Like what I need.

I have to lean heavily on my cane and can't help worrying that I did real damage today. I disappear into the bathroom while the others crowd around the kitchen table. I tug my jeans down, expecting to see some sign of injury, but the scar is still just a scar, pink and puckered and normal. I find a bottle of Advil in the medicine cabinet and take four with tap water.

When I come out, I find the others are telling Lyssa's increasingly horrified parents about what happened to Wedgie. No one mentions Lyssa's speech.

"Did you file a police report?" Rick asks as he dishes up heaping plates of pasta.

"I want nothing to do with the police," I say. "If it weren't for them, none of this would even be happening."

Peter runs a hand over his short beard. "I think you should have this on record," he says. "At least with the school."

"They're not doing anything," Lyssa says. "There's been other stuff. They don't care."

"What other stuff?" Peter asks.

"I'll tell my lawyer," I say quickly, wanting to forestall a complete rehashing of my humiliations.

Peter looks concerned, but doesn't press. He offers to have a go at fixing my side mirrors after dinner and the rest of the meal passes with small talk and Shoebox making his rounds beneath the table, begging for bread crusts. I give him my whole slice. I'm too keyed up to eat much anyway.

37

"Cecelia Stanton and Alyssa Dante-Arroyo to Mr. Baker's office. Cecelia Stanton, Alyssa Dante-Arroyo to the office, please."

The week before Christmas vacation, the bored voice of the school secretary shatters the test-induced silence in Psychology. Like Pavlov's dogs, everyone turns to look at us, practically drooling in anticipation of gossip.

"You can finish your test when you get back, or after school," Mr. Lynch says as we go.

"This is probably gonna suck," Lyssa says matter-of-factly when we reach the hall.

We walk slowly, out of both necessity and a desire to delay the inevitable. After a couple sessions with Jacqui and lots of hot baths, I'm finally feeling like I didn't break myself, but I'm still not at full speed.

Who am I kidding?

I wasn't at full speed before the setback either.

Jacqui was extra pissed when I hobbled into the first post-Wedgie appointment and gave me a huge lecture about not getting in the way of my own recovery. I was officially banned

211

from the reckless kicking of things, but since my punishment consisted of an hour's soak in the hot tub, I figured I got off easy.

Today doesn't look nearly as good.

Mr. Baker is already waiting for us when we arrive. He points at me, then to the bench outside his office door. "Sit."

I do.

"You," he says to Lyssa, "inside. Now."

The heavy door slams behind them.

The wooden bench digs uncomfortably into my back, reminding me of the pew-like benches at court. That thought doesn't relax me at all.

Next to the bench is a ballot box with a poster soliciting early nominations for the Winter Gala pageant. It feels foreign that there are actually people whose biggest concern right now is whether they'll be allowed to compete for Winter King and Queen.

I wonder if they appreciate how lucky they are.

I strain to hear what's being said in Baker's office, but despite the raised voices I can't quite make out words.

Finn rounds the corner, a pink pass in his hand. He looks panicked. As soon as he sits, his knee starts jackhammering up and down. "What the hell did you guys do?"

"I have no idea."

"We heard them call you down here. Is it about the car?"

"I just said I don't know." I have a feeling his fear is directly tied to our knowledge of his library scheme.

He folds his crumpled pass into a shrinking square. "If it's, you know," he says, confirming my suspicion. "What are you—"

Before he can finish, Mr. Baker's door opens and he steps out. He jabs a finger at Finn. "You, what are you doing here?"

"I have a pass?" He waves the pink square at Mr. Baker like it could be an answer.

"Get back to class," Baker snaps. "Seelie, inside."

Finn shoots me a pleading look and I follow Mr. Baker inside.

Lyssa is in one of the wooden armchairs in front of Baker's sprawling mahogany desk. She has it pushed as far across the office as possible. Her body is thrumming with tension, all the way from her long, thrust-out legs to her rigid jaw. My stomach clenches.

"Take a seat," Baker says. Instead of going to sit behind his desk, he leans on the front of it and folds his arms.

I perch on the edge of the other armchair, cane held upright between my knees like it might offer some protection.

"Tell me about last Friday," Baker says.

My heart is racing. I turn to look at Lyssa but Baker holds up a hand.

"Tell me," he says. "Not her."

"She didn't do anything," I say. My face is hot. "Why is she in trouble?"

"Nobody said she is." But that's a lie. Lyssa's face says it loud and clear. "Just tell me what happened."

So I explain how we found Wedgie and what was done to the Bug. I don't mention Lyssa's speech. I don't know how to feel about the things she said. Thinking about it makes me feel like I have a head full of hornets, but maybe in a good way.

"Why didn't you call administration?" Baker asks.

"What for? This isn't the first time something like this has happened. You're not doing anything!" I'm getting loud, but I can't help it. I grip the cane tightly, trying to keep it together. "It doesn't matter. It's just a car."

But it does matter.

"You heard Ms. Dante-Arroyo verbally threaten the student body?"

"What are you talking about?"

"I have a video sitting in my inbox that clearly shows Lyssa making threats. Unspecified threats, but still threats." Mr. Baker looks tired.

"I'm suspended," Lyssa says from the back of the room. "Guess vacation starts early this year."

I gape at Baker, dumbstruck. "She's suspended for trying to defend me? How is that fair?"

"It's not," he admits. "But I'm between a rock and a hard place. If that video gets out and then there's a fight, that's a huge problem."

This can't be happening.

"What about the people who did this? You know it was Trevor and his friends. What about them? Are they suspended too?"

"Do you have proof?" He sighs and scratches his bald head. "Look, I know this isn't easy. Without proof, I can't do anything. That's the problem here. Do I believe they did it? Yes. Will I be talking to them? You bet. But in the meantime, I actually do have proof Lyssa made threats, however well-intentioned they may have been, and I'm required to act on it."

I can't believe this. School has been hard enough to face with the faction intact. How can I do this without Lyssa?

38

"What happens if I stop going to school?" I ask.

Cara looks at me like I'm an idiot, but it's an honest question. I wait.

"It's a condition of bail. So aside from screwing up any college plans you may have, you could be sent back to jail. Your trial is still weeks away. I don't think jail is where you want to spend those weeks," she says. "Where is this coming from?"

We're sitting in my kitchen for our last meeting before she returns to Boston for the holidays. Mom still isn't here, which is why I felt okay asking the question. Among the papers on the table is the mystery note and I carefully line its edge up with a crack in the table.

"Did something else happen?" she asks.

What's happened so far isn't enough? Really? I shake my head. "Never mind. It's fine."

"Vacation starts in two days. That will help."

Not likely. From the living room, the Christmas tree fills the house with the scent of pine and the promise of forced family interaction. 'Tis the season.

I smooth the ruffled edge of the note down. I press each torn piece flat, one by one. I hate people who leave the fuzzies on the sides of their papers. "What if I got my GED?"

Cara doesn't answer right away. She's quiet long enough that I glance up from the note. She's casual today, dressed in dark jeans and a black sweater. Her shoes are still crazy, though: shiny red ballet flats, like she's trying to get to Oz.

"Is it that bad?" she asks.

I nod. The note blurs when I look down.

I don't know if it's Finn's drug bomb or Lyssa's suspension or the culmination of all the things that have gone wrong since that day in October, but I'm so, so tired.

"I can't keep doing it." I don't just mean school. I'm sick of walking around worrying about what's going to happen next, sick of pretending everything is fine, that the weight of my secret isn't smothering me.

"You can," she says. "And you will, because you must."

I grit my teeth. She doesn't get what it's like to have to show up every day to a place that already hated you even before you became a killer. She would've run with the Madisons and Trevors in high school. She doesn't know how soul-sucking it can be on the other side.

"High school is a shitty place," she says, as if reading my mind. "I know that. Trust me, I know that. But you have to get through it. This is literally your life that you're fighting for. If you violate the terms of bail, if you show the court you don't care about getting your life back, you will lose it. That's a fact. Trials are about presenting the evidence, but they're also about telling stories. You need to be the hero in this one, and the hero doesn't give up."

"Do you really think we're going to win? Everyone already thinks I'm the monster."

"Not everyone. I don't. Your friends don't. Detective Mellers doesn't."

"Really?"

"Really. I'm considering calling her as one of our witnesses."

I mull this over. Mellers's partner spearheaded the campaign to lock me up. Can she really be trusted? "Will I have to testify?" I ask.

"Do you want to?"

The thought of sitting on that witness stand fills my insides with rabid butterflies. "Do I have to?"

"Technically, no," she says. "You have the right to remain silent. We can try the case without your testimony, but I don't see a compelling reason to keep you off the stand. While you're on break, I want you to give some serious thought to testifying. I won't force you one way or the other, but I'll need your decision the next time we meet."

"Okay."

I hear the jangle of keys at the door and the walls slam up in my brain. Mom comes in with both arms weighted down with grocery bags because she refuses to make multiple trips back to the car.

"Ms. Dewitt, hi. I didn't know you were coming today," she says, dumping the bags on the counter and shooting eyeball daggers at me.

"We were just going over some small details," Cara says. I pray to an assortment of gods and demons that she doesn't

217

spill what I said about quitting school. "I'll be back in Boston until after the holidays and wanted to touch base before I left."

"Have there been any developments?" Mom asks as she puts groceries away.

"Nothing new. Like I said, this was mostly to touch base." Cara is gathering up her papers. Before she takes the note, she taps it twice. "Remember, try to find out who wrote this."

I nod.

"Wrote what?" my mother asks, coming over.

"Nothing," I say. Cara is putting the note into her folder but my mother startles her by snatching it.

"Mrs. Stanton, I'll need that back." Cara holds a manicured hand out while my mother reads the page.

Mom hands it back. "That's good evidence, right? Seelie, did one of your friends give you that?"

I hate that she's horning in on my business. "You just heard her say we don't know who wrote it. It's not a big deal."

"I'll be available by phone or email if you need me for anything," Cara says, clearly not wanting to get involved in a mother–daughter spat. "Otherwise I'll be in touch after New Year's."

I see her out. Before I can make it upstairs, Mom calls me back to the kitchen.

"Help me make supper," she says. "I want to talk to you."

"I have nothing to say." This feels like a trap. We rarely have dinner together on days the restaurant is open.

"I got a call from your school today." She deposits a bag of salad fixings and a bowl in front of me. "Anything you want to tell me?"

"Nope." I tear chunks out of the lettuce, imagining it's Trevor's head, and throw them into the bowl.

"Nothing at all? Not a compelling reason for why you haven't been to history all month?"

"I'm doing an independent study," I lie, slicing into the cucumber with a razor-sharp Wusthof.

"Then why does your teacher keep reporting you absent?"

"Because he's an idiot and probably forgot." It's the kind of thing that could be true about Wilkins.

"Seelie, this isn't the time to be causing trouble at school, you know."

"I'm not the one causing trouble at school," I say and instantly regret revealing even that much.

"You're the one I'm getting calls about," she says, oblivious. "I really don't have time for this, Seelie. Between all your legal drama and trying to keep the restaurant above water I'm at the end of my rope here. Just go to class like a normal person, please."

I set the knife on the counter. Deep breath. Don't flip out. "My legal drama? What planet do you actually live on?"

"One where people are expected to take responsibility for their actions. I don't know exactly what happened in that barn, but there are consequences to every action. You need to learn to think before you act."

I step away from the counter, away from the knife. It takes a conscious effort to close my jaw.

"Are you saying I brought this on myself?" My legs are forgetting how to stand. I collapse into a chair at the table. "Is that what you're saying? That I somehow deserve this?"

She sighs. "All I'm saying is go to class, Seelie. Don't make things harder than they already are."

At this point, I'm not sure how much worse things can actually get.

39

It's during Christmas vacation that I learn just how cataclys-mically worse things can get.

I don't know how I know, but I know.

I think I've known all along.

Proof is a formality.

I haven't started Wedgie since the day I drove her home from Lyssa's, but I do it now. Snow has fallen overnight but I don't brush it from the hood.

I drive the twenty minutes to Walmart, because even though Walgreens is closer, I want self-checkout. I walk through the brightly lit store in a daze. People look at my scarred face and for once I don't turn away.

Let them stare.

I killed a man.

And I'm being punished.

40

I pee on the stick.

    The pink plus sign destroys me.

41

My first thought is of evisceration: I want it out and I want it out now.

It's like I'm being attacked all over again from the inside out. A hostile takeover of my whole self.

My second thought, when it finally comes, is that maybe I'm finally out of tears, because I'm not crying.

I sit on my bed for a long time with my phone in my lap, ignoring the texts that occasionally vibrate it.

I have to take care of this.

I have to take care of this now.

I google *abortion clinic near me.*

A phone number and address appear for a Springfield Planned Parenthood. I tap the number before I can overthink it.

A recorded message starts at once, giving me language options and asking me to choose a reason for my call. "Impending loss of sanity" isn't on the list, so I press zero to speak to a receptionist.

"Planned Parenthood," says a cheerful female voice. "How can I help you?"

Good question.

"I need to schedule an abortion," I say. My voice sounds hollow and distant, but unexpectedly steady.

Maybe I'm in shock.

"Okay, I can help you with that," she says. Like it's normal. Like it's not the end of my world. "Can I get your name and address first?"

I give them.

"And did you want in-clinic or medical?"

"I don't know," I say. I should've looked this all up before I made the call. Why didn't I look this up? "Is one better?"

"They're just different, but many women find the pill to be less invasive."

"Are there side effects?"

"The most common side effects are cramping, nausea, and vomiting, but that rarely extends more than three or four days."

Nope.

Can't do it.

I don't want to have to explain my stupid phobia to her. Now that I know why my stomach has been such a mess, it's a miracle I haven't been sick yet. I don't think I could force myself to take a pill that was almost guaranteed to make me vomit. "In-clinic, please."

"Okay. And do you have insurance?"

I hesitate, knowing that this could be a problem. "I do," I say, "but do I have to use it?"

"Well, many insurance plans cover our services," the woman says, sounding confused. "It makes it more affordable for you."

My mother can't know about this. About any part of it.

"If I don't use it, how much will it cost?"

"We offer a sliding-fee scale based on income. What do you do?"

I almost say horse care, but I don't actually do that anymore, do I? "I'm just a student."

"Ah," she says, as if that clarified something. "You're under your parents' insurance?"

"Yes."

"Massachusetts requires that parental permission be obtained for all abortion services," she explains.

"I can't tell anyone." All the blood has drained to my toes.

"Under certain circumstances, a judge can excuse you from the requirement."

That would be so much worse than telling my mother. That could ruin everything.

Fuck.

Fuck, fuck, fuck.

This can't be happening.

My room is starting to spin.

"Or," she says slowly when I don't answer, "there are certain states, such as Connecticut, that don't require parental consent. Maybe you called the wrong office?"

I hang up and search for Connecticut abortion centers. The nearest clinic that pops up is not Planned Parenthood, but a private clinic. I click through to their FAQs, looking for pricing. A private clinic has to cost more. But no. At the bottom of the page is a line that says, *Thanks to generous funding from MaryAnne and Charles Cranston, we are able to fully subsidize certain services for the survivors of sexual trauma.*

I click the "certain services" link. I read the page and know I've found the right place.

The lady who answers the phone has a lilting West Indian accent that sounds too carefree for such serious business. She takes down my information with friendly efficiency.

"Do you know approximately how far along you are?"

I know to the hour, but I just tell her, "From October twenty-first."

If the specificity of the date weirds her out, she doesn't say anything. Keys clatter at the other end of the phone. "Hmm. Okay. That puts you out of range for medical. I do have an appointment available the day after tomorrow for a surgical, though."

"I'll take it."

"Plan to be here for approximately four hours. If you have sedation, you'll need to bring a responsible companion to drive you home, and don't eat or drink anything after midnight before your appointment."

"Okay." I should be writing this down. I'm not.

"Our clinic has secure parking directly adjacent to the building, but the city does allow protesters to congregate on the sidewalks surrounding the parking lot. Try to ignore them. They're not allowed onto our property and they know it. There's a security guard posted at all times to ensure our patients' safety."

When we hang up I go back into the bathroom. The test is still on the counter, mocking me with its fading pink plus sign. There's got to be an untapped market for pregnancy tests aimed at people who have no desire to be pregnant. Like instead of this

226

cheerful plus sign, it would say, *Yup, You're Screwed* as soon as it detected the invasion of unwanted pregnancy hormones. Or maybe *Don't Panic* (in large friendly letters) would be more helpful. And if you're not pregnant, the test would just flash little thumbs-up signs at you.

I wrap the stick in half a roll of toilet paper and take it downstairs. I don't want to leave it in the exposed bathroom trash in case my mother sees it. I shove it deep into the kitchen trash, piling empty yogurt containers and other gross bits of rubbish on top of it. Mom is bound to notice if I take the bag out to the dumpster since I haven't done it since the attack, so I leave it, hidden in plain sight.

Back in the bathroom, I pull Mom's bathrobe off the hook behind the door to reveal the full-length mirror I normally avoid like the plague. I pull my hoodie up and take a long, hard look at my stomach, searching for a sign of the horror that lurks inside.

I'm big. There's no denying that, so my belly has always been pretty round and soft. I know there's muscle under there somewhere from the long hours in the barn, but it's well hidden. I run a hand over the skin with the same reserve I would use for petting snakes. I don't love this part of me on a normal day and I dislike it that much more knowing there's an invader festering beneath the flesh. I prod my gut, wondering exactly where this final assault has been hiding. Just above the band of my underwear my stomach feels firm and there's a strange tautness to the usually squishy flesh. It must be there, then. But unless you were looking, really looking, you'd never know.

Somehow that almost makes it worse.

I lay both hands against that spot, like women do on TV, and wait to feel something stir.

Nothing does.

42

There are eleven unread texts on my phone.

I ignore them all and open a new message to Ashlyn.

ME: **I need you to come over right now. Alone.**

ASH: **U OK?? Been trying to reach u all morning**

ME: **Just come over.**

ASH: **K. 10 min**

I wonder if I'm making a mistake, but I have no choice. It obviously can't be Finn, and Lyssa . . . I don't want Lyssa to know about this. Not ever. Especially not when it feels like we're dancing on the edge of something I've wanted for so long.

I'm pacing the living room, knowing it's bad for my leg but feeling incapable of sitting still, when I'm suddenly wracked with full-body shakes like I haven't experienced since the hospital.

That can't be good.

My breath is raspy in my ears and everything I look at is a little too . . . sharp.

I see Ashlyn pull in with her mom's minivan and try to get back some of the preternatural calm that got me through the phone calls this morning.

It takes several tries to unlock the door for her because my hands are trembling so hard. I lean my forehead against the cool wood of the door as I steady myself. When I hear her footsteps on the porch, I step back, hoping I don't look as frayed and tattered as I feel.

Okay.

I'm okay.

"Oh god, what's wrong?" Ashlyn asks the instant she sees me.

I lock the door behind her and steel myself.

I can do this.

I have to.

"Let's go upstairs," I say.

In my room, she deposits her purse in the nest chair and sits on the bed.

I lock the door even though we're the only ones here.

I can't help it.

I sit next to her, keeping my feet flat on the ground. Ashlyn draws her legs up under her and turns to face me. From the corner of my eye I can see her studying me. From that side she can't see the scar. From that side, things look normal.

"What's up?" she asks.

My hands start to shake in my lap. I clench them together, digging my right thumbnail into the soft web of my left hand.

"I have to tell you something."

Blood roars in my head.

She scoots a little closer. "Seelie, what is it?"

"I have to tell you something," I repeat to my hands. "And I need a favor."

"Anything. Of course."

"Actually, two favors." I look at her now. She has to understand how important this part is. "First you have to promise you won't tell anyone what I'm about to tell you. Not even Lyssa or Finn."

She considers this, not agreeing automatically. She knows I'm asking her to commit a sin of omission. "Okay."

"Swear. No matter what." My eyes bore into hers. "Not a word. Not to anyone."

"I promise." The furrow between her brows deepens.

I look back at my hands. I don't know how to do this.

I open my mouth only to find myself deserted by the truth. It's that word I never wanted to say to anyone, even to myself, even in my head.

Ashlyn doesn't rush me.

The stillness in the room is like the stutter between earthquake tremors.

I bring it all tumbling down.

"Shane raped me." A tiny trickle of blood appears on my web.

I hear Ashlyn's hands clap over her mouth but I don't look up.

I rush to fill the exploding silence.

"I haven't told anyone. Not even the police. Or Cara. You can't tell the faction." I turn to her now, imploring. "You can't tell anyone."

Her eyes are full of empathy and she throws her arms around me.

"I'm so, so sorry," she says into my hair. "Oh Seelie, god, you didn't have to carry this around by yourself for so long."

And in that moment I believe her. It gives me the strength I need for the next part.

I pull away, wiping my eyes and exhaling a shaky breath.

Now or never.

"There's something else."

"The favor."

I nod.

My fingers are at war again in my lap. "I'm pregnant."

Ashlyn rocks back as if the word were a blow. She looks stunned.

Again, words tumble out of me to fill the vacuum. "I'm going to get it taken care of. I have an appointment and everything. It's all set. I just need a ride because of the medication and I know it's a huge favor and it's all the way in Manchester but I didn't know who else to ask."

"Oh god," she whispers. The sadness on her face is so profound that it hurts.

"The appointment is on Friday. In the morning."

She doesn't answer and I realize how wrong I was to tell her, to tell anyone.

"Don't do this, Seelie," she says softly. "Don't do it, you've already been through so much. Don't put yourself through this too. You'll regret it. There are other options."

Now it's my turn to be stunned as she struggles to fill the void.

"You have choices." She's on her knees now, beseeching as she grasps my hands. "Please don't do this."

The tectonic plates of our friendship shift.

I fall headlong into the chasm that opens between us.

"I understand if you don't want to keep it," she continues, oblivious to the knife she's twisting in my heart. "I really do. I don't blame you at all. But adoption. You could give it away."

"Stop." I withdraw my hands from hers. "I can't listen to this. Not from you. Just stop."

How could I have been so wrong? How could I think thirteen years of friendship could override a lifetime of her beliefs?

"I know you're confused," she says, reaching for my hands again, but I get up. I can't stand to be near her right now.

"I'm not confused. This is the least confused I've been about any part of this entire catastrophe. He raped me, Ash. How can you sit there and tell me to keep it?" She looks like she's going to cry but I don't care. "It's like he's still hurting me. Still. Don't you get that? He's been inside me for two months, poisoning me."

"I didn't tell you to keep it," she says quietly. "I said adoption."

"I can't do it. I can't let him live inside of me for nine months. I can't."

"Seven," she says, like that makes a difference. I know her anguish is real, but she's being blind. Why is she being so blind?

"You don't understand. No one can know about this," I say. "No one can know what he really did to me. How can I keep that a secret if I have his fucking baby?"

"Why do you have to keep it a secret?"

Panic floods my system. "You promised. You promised you wouldn't tell anyone."

"I won't, but why can't you?" She unfolds her legs and reaches for me, but I stay back. "Please sit with me. We can talk about this."

"If you're gonna try to talk me out of doing what I need to do, there's nothing to discuss."

We stare at each other from across a vast sea of differences. Tears slide down Ashlyn's face as she stands and my own eyes well in traitorous sympathy.

"I asked you for help," I say hoarsely.

"I love you like a sister, but I can't watch you do this," she says. "Please just think about it. You can change your mind. It will be okay."

She hugs me then and I cling to her, knowing this might be what goodbye feels like.

43

The protesters rattle homemade posters at me, united in strident indignation. One sign has a giant picture of a mangled fetus on it, but most are slogans painted in uneven letters: *Abortion is MURDER*; *Adoption is a Better Option*; *STOP KILLING BABIES*; *Your mother chose life!*

But I didn't choose any of this.

Wedgie's windows are rolled up against the cold and their chanting, but I have to drive past them and they crowd my car, shouting, "Murderer! Murderer!"

If only they knew.

I park as close to the door as possible and hurry inside. A security guard with arms as thick as my thigh looks up from his breakfast sandwich as I slip inside, fragments of the protest seeping in before I can shut the door, like malevolent ghosts refusing to rest.

The tiny antechamber smells of sausage and fried potatoes.

"Good morning," he says and his smile is so reassuring that it has to be the thing that got him hired. "You make it here okay?"

I nod.

"Name and appointment time?"

I give them and he checks it against his clipboard. "First of the day," he says and the smile is back. I wonder if all clinics have someone like this as their guardian.

I hope so.

The waiting room is empty but for a handful of lonely maroon chairs scattered atop industrial blue carpet. The lights are dim despite the early hour, but it makes the space seem somehow cozy.

The receptionist hands me a mountain of paperwork attached to a clipboard. I curl up in a chair and prop the clipboard on my knees. The pile of forms details the procedure and requests consent and a lengthy medical history. I only half-read them, filling the blanks in automatically with tight, cramped letters.

The last one asks if I would like to authorize the clinic to discuss my health with anyone else, check yes or no. I almost check no, but scribble in Cara's information.

Just in case.

Ashlyn might not have been wrong about everything. Maybe I don't need to keep it a secret. I found dozens of articles online about DNA evidence in court trials. Maybe this worst part could be the thing that saves me.

///

I'm taken from the main waiting area and deposited into a small, sunny room and left to wait some more.

It's only after I've memorized every birth control and sexual-health poster in the room that the door finally opens.

"My name is Jasmine," says the lady who comes in. She's about my size, with a head full of curly dreadlocks and a calming

236

demeanor that rivals the security guard's. It must be a job requirement. "I'm one of the nurse-counselors here. We're going to go over a lot of things before we get started, including any concerns you have. I want you to know that if you start to have any doubts about your decision, you can call off the procedure at any time."

"I won't." I don't want to be talked out of this. I don't want to wait.

"Can you tell me a little about your situation?" She opens a manila file folder, shuffles pages.

Can I?

I look out the window at the shrunken protesters, mouths moving on mute, signs thrusting for the sky.

"I was raped." It's easier to say this time, to this kindly stranger, knowing that no reaction will be worse than Ashlyn's. "I need to get rid of it. That's my situation."

"I see," Jasmine says and her complete lack of shock is encouraging. She's checking something in her file folder. "I'm terribly sorry you had to go through that. Were you offered any medication to prevent the pregnancy when you went to the hospital?"

"No." Not a lie, but not the whole truth either.

She frowns and writes something in the file and it hits me that this is my own fault. I could've avoided this entire experience if only I had told the doctors the truth. She doesn't seem to notice my distress as she pulls out my medical history papers and goes over each question, verifying the answers I filled in. The poison in my belly grows heavier with every second that ticks by beneath this layer of redundancy.

"Is anyone pressuring you to have an abortion?"

"No."

"Did you bring someone to drive you home after the procedure?"

I swallow. "No. I'm doing it without sedation."

Again, she is so very calm. "Some women find being awake difficult, and that's without having been sexually assaulted. But if you're sure that's how you want to proceed, I'll need you to sign this form waiving any sedation."

I sign it.

I need to do this.

At last, she asks the question I've been waiting for: "Are you familiar with the additional services we can offer for sexual-trauma survivors?"

I nod, because that's half the reason why I'm here, and sign those papers too.

"Okay, the last thing we need to do is get blood and urine samples," Jasmine says, turning to get a plastic cup out of the low cabinet behind her chair. She places it on the table. She snaps on a pair of blue latex gloves. "I'll just need to prick your finger for the blood sample."

I hold my hand out.

It doesn't shake.

"This is for the rapid HIV test," she says. "It will take about thirty minutes to process, during which time we'll get you changed and get the urine sample."

HIV.

I never even considered HIV.

She sends me to a large bathroom with a basket and the pee cup. The basket holds a robe and a thick white blanket.

I change slowly, trying to eat up as much of the wait as possible. I'm allowed to keep my shirt, socks, and the ankle monitor on, so there's only so long I can drag it out. I fold my pants around my underwear and put them in the basket, pee in the cup so they can confirm what I already know, and wrap the robe around myself.

Twenty-four minutes left.

Goose bumps prickle my legs and I wrap the blanket around my waist like a cocoon.

Jasmine fills the remaining time with gentle cautions about practicing safe sex in the future and the importance of seeking support following the abortion. If she notices the tracker strapped to my ankle, she has the kindness not to mention it.

Nineteen minutes later she asks if I am prepared to hear the test results and all I can do is nod.

44

"The results are negative."

I almost slide off the plastic chair in relief. He didn't kill me.

How many people must sit in this same room, wearing the same robe, with the same stiff white blanket over their legs and be told that they're not so lucky?

What does it say about the universe that I can count myself among the lucky? Mutilated, pregnant, and looking a murder charge square in the eye, but hey, at least I don't have AIDS. That's what counts as lucky these days?

There needs to be a better scale for such things.

Jasmine takes the basket that now holds my bag, sneakers, and the pants with my purple undies tucked deep in the leg, and leads me, shuffling in my blanket skirt, to a room that finally looks like a doctor's office.

A paper-covered exam table sits in the center, dual praying-mantis arms jutting out from one end. Various monitors and machines line the room. The lighting is, like in the waiting room, strangely dim for a medical setting.

"You can take a seat on the table," Jasmine says, as she places my basket of belongings on an empty chair.

I sit on the long edge of the table, away from the praying-mantis arms.

"Other way," she says gently.

Right.

I reposition so my legs dangle between the metal protrusions.

There's a knock on the door and a tall, serious-looking woman comes in.

"I'm Dr. Janowitz," she says, extending her hand. She exudes quiet competence. "Are you ready to get started?"

I nod. My head gets the slightest swimmy feeling.

"We're going to start with an ultrasound to see how far along you are and to make sure there aren't any complications we need to be aware of." She pulls a machine over on a rolling cart, angling it so she can see the screen. "If you could scoot back on the table and pull up your shirt, we can get a look. This might be a bit chilly."

She squirts a stream of frigid slime onto my belly and goose bumps erupt across my skin. I try not to shiver as she runs a probe over every inch of my stomach. Jasmine stands at my side, smiling encouragement at me.

"Looks like we're just shy of ten weeks," Dr. Janowitz says, wiping gel from the device. "Would you like to see?"

The swimming in my brain gets worse. Do I want to see the horror Shane Mayfield implanted in my guts?

"Definitely not."

If my answer surprises them they don't show it. These people are the very definition of unflappable. Jasmine hands me a wad of scratchy paper towels to wipe up the excess gel while the doctor finishes with the ultrasound machine. I pull my shirt back down and cringe as the fabric finds an errant trace of the goo. I sit up and rewrap my robe. Jasmine is busy at the counter, arranging something on a tray.

"Now I'm going to need you to put your feet in the stirrups and slide to the edge of the table," the doctor says. She pulls a wheeled stool over and a tall, flexible light. Jasmine places her tray of tools on a cart near the end of the exam table. "We're going to start with a local numbing injection."

The stirrups are nothing like the ones on saddles and they're cold beneath my socks. My knees yearn for each other.

Breathe in, breathe out.

This is how I save myself.

"Do you want me to hold your hand?" Jasmine asks.

I look at her like she's crazy.

She smiles down at me. "Some people find it helpful. I'm here if you need me."

What I need is for this to be over. The mantis arms of the table leave me too exposed and vulnerable.

Dr. Janowitz positions the light so she can see the truth.

My heart grows bat wings and tries to fly away.

She talks me through each step, calm and quiet and very, very gentle. She's a good doctor even if I'm not a good patient.

I lie with one hand behind my head in a ridiculous parody of relaxation. I dig a fingernail into the nape of my neck but it's a poor distraction.

I look everywhere but at my raised legs.

One of the ceiling tiles has been replaced with a picture of flowers and baby animals. It looks like the puppies and bunnies are peering down to observe the proceedings and I wonder who thought that was a good idea.

From the other side of the world, Dr. Janowitz says, "Only a few more minutes now. You're doing great."

I close my eyes, pretending I don't exist below the ribs, and take my brain away.

//

I'm woozy when I stand, like maybe the lidocaine has worked its way down into my legs.

I hold the edge of the table while I wait for the room to stop tilting. Maybe I should've brought my cane.

"Are you okay to walk?" Jasmine asks. She's reaching out like she might grab my elbow if I fall. I can't fall. I can't let anyone else touch me today.

"I'm fine." A lie. I don't even remember getting to my feet.

I follow her to the recovery room, where she settles me into an oversized leather armchair. At the other end of the row of chairs is another girl, older than me and playing on her phone like she's in her own living room.

I'm glad she's not looking at me.

Jasmine drapes the white blanket over my legs and places a flannel-covered heating pad on my belly. She gives me a juice box and opens a small, cellophane-wrapped packet of graham crackers like it's kindergarten snack time.

"You just rest awhile." She clips a plastic monitor to my finger and checks the machine it's wired to. "If you need anything or start to feel funny, you let the nurse at the desk know. I'll be back to check on you in a few minutes."

The calories in the apple juice are like magic. The fog in my brain fades. My lower body comes back to me and it's okay. It's empty and clean and finally okay.

45

Ashlyn doesn't come to lunch anymore.

"What's going on with you two?" Lyssa asks.

"What? Nothing." An obvious lie. We still have classes together, but we orbit around each other, gaping black holes where friendship used to live.

"Bullshit."

"Nothing's wrong, really."

She crunches a nacho. "Is it Finn?"

I almost choke on my soda. "Is what Finn?"

"She still thinks we ganged up on him, right?"

"What are you talking about?"

"Oh come on. I know you're not over that yet and I sure as hell ain't either. But she fell for his little confession, hook, line, and lead weight."

I shake my head. The truth is I don't know how I feel about Finn. Since confronting him, I haven't once seen him in the library. I want to believe he's dropped it, but Lyssa's right. It does still bother me a little. The fault lines in our group are getting worse.

"It's not Finn." I can't bring myself to pile another lie on. I shrug. "I don't know."

Over her shoulder I can see a squadron of girls taping posters to the wall. Winter Court campaigning has begun in earnest now that the gala is right around the corner. Right after I have court.

"Fucking Winter Court," I mutter, glad to be able to move the conversation away from Ashlyn and me.

"No shit, right? Who cares about winning stupid plastic crowns that much?" She says it loud enough that the girls behind her turn around. Great. They glare at us before flouncing off, leaving their campaign choice for all to see.

"Oh god." I clap a hand over my mouth. I can't rip my eyes from the poster.

"What? What is it?" She cranes her head around and understands immediately. She turns back to face me, almond eyes wide. "Holy fuck."

The sign behind our table features a huge photo of the girl I hate most in the entire school, surrounded by hand-painted hearts and huge bubbly letters: *Nominate Madison Tierney for Winter Queen.*

Each *i* is topped with a circle, the tails curling up like cheerful little cherry stems.

///

It takes an entire week to catch Madison alone. It's right after lunch and I'm in my usual hideout on the upstairs balcony when Mrs. Givens brings her class into the library to get research materials. I spot Madison at once and when she asks to go to the

246

bathroom halfway through the period, I abandon the GED prep book I'm studying to go after her.

I've been rehearsing this moment in my head since I learned it was her, but when I follow her into the girls' room, every prepared speech I had evaporates.

Madison stands in front of the mirror, purse plopped in the sink. She's crushing her lashes in an eyelash curler, mouth hanging open, and she doesn't acknowledge me when I come in.

"I need to ask you something," I say. I stay near the door, not wanting to put my reflection next to hers in the hazy mirror. My face is already hot.

She doesn't say anything, just does her other eye and blinks several times. She swipes on lip gloss and then finally turns to me.

"Look, if you want to learn about makeup, why don't you watch YouTube like a normal person instead of stalking me in the bathroom?" She zips up her pink Michael Kors purse and slings it over her shoulder.

I don't move from the doorway.

"What are you doing?" She looks uneasy, like maybe she knows exactly what I'm doing.

I pull my phone out, open the image of the note. I hold it so she can see the screen. "You put this in my locker."

It's not a question.

"No, I didn't," she says, crossing her arms under her ample boobs. "Get out of my way."

"What did he do to you?"

"I don't know what you're talking about." But she does. A

split-second flash of fear contorts her cover-model face and betrays her.

"You left me this note. You wanted me to know."

"I don't know what you're talking about."

"He hurt you too, didn't he?"

She reaches forward so quickly I think she's going to hit me, but instead she flips the lock on the door. She's very close to my face and I'm suffocating in the cloying floral scent of her perfume. But I won't let her intimidate me. Not anymore. I've faced down worse than Madison Tierney.

"Tell me," I say gently.

"It's not like with you," she snaps, stepping back. She gestures at my face and sneers. "He didn't mutilate me or anything."

I ignore that. "What did he do?"

"Nothing. He could just be a dick sometimes, you know? It doesn't matter."

"It does."

She shakes her head.

"Then why did you leave me the note?"

"I don't know!" She flings her hands up and stalks to the other side of the bathroom. "It was stupid."

"You thanked me for killing him, Madison. There must be a reason."

"Why does it even matter?"

"Because it could help keep me out of jail for doing something I had to do! For something you thanked me for doing!" I slam my palm against the wall. I have to calm down. Lowering my voice, I tell her what Cara told me. "This could help establish a pattern of violent behavior."

"You think I'm going to help you in court? Are you crazy?" She snorts.

"Then why thank me? Why get involved at all?"

"I was just glad he got what was coming to him. That's where it ends."

"I won't use your name. I swear." I need her to talk to me.

She's quiet for a long time, leaning against a sink with her arms wrapped around herself. I jump when someone tries to open the door behind me, but after rattling the handle, whomever it is gives up. I look back at Madison and am surprised to see her bottom lip quivering. She fixes her gaze on the ceiling and draws in a shuddering breath.

"It happened last year. I was at Trevor's house, waiting for him to come back from practice. I was hanging out with Shane. I kinda had a crush on him, even though I was going out with Trevor, right? So we had a couple beers and no one was there, so when he tried to kiss me, I let him." She tells all of this to the pocked ceiling tiles. I don't dare make a sound. "I was drunk and I let him kiss me. I let him. But then he wanted me to, you know, and I didn't want to, but I let him make me anyway. I mean, it was only a blow job, right? I didn't want to make it a big deal. But it kinda was, you know? And I let him make me do it. I mean, it could've been worse. I'd heard he'd done things to other girls too, so it could've been worse."

Yes, it could've been worse. But it was still bad enough that I ache for this girl I hate.

"Thank you," I say softly. "For telling me."

She swipes furiously at her eyes and storms over. Her finger is right under my nose. "You listen to me," she says. Her voice is granite now. "If you can use this to help your defense, fine, because I do think you did the right thing, but I'll never say so in public. You so much as breathe a single, solitary word that connects me to this, I'll deny it and I'll destroy you. Shane might've fucked you up, but I will end you."

"I know." I understand the need for secrets. And like it or not, Shane has linked us together now. "I would never do that."

"Make sure of it." She unlocks the door and I step aside so she can pass. She stops in the hall and turns back.

"Good luck," she says and disappears down the hall.

46

I tell Cara I want to testify.

47

The familiar cacophony of Cranberry Creek is a comforting distraction from the turmoil in my brain. Lyssa and I managed to snag our favorite booth in the corner, despite only being a party of two on a busy Sunday morning. The decor here is pure country chaos: vintage advertisements, photos, license plates, and farm tools line the dining room and a huge moose head hangs from the wall above us, sporting a rakish deerstalker hat and watching the waitresses bustle around the busy restaurant.

"I can't believe Finn went to church," Lyssa says. "Again."

I feel a pang at this news. I didn't know he had. I stab at the huge pile of bacon-and-cheese-covered hash browns that sits between our identical plates of pancakes.

Her phone vibrates but she doesn't notice it as she gestures around the restaurant with her fork. "I mean, who in their right mind would ditch us—and breakfast—to go sing stupid songs and partake in crappy cannibalism?"

"Maybe those wafers are better than we know."

"But not better than pancakes. Or cheesy potatoes."

"True story."

It's weird being out to breakfast with just Lyssa. We used

to do this at least two or three times a month, but it's always—always—been the four of us. I wonder if we'll ever be the four of us again.

Lyssa's phone skitters across the table as it lights up again. "Speak of the devil," she says, checking it this time. Her forehead wrinkles as she reads the text. She slides out of the booth. "Be right back."

"Is everything okay?"

"Yeah." She grins. "Finn's apparently having a come-to-Jesus moment. He's probably got the stigmata or the sacred syphilis or some shit."

I finish most of my pancakes by the time she gets back. And more than some of the hash browns.

"Dude, you ate all the bacon," she says, dropping back into her seat.

"You took forever. I was bored." Something in her eyes worries me. "Is everything okay?

"Five by five." She shovels a forkful of potatoes into her mouth and asks, "Have you talked to Madison yet?"

"I have," I say slowly.

Her eyes widen and she swallows. "And? Why didn't you say anything?"

"And she won't help."

"What do you mean? She admitted to writing it, though?"

"She did. But she said it was a mistake." I won't betray her secret, not when I can't even share my own, but adding this deception to the many swirling through our group is almost more than I can bear. I pulverize a slice of apple with the edge of my fork.

"But what did she say?" Her phone buzzes on the table but her eyes are searching my face.

"She said she can't help." It's not a lie, but not the truth either. I can feel my face flushing beneath her scrutiny.

She puts her fork down. "What aren't you telling me?"

I press my lips together, forcing the words to stay down.

"What aren't you telling me?"

"I can't," I say and it shreds my heart. "I promised I wouldn't tell."

"So what?" She looks genuinely puzzled. "It's just Madison. Who cares? Did you get something useful or not?"

I nod.

"He hurt her?"

Another nod.

"Like you?" She raises an eyebrow, not buying it.

"Sort of."

"What did he do?"

"I can't tell."

"Why the hell not?"

"I promised."

"Seelie, that's bullshit. This has the potential to help your case but you promised that slithery bitch you wouldn't tell? Are you stupid?"

My cheeks scorch. "You don't get it."

"Then make me!" Silverware rattles as she bangs the table and people turn to stare. "Stop shutting me out."

This has suddenly become about more than Madison.

I can't speak.

She rubs her face, pressing at her eyes until she must see

stars. I watch her jaw muscles strain against the confines of her skin and I sit very still.

"I'm asking you to tell me what she said. That's all."

"I can't." Barely a whisper.

"I'm asking you to choose us, you and me, over you and her. Please. You owe her nothing."

"Lyssa," I say, but she already knows I'm not going to tell. She shoves her bangs off her forehead and stands up.

"Fine. I get it." But she doesn't. She pulls a Tyvek Wonder Woman wallet from her back pocket. "I'll go pay, then I'll take you home."

She stands, not even waiting for the check, and stalks to the register near the bakery case. I can't help noticing that the customary white box we usually fill with pastries doesn't appear on the counter and this makes me sadder than it should. I don't want Lyssa to be mad at me, but what happened to Madison isn't my story to tell.

Her phone buzzes against her plate again and I see Finn's name appear on the text notification. Without thinking, I double-tap to open the message.

Everything tears apart in an instant.

There are six texts from today, none of which Lyssa has replied to.

FINN 12:01 AM: **Going to church with Ash. We can't make breakfast.**

FINN 12:46 AM: **I think I fucked up**

FINN 8:52 AM: **I think I fucked up. Need to talk**

FINN 9:04 AM: **Ash is in confession. I don't know about**

255

this whole church thing but I know about the faction. Confession: I think I'm the reason S got hurt. Need to talk.

FINN 9:26 AM: **DON'T tell her. Or Ashlyn. I didn't know it was laced I swear. I need to fix this. Somehow.**

FINN 9:39 AM: **I don't know how to fix this.**

I don't notice Lyssa is back until she's taking the phone from my hands.

I hold onto it, staring up at her. "What is this?"

"Nothing you needed to see." She gently pries the phone free. The anger that filled her face moments ago is overlaid by a fathomless sadness.

"I saw it was Finn." I desperately want to unread the texts. "I was going to give him a hard time about church. I didn't know . . ."

"I know." She gets my coat from the peg near our booth and holds it open for me. "Let's just go."

I still don't move. Denial sings a siren song I want to surrender to. "You said everything was fine," I say dumbly. "You lied to me."

"Pot and kettle," she says, pulling me up. "C'mon."

"Were you gonna tell me?" I fumble with my coat. "What does he mean? How is it his fault?"

I follow her out to the Jeep. My teeth are chattering. All my bones are.

Lyssa puts the heat on full blast but we stay in the parking lot.

"What did he mean?" I ask again. When Lyssa doesn't answer, I fish my phone out of my bag. No missed texts or calls for me. I pull up Finn's contact information.

"Wait."

I look up at Lyssa, my thumb hovering over the call icon.

"I want to be clear," she says, eyes boring into mine as she reaches for my phone. Her soft fingers close over mine and there is no part of me that wants to take my hand away. "This is me, choosing you and I over me and Finn."

My breathing stops as she struggles with something she doesn't want to say.

"Finn thinks he sold Shane the pot he smoked the day he attacked you. It was laced with PCP."

48

I try to absorb that, but it doesn't make sense.

"Why?" I ask. "Why didn't he say something that night we found out?"

Lyssa sighs and releases my hand. "He didn't know. Fucking idiot. Apparently he really doesn't use his own product or he would've known. He's been selling the same batch for the past few months and someone said something to him about it."

My head is spinning. "So he's still dealing?"

"Yup." She slams the Jeep into gear and pulls out of the lot.

I lean my head against the window and watch the trees smear together. A hush settles between us like an unwelcome passenger. There's a part of me that wants nothing more than to open the door and topple out. Just be done. But of course I don't do that.

We're at my house far too soon.

Lyssa parks, but hits the button to lock the doors. I don't move.

"I chose us," she says quietly. "Your turn."

She doesn't know what she's asking of me.

I shake my head and the truth rattles in its cage. I try to figure out a way to free it, but I can't. It will destroy everything.

I've already lost Ashlyn and probably Finn now, too. I can't lose Lyssa. And I will. If I tell her everything, it will be our undoing. It will become who I am. The victim. The murderer, times two. And worse, a liar. Whatever we are is too fragile for the weight of such secrets.

"When did you decide you couldn't trust me anymore?" she asks.

My throat closes up. She's wrong. God, why can't I tell her how wrong she is?

I am so afraid of what the truth will do to us.

She shakes her head and when her bangs fall into her face something small and vital snaps in my chest. She should just rip my heart out with her bare hands. It would hurt less than this.

"Of course I trust you," I whisper and I don't stop myself from smoothing those errant black strands off her face. I tuck them behind her ear, running my fingers around its delicately curved edge, thinking there has never been such a perfect ear.

"No, you don't," she says, pulling away.

Her complete conviction guts me.

Snowflakes fall and die on the windshield as the silence echoes around us. Lyssa strangles the steering wheel, the skull-patterned cover twisting like skin beneath her ragged nails.

Everything inside me is coming unraveled.

"We never had secrets before." She stares at the windshield like she can't bear the sight of me, her profile a stony mask. "Now you're lying to me about what happened with Ashlyn—and she's barely speaking to me either, by the way—and you're covering up for Madison, of all people. Madison. I just don't get it, Seelie. What did I do to get shut out of your life?"

"You didn't do anything," I say, choking on everything I can't bring myself to tell her.

"Then let me back in." She turns her whole body to me and it's not anger twisting her face, it's pain. "I love you. You know that, right?"

My stomach takes my heart hostage and I'm drowning. When her hands envelop mine they only pull me further under. I am choking on unsaid things.

"I would do anything for you," she says, squeezing my hands. "All I'm asking you for is the truth."

I am lost in the warmth of her palms. I want to stay here forever, basking in the heat that spreads from our hands through my veins. I want to climb into a world where this is normal, where she holds my hands and looks at me like I'm something worth keeping.

Destroying this moment is the most heartbreaking thing I've ever done, but I do it. I have to. I don't want her to know what he's taken from me. Even though she might understand, if I put it out there, she will never un-know the truth of what he did to me and I won't let that be what she sees when she looks at me.

"I can't." The words are too weak to disturb the fuzz on a dandelion corpse, but they lay waste to everything we are and could've been.

When she withdraws it's not just her hands; her entire being pulls back. Everything about her closes right up.

"Okay," she says from so, so far away. "Whatever you think is best."

My hands clutch at each other in the absence of hers, but

it doesn't help. "Please understand," I beg. Every fiber of me wants to reach for her, to get her hands back. To get her back.

"That's what I'm trying to do. Christ, that's all I've ever been trying to do." She shakes her head and hits the button to unlock the doors. "Forget it. Just go."

"Lyssa, please." I can barely see her through the ocean of tears.

"Whatever the truth is, it's not worse than being lied to," she says.

It is.

Ashlyn proved that.

I don't look back as I walk away from Lyssa. I can't bear to see the wreckage in my wake.

49

Lyssa doesn't show up to get me before school Monday morning. I didn't expect her to, not really, but I hoped. Really hoped. As I dressed I almost convinced myself that it had somehow all blown over and she'd be waiting for me outside, same as always. But she doesn't come, and who am I to expect her to anyway? She has every right to hate me. She was right about everything. I have been shutting her out. I have been lying, both by omission and outright, because what I feel for her now is not the same as what I felt a year ago. We are not just friends. We are something more. Or we were. Or could've been.

I don't bother going to school. The trial is in three days. I think the court will agree that's a valid reason for being absent.

I call the office and when the school secretary picks up I say, "Hi, this is Rebecca Stanton. I wanted to let you know my daughter, Cecelia, will be out for the rest of the week."

Maybe forever.

"The reason for the absence?" the secretary asks.

Really? As if she doesn't know exactly why I might be ditching school.

"Family emergency," I say and hang up.

I text Cara and tell her I'm home. She's supposed to be coming over tonight to work on trial prep but I would rather do it while my mother is still gone. She texts back to say that she's in jury selection and will come by when she's done at the court. She doesn't admonish me for skipping school and I take that as a good sign.

But as I absorb the words *jury selection*, it's all I can do to keep breathing.

Three days from now I will be sitting in court.

Three days from now the rest of my life could be taken away by a jury of my peers.

Only they won't be my peers. They'll be adults. Strangers. But maybe that's better. My real peers have been finding me guilty every day since I returned to Amesford High.

///

I can't help checking my phone every few minutes, foolishly hoping to find a text or missed call from Lyssa or Finn. Of course, there's nothing.

Shane may not have killed me, but I've still lost everything that matters.

And that royally pisses me off.

The squeal of brakes wrenches me from my angry reverie. I peer out the living room window, expecting to see Cara's car, but it's only the square white mail truck stopping at our box.

The mail truck.

Of course.

I shove my feet into the polka-dot rain boots my mother

keeps by the door and am at the mailbox before the truck makes it to the next house.

Catalogs, bills, and yes, there, a large manila envelope with Cranston Laboratories printed in the top-left corner.

I take the envelope to my room and tear it open. My hands shake as I scan the cover letter, but it's the report I care about. The charts are filled with numbers and letters that might as well be hieroglyphics, but it doesn't matter. They'll make sense when they have to.

If they have to.

///

Jury selection turns out to be an all-day affair and Cara doesn't show up until nearly four o'clock.

She pulls a chair away from the table and places it in the middle of the floor. She gestures for me to sit.

"This is going to be the hardest thing you've ever done." Her blunt honesty is like yanking off a Band-Aid.

I never once thought it was going to be a cakewalk.

"I don't want to sugarcoat it," she says, staring down at me. "The prosecution is going to try to tear you apart. Their goal is to discredit you, to trip you up, and they are very, very good at that."

This isn't news. We've talked about this before, but there's a certain intensity to her now that makes my palms sweat. I wipe them on my jeans, wishing she would just sit down with me instead of pacing around my chair.

"They're going to try to rattle you," she says from behind me. "They're going to call you a murderer."

I flinch at the word as she comes back around the chair.

"And you can't react."

I try to make my face empty and hope she didn't see. "I won't."

"You're a murderer," she says, looking right in my eyes. I clench my teeth. "You're a murderer. You're a murderer."

Tears fill my eyes.

"No, I'm not," I whisper.

"You're a murderer," she says over me.

I bite my lip when it starts to tremble.

"You're a murderer."

I block her out. I take my brain away. I don't let her words penetrate as she stalks around the kitchen, repeating the accusation. Finally she stops saying it, just stands and gazes down at me, arms crossed. My jaw is still clenched tight, but I raise my now-dry eyes to meet hers.

"You're not a murderer," she says gently. "But sometimes you think you are, right?"

She already knows the answer. My cheeks flush with silent self-recrimination.

She nods. "I know you do and it's normal to be conflicted about taking a life, even when you had no other choice, but I need you to get a lid on that guilt. That will be your undoing."

"I didn't do anything wrong," I say.

"Exactly. When you answer the prosecutor's questions I want you to remember that. You need to stay calm, you need to stick to the facts, and you need to keep your anger in check. They're going to want you to explode and you can't give them that. You need the jury on your side. When you get questioned, you answer to them, not to the prosecutor. Make eye contact with them. They need to see you as the survivor you are."

She resumes her lion's pacing and runs me through a rapid-fire series of questions so I can practice staying focused and unflustered. It's hard, even here in the safety of my own kitchen.

When my mother gets home, she doesn't interrupt us, just watches from the doorway. It gets harder to answer Cara's practice questions under her scrutiny but I force myself to do it anyway. It's not going to be any easier in three days when the whole world is watching.

50

The next day of prep covers everything from body language and trial etiquette to what will happen if the jury comes back with a guilty verdict.

It's not something I want to think about.

At all.

I know it's an outcome I need to be prepared for, but the mere thought of being led away in handcuffs makes me dizzy. It's too much to take in. I mean, I could go to prison. For life. All depending on what twelve strangers decide for me.

It seems like a horribly flawed and unfair system.

"Tomorrow we'll run through everything one more time," Cara says as she gathers her things to go. She looks exhausted and wired all at once.

"No."

She stops. "What?"

"I said no. I want tomorrow. You were right, they could come back guilty. We don't know. I could lose the rest of my life in two days." I bite down on the edge of panic that creeps into my voice. "I want tomorrow for myself. Please."

Everything about her softens. "Okay. Tomorrow is yours.

You're as prepared as you're going to be. If you feel like you need me for anything tomorrow, you call. Anything. Otherwise, I'll see you Thursday morning."

"Thank you."

It feels like a stay of execution.

//

One day.

My last day of freedom dawns cold and crystal clear. The sky is a painful blue.

I check my phone and while the absence of messages from the faction crushes me, I am relieved to see an email from Elaine.

Seelie,

Of course you are welcome to any of the horses, any time. I can't imagine how difficult this is for you right now, but I am confident you will come out of things just fine. I hope you find some small comfort from the horses. As Benjamin Disraeli said, "the canter is the cure for all evil." Perhaps you too will find it helpful. I will be gone for the better part of the day, so feel free to bring someone with you if you wish.

Perfect.

//

I take Tulsa from his paddock and spend a solid hour grooming him. He leans into the curry comb and I don't stop brushing him until he shakes his whole body like a wet dog and gives a happy snort. When I saddle him I'm aware that it may be for the last time ever. Cara said if I get sentenced to life, the very earliest I could hope for parole would be in twenty-five years.

Tulsa will not be alive in twenty-five years.

I know getting on will be the hardest test of my leg yet, so I drag a hay bale out to use as a step. I take the reins in one hand and put my left foot in the stirrup.

Moment of truth.

It doesn't falter.

The snow on the trails is pristine. With no leaves to block the sun, the white path sparkles like diamond dust. Tulsa prances and huffs big puffs of frosty breath, excited to be out in the open.

I am too.

We spend a few minutes walking to warm up, then I stand up in the stirrups, testing my leg again. It holds. I can do this.

Crouching low over his fuzzy neck, I squeeze his sides with my heels and he bounds into an exuberant canter. We race across the unmarred snow and for a few blissful minutes we manage to outrun everything in my head. All the doubt and fear and anxiety get trampled under the relentless pounding of his hooves.

We gallop flat out until both of us are spent. I can feel the gelding's heart thudding beneath my legs, quick as my own. My thighs burn, but it's as much from not being on a horse in so long as it is from anything else. I'd forgotten what good pain feels like.

My thoughts catch up on the long walk back to the barn but I don't fight them. It's now or never. Decisions have to be made.

The last time I rode these trails was the day of the attack, the day I almost lost everything.

It seems only fitting to be on the same path when I decide to take it all back.

The sun is starting to sink behind the skeleton trees when we make it back to the cozy oasis of the barn. I untack with the same care and deliberation I used getting Tulsa ready and set up bran mashes for all the horses before bringing them in. It doesn't matter that it's not my job anymore, I want to do it. I spend a few minutes with each of them, feeling a sense of peace settle around me like a shawl. One way or another, it ends tomorrow.

I stand at the door of the barn for a long time, memorizing the scent of the horses, the quiet snuffling sound of their eating. This is a scene I want to be able to come back to in my head, if things don't go right.

I'm about to turn off the lights and leave, ready to face the last part of my last day, when I hear a creak from above.

From the hayloft.

I freeze and nothing in the world could prepare me for what I see.

51

Trevor Mayfield staggers down the steep hayloft stairs.

The barn spins like a Tilt-A-Whirl.

This can't be happening. I clutch the wall, afraid I'm going to fall right over.

My legs are liquid; fluid, soft things that can't hold me. I cast around, eyes seeking a weapon, a retreat. The tack room door is right there. It locks. I could hide there, call for help.

Trevor stops halfway down and he's holding the wall too, like the pair of us are all that's keeping the building upright.

Seeing him like that, barely able to stand, shakes something loose in me and I realize he's not a threat. If I could save myself from his brother then I can save myself from anything. I'm not some weeping damsel in distress and I don't need a hero. I can be my own damn hero.

I stand tall, cross my arms over my chest, and decide there is no way I'm going to let him ruin what could be my last day of freedom. The Mayfields have taken enough from me; they won't get today too.

"What are you doing here?" I demand.

Trevor jolts at the words and it seems like he might fall

headlong down the stairs, but he manages to stay upright. When his eyes finally settle on my face it's like he has to work to keep them there. He staggers down the remaining stairs, stumbling only when he reaches the bottom. He lands heavily on the last step and sags against the wall.

"I had to see," he slurs. "I had to see where it happened."

I don't know what to say to that and don't answer.

Trevor looks up at me from the dusty step and his entire face crumbles. "I miss my brother." Tears spill down his splotchy cheeks.

He cries with his entire body, as a child would. This is not the cocky, self-proclaimed king of the junior class that I know and revile.

This is grief personified.

"Why did you take my brother away?" he asks. His face is a mess of tears and snot but he doesn't seem to notice.

I don't know how to answer that. I don't even know if I should.

"He was my best friend, you know," he says, the words stumbling into one another. "He looked out for me. Taught me how to play basketball and how to drive. When I crashed into the mailbox, he told Dad he did it so I wouldn't get in trouble. That's the kind of guy he was. A good guy. A really good guy."

Trevor leans forward to pull something from his back pocket and I go rigid. Stupid, stupid. I should've run when I had the chance. But it's not a knife he takes out. It's a tarnished silver flask. He upends it, sucking out the last drops of whatever Dutch courage he filled it with.

"I want my brother back." A fresh wave of tears hit him and the empty flask tumbles from his hands. "I just want him back."

"I know," I say, because it's true and because he's very, very drunk.

"I hate you. I hate you so much," he sobs. He's leaning heavily against the wall. I have no idea what to do with him. "He was my best friend."

"I know."

He lurches to his feet. "I hope you die," he says, and it sounds so pathetic I can't even fault him for it. He pitches hard into the wall and stays there.

I know what I have to do with him.

But I really, really don't want to.

"C'mon," I say. "I'll drive you home."

///

The fact that Trevor doesn't puke in Wedgie is nothing short of a miracle.

I leave him unceremoniously at the end of his driveway, which is less than five minutes from the barn, and continue home with my mind reeling. Trevor Mayfield was inside my car. I was *nice* to him. What is wrong with me?

My mother is waiting at the door when I get home.

"Where have you been?" she asks, as if my boots and riding pants don't make it obvious.

"Riding," I say. I'm not going to let her rankle me. Not today.

"Shouldn't you have been with Cara?"

"No, we already took care of everything."

"Then come sit down. I want to talk about tomorrow."

273

"I have to change." I go upstairs before she can stop me.

I take a ridiculously hot bubble bath. One way or another, this will be the last time I have to bathe with the weight of the waterproof GPS tracker around my ankle.

I dress in comfy clothes: yogas, a hoodie, and dinosaur socks. I don't need to be fancy tonight.

Tomorrow, however.

Cara wants me to wear a skirt, of course. But the skirt doesn't have any pockets and tomorrow I want pockets. I pull out a pair of black pants and consider shirts. I really should've gone shopping for this. How did I not manage to get something appropriate to wear?

I settle on a drapey, dark purple sweater that manages to look nice and be cozy at the same time. I can put a black tank top under it and call it done. Cara will probably wish it were brighter, but I'll be more comfortable wearing this than funeral clothes.

I toss it all in a bag, along with the envelope from my desk. Just in case.

I look around my room and the fact that I might never sleep in it again almost wrecks me. Fluttery fingers of panic pull at my brain but I brush them aside. I can't give into that. Not yet. I'm not finished with this day.

With a final look around, I close the door and go downstairs.

"Seelie," my mother says with a sigh before I even hit the landing, "I thought you were just changing. I said I wanted to talk to you."

I fish my keys out of my bag and the jangling draws my mother from the kitchen.

"You're leaving again?" she asks. "Don't you think you should be spending this time with your family?"

"That's what I'm doing," I say.

"We need to talk about what's going to happen."

"I'm sick of talking about that. I have something I need to do." I don't raise my voice, but I'm making it clear I won't be stopped. Before I step around her, I meet her eyes. "I'm sorry I was never what you wanted."

She unfolds her arms and something—an explanation or maybe a protest—dies on her lips.

"Bye, Mom."

52

A certain sense of inevitability propels me toward Lyssa's house.

I haven't texted her to say I'm coming because I don't want her to tell me not to bother. I need to do this. But I realize my mistake when I get there and see her Jeep idling in the driveway. She must already have plans.

Tough.

She comes out the front door with a large, flat package tucked under her arm and pulls up short when she sees Wedgie blocking her in. I kill the engine and get out.

Here goes everything.

"I was just coming to see you," she says.

I stop. "You were?"

"Yes." She sets the package against the front of the house and jogs to the Jeep. She turns it off and comes around to where I'm still standing, stupefied. This was not remotely how I expected this to begin.

"I thought you were still mad at me," I say.

"I am. I mean I was." She runs a hand through her hair. "Come on."

She leads me to the porch, which is free of snow and lit by

the two sconces flanking the door. A bench swing hangs at one end and I perch on the cold wooden slats, trying not to shiver. She doesn't sit with me. Instead she paces the narrow width of the porch and I wonder what it is lately that makes people incapable of sitting when they talk.

"Look." She stops in front of me. Another pass through her hair makes the long pieces stand in a million directions. She's nervous and that somehow makes me feel braver.

"I have something to tell you," I say.

"I don't care." Both hands rake through her hair this time. "I don't care if you have secrets. I don't care if you lie to me, or shut me out. I don't care if you think you're broken. All I care about is you. I always have. More than anything else in the world."

A rush of tears fills my eyes. This isn't right. Why is she doing this now? Why didn't she just let me go first? I don't want to listen to these kind words because I don't want to hear her take it all back when I'm done talking. She retrieves the package she propped near the door and returns, dropping to a crouch at my feet.

"I was going to give you this tomorrow, after you won. But then I thought tonight would be better." She holds the parcel up like an offering. "For luck. Or maybe clarity. I don't know."

The package completely covers my lap. I slide my hand under the edge of the brown wrapping and pop the tape with shaking fingers. I know what it is. I fold the paper back to reveal a framed drawing.

The drawing.

It's finished now, of course. Details that were only roughed in before are complete and the colors are vivid even in the soft porch light. It's almost exactly as I remember it: the scarred warrior woman riding Roman-style on two hell horses, the demon parrot, the blood-red letters of the title. I study it in the amber glow and notice the touches she's added to the girl. On her left leg, above her knee-high boot, is the dark stain of a healing wound. She still wears the eye patch, but now her face is a galaxy of freckles and the scar is just a jagged tear in the fabric of that starry space. It looks like it belongs there.

Lyssa watches me expectantly. Anxious anticipation radiates from her in palpable waves.

I trace my fingers over the crimson letters. *The Mighty Cicatrix.* "What's this mean?"

"Scar. It's an old word for scar. I think it's beautiful," she says and then looks unexpectedly shy. "It's how I see you."

I run my finger from the letters to the warrior's face, touch the scar. Finished, it no longer looks like a portrait of a villain. It looks like a hero.

"I'm a mess, Lys," I whisper. "I'm not like her."

"You are, though. You just don't get it. You think you're damaged, but you're not."

It's freezing out, but I'm suddenly burning beneath my coat and scarf.

"You think this—" She touches my thigh and her fingers land precisely where the knife went in. It sends a radiant jolt through me. I keep very still even though my heart is galloping like a spooked horse. "And this—" She traces her thumb down the canyon that bisects my face. I want to cry when she does it, her fingers ever-so gentle as she cups my cheek. I close my eyes and she keeps her hand there, completely unbothered by this most hideous part of me. I can't help leaning into the heat of her palm even as I long to hide my face from such tender contemplation. "—make you broken. But you're wrong. They make you better. They tell the world how strong you are, how brave."

I open my eyes and find hers drinking me in. With a shaky smile, I cover her hand with mine.

It's time. Even if she never looks at me like this again, it's okay. This has to happen.

"I need to tell you something."

///

I tell her everything.

My whole truth.

She doesn't interrupt me, even at the worst parts.

When I finish she stands and pulls me to my feet and into her arms.

We are not ruined.

///

Shoebox lies in the middle of the futon and I have my feet propped on his furry back. Lyssa is on the other side of him, looking entirely too pleased with herself.

"You really hit him?" I ask, laughing.

Lyssa shrugs. "He deserved it."

"But it's okay now?"

"I don't know. He feels really guilty. Like, really guilty. But I, yeah, I think he's done dealing after all of this."

It turns out that when Lyssa dropped me off after breakfast, she went and sat at the entrance of the trailer park where

Finn's grandparents live and waited for hours until he showed up. When he finally got there, she had spent an eternity stewing in rage and frustration, so before Finn could say a single word, she hauled off and punched him. Hard.

While Lyssa showers, I text him.

ME: **This wasn't your fault. It wasn't the drugs fault. It was only Shane's fault. Really.** ♡

After a moment the typing bubble appears, but vanishes after a few seconds. I'm okay with his silence, because at least I know he saw it. I only hope he believes it.

I realize he's not the only one who has to believe it, though. Everyone does. I open a new text.

ME: **I know its late and this is random but it wasn't the drugs that did this. Shane did it. You'll make that clear, right?**

CARA: **Don't worry. Get some rest. I'll see you in the morning.**

I hear the shower turn off and type out one more message, this time to Ashlyn.

ME: **I'm sorry I asked you to pick between your beliefs and me. That wasn't fair. I love you and I'm sorry.**

Lyssa comes back in surrounded by a cloud of clean-girl smells and I put my phone away, content that I've said all that needs saying. She nudges Shoebox off the futon and opens it flat. The stubby dog hops back on before she can finish. We don't talk about what might go wrong tomorrow as she pulls pillows and blankets off the loft for me.

I take one last look at the Cicatrix picture before Lyssa shuts off the lights. She's drawn like she's never lost a battle in her life. Like she's never lost anything at all.

I know I should sleep but the thought of ending this last day is more than I can bear.

"Lys," I say into the shadows. There's a glowing twist in my belly as I ask, "Will you sleep down here tonight?"

"Yeah, of course," she says and pulls down the other pillow, which she flops at the opposite end from mine, the way Ashlyn and I do during sleepovers.

"No," I whisper and the tickle in my belly intensifies. "On my side."

"Oh," she breathes. She hesitates and the silence is punctuated by the thudding of my heart. "Are you sure?"

"Yes."

Just in case.

She folds herself around me, sliding one arm under my neck and the other around my waist. My fingers curl around her wrist in the dark and she pulls me into her. A blissful warmth spreads through me like melted chocolate.

"This is okay?" she asks and her whispered breath fills my ear, making me shudder.

I burrow into her. "More than okay."

She presses her lips into the hollow just below my ear and squeezes me tighter.

I roll into her, so my face is tucked into her neck. She smells of mint shampoo and everything I ever needed. "I was so scared to tell you," I whisper. I can barely hear myself, but I keep going, the words tumbling over themselves in a breathless rush against her skin. "So, so scared. It was like he ruined me and how could anyone ever want me after that and I—"

I stop.

I don't have to explain.

Not to her.

I push myself up and make a decision that needs no thought. My lips find hers in the dark and we twine into each other. Her mouth is soft and sweet and I fall into her, into us, and no matter what happens tomorrow, this is okay.

We are okay.

53

The sky is an iron sheet of clouds that I try not to read anything into.

Even though we're early, the parking lot of the court overflows with cars and news vans. This is a big deal. I'm a big deal.

"Calm is the key word today, people," Cara says when we make our way toward the court. "The cameras will be there, just like always. Don't engage with them, but don't let them push you around."

"Can I push *them* around?" Lyssa asks, winking at me. Cara glares at her and Lyssa raises her hands in surrender. "Okay, guess not."

Peter and Rick trail behind us, a stripped-down version of our usual army.

"This is going to be a circus compared to before," Cara says. She turns to Lyssa's parents. "If I were you, I'd take Lyssa and wait right by the door if you want to get seats behind us."

"I don't want to leave Seelie," Lyssa says, always the protector.

"It's all right," I tell her, putting a hand on her arm. "You have to."

She's not happy about it, but she can't save me today. Only I can do that.

As we reach the steps that will take us into the fray, I notice two people running toward us and stiffen, expecting reporters. But then I realize that it's Ashlyn and Finn, bundled up against the morning chill.

I stop, shocked. "You came," I say, unable to keep the smile from my face.

"Of course we did," Ashlyn says, her pixie face pink with cold beneath a slouchy blue beanie.

Finn looks at me like a dog expecting to be kicked. The yellow remnants of a fading bruise color his left cheek. I hug him. "It's okay," I tell him. I feel him nod against my shoulder and let go. He takes Ashlyn's hand and the relief on his face is so profound I think he might melt.

"Okay, this is touching, but we have places to be," Cara says, but she's smiling. She repeats her warning about the media. "We can talk to them after we win."

We march up the stairs. It's time to fight for my life.

Again.

The press swarms us like fire ants. Lyssa tries to step in front of me, but I don't let her. Instead, I walk side by side with Cara, leading the charge as cameras flash around us. Reporters shout questions at us and I keep my head up.

Let them take their pictures.

///

In the shabby courtroom people are crammed into the hard wooden pews, shoulders and thighs touching their neighbors like a fire-code violation waiting to happen. The heat rising from all those bodies makes the air suffocating and stale.

My peers may not be in the jury box, but they are here, school day or not. I catch sight of Ryan, Jason, and Madison, who refuses to meet my eyes. Most of the basketball team is here and so are several teachers, including Mrs. Givens and Mr. Ricketti. School must be a ghost town today, at least for the upper grades.

Jacqui and Nurse Francine sit together near the back.

Trevor and his parents are directly behind the prosecution's table, where a huge portrait of Shane is propped on an easel. It's an old picture, the same one he used in the yearbook, and he looks like a Hollister model. Trevor, on the other hand, doesn't look nearly as put together. His eyes are ready to fall out of his head and I wonder if he has any recollection of what happened yesterday. I sincerely hope not.

Judge Ballard, dwarfed by his billowing black robe, is presiding. It seems like a lifetime ago that I stood before him to be arraigned. He invites the prosecution to begin opening statements.

Mr. Blakely smooths his somber black suit and approaches the lectern. He stands silently for a moment, looking out at the twelve strangers sitting in the jury. I can feel the sea of people behind me, their anticipation a living, breathing thing.

Here we go.

"Ladies and gentlemen of the jury, I would like to ask you a question. What does heartbreak sound like?" The prosecutor pauses, laying his hands flat on the lectern's surface. "It's the sound of a mother hearing that her beloved oldest child has been murdered in the prime of his young life."

I let the words wash over me. Some of the jurors flick their eyes to where I sit. There are seven men and five women. This strikes me as wrong. One of the men is old enough to be a grandfather and is wearing a bow tie with his checkered shirt and cardigan. Will he understand what it's like to be a teenage girl faced with a monster? Will the middle-aged guy with the suit? Or the heavy Latino man? Will the shrew-faced woman understand, just because she's female? What about the two girls who look like they could still be in college? Will they see the truth or will they be blinded by Shane's golden good looks?

"On the afternoon of October twenty-first, Shane Mayfield passed a horse farm down the road from where he lived with his parents and little brother," Blakely continues. "This was a popular young man who was friends with everyone, so when he saw an old classmate riding, he stopped to visit. You will hear a witness tell you it was not unusual for Ms. Stanton to invite young men to visit with her at the barn. This should have been no different than any of those other visits. But Detective Troy will testify that on that clear and sunny October afternoon, something went horribly wrong. There is no denying the fact that Ms. Stanton sustained injuries that day, but you will be presented with evidence that shows you that she willfully and very intentionally set out to kill Brenda Mayfield's poor son with a hammer—a hammer—on that lovely autumn day. She may look like an average school girl, but rest assured, the evidence will show that she is a cold-blooded killer."

Mr. Blakely returns to the prosecution table and sits. Cara rises and strides over to the jury box. She doesn't hide behind the lectern. In her pumpkin-colored silk blouse and impeccably tailored skirt suit, she looks like she belongs on a runway instead of standing in this tired wood-paneled courtroom. Her gray heels are almost subdued, at least until she walks away and reveals a flash of the orange soles. She's still Cara, even on trial day.

"This is a story about survival," she says softly. The jurors shift forward in their seats to hear her. She gestures with a manicured hand at me, gives me a reassuring smile, and turns back to the jury. "Seelie Stanton is just seventeen years old. She's in eleventh grade. She loves horses. She loves her friends. She puts peanut butter in her cocoa and she likes bad eighties movies." Some of the jurors almost laugh at this. "She dreams of galloping down sandy beaches. She dreams of croissants in Paris and cream teas in London. She dreams of college. She dreams."

She looks back at me. The jury follows her gaze and I meet each of their eyes as Cara continues. They stare openly, but it helps to know that when they look at me they also see Lyssa, Ashlyn, Finn, and their families behind me. My mother. They see people who love and support me. And thanks to Cara's words, now they see me. A person.

"You will hear from Seelie herself how Shane Mayfield turned her dreams to nightmares. He brutally attacked her and left her faced with a choice no seventeen-year-old should ever have to make. Seelie made a split-second decision that would change her life forever. She did what she had to do in order to survive. Even as she was bleeding and terrified, she knew she wanted to live. Had to live. She fought back against a monster who was bigger than her, stronger than her, and high on illicit drugs—and she won. She won. When you look at the girl seated here before you, you are not looking at a cold-blooded killer. You are looking at a survivor."

54

"The prosecution would like to call Elaine Burgess as its first witness," Blakely says when he resumes his place at the lectern.

When Elaine takes the stand, it's the first time I've seen her since the attack. She looks old. Her gray hair is pulled into a low ponytail that brushes the collar of her floral shirt.

"Mrs. Burgess, can you tell the court how you're acquainted with Ms. Stanton?"

Elaine smiles at me, but her eyebrows knit together in a way that lets me know she's not happy. "She has worked for me at my farm for nearly three years taking care of my horses."

"And to your knowledge, has she ever had anyone accompany her to your farm while she performed her duties?"

The wrinkle deepens on her forehead. "Yes, but—"

Blakely raises a hand to shush her and interrupts. "Has she had male visitors at your farm?"

"Yes," she says. She points behind me. "She's brought that boy with her before. Finnegan."

"Is she ever left unsupervised on your property?"

"Yes, quite frequently. She knows her job and I trust her completely."

"That means she could've had visitors that you didn't know about?"

"Well, yes, but—"

"No further questions," Blakely says before she can explain.

Cara approaches the witness stand. "Elaine, did you know that man?" She gestures to the photo of Shane.

"I did. Everyone knew him," she says, disdain plain on her face. "He used to tear up and down my street in that godforsaken sports car of his at all hours of the night."

"Did you ever have him on your property?"

"Absolutely not."

Cara asks the next question gently, and though I'm prepared for it I can't stop the blush from burning my face. "Does Seelie have many friends?"

Elaine shakes her head. "No. Not many. Just a few very good ones." She smiles at me and I feel slightly less like a loser.

"So it's not likely that she would ever invite Shane Mayfield to visit while she rides?"

"Absolutely not."

"Objection!" Blakely protests. "Speculation. The witness has no way of knowing what happens in her absence."

"Sustained," the judge says, tapping his gavel.

"I have no further questions," Cara says. "Thank you, Elaine."

The next witness to take the stand is Detective Troy.

"Detective Troy, please walk us through the events of October twenty-first," Blakely says, setting a briefcase on the lectern.

Troy leans forward and places his arms on the rail of the

witness box, comfortable in a way I can't be. "At approximately six o'clock on the evening in question, a 911 call was placed summoning police and ambulances to 143 Summers Road in Amesford. When we arrived on the scene we found the victim lying in a pool of blood in the hayloft. He had sustained severe trauma to the head. Worst I've ever seen."

"Your Honor, the state wishes to enter into evidence photos of the victim's condition to corroborate Detective Troy's testimony," Blakely says.

"Proceed," Judge Ballard agrees and then addresses the jury and gallery: "These images are graphic and may be upsetting."

Blakely pulls a file out of his briefcase and removes several eight-by-ten-inch photographs. Cold sweat chills the back of my neck. I don't want to see these. I don't want my friends to see these. Blakely presents the photographs to the jury, some of who recoil in shock, then turns so the entire court can see the horror. There are gasps and murmurs among the audience, a strangled sob from someone. I try not to see the pictures, but it doesn't matter. The pulpy image of Shane's head is tattooed on my brain forever.

I desperately want to turn around and make sure my friends haven't seen, make sure they're still there, but I can't. It was one of Cara's rules: no turning around. I'm terrified of what their reactions are. It's one thing to know I killed a man, it's another thing to see his battered, broken body.

"Order," Judge Ballard says, banging his gavel, and the court hushes.

"Detective, please continue," Blakely says when he's satisfied everyone is suitably scarred by the photos.

"The victim was obviously beyond rescue at that point," Troy says. "We found the murder weapon within a few feet of the body and had it dusted for prints."

Blakely reaches back into his briefcase and holds up a large ziplock bag with the black mallet inside. "This is the murder weapon?"

"Yes. The defendant's prints were all over it."

"And it's true you received a confession?"

"Yes. She said, 'I hit him until I knew he wasn't going to get up.' She admitted to hitting him as many as six times after he was incapacitated. When asked if the victim had verbally threatened her life, she admitted that he had not."

"He had not threatened her life," Blakely echoes, looking at the jury. He nods at Troy. "No further questions."

Cara's entire demeanor is different when she gets up. She is no longer the kind woman telling the jury a survival story. She's a predator standing before Troy with her hands on her hips. "Who called 911?"

"What?"

"Who made the call?"

"The defendant." Troy pulls away from the rail and leans back in his chair.

"Is it common to have murder suspects call the police?"

"This one did."

"That's not what I asked. I said, is it common for murder suspects to call the police?"

"No," he says grudgingly.

"Your Honor, I would like to play the 911 call from that

night," Cara says, turning away from Troy and dropping her arms.

"You may proceed."

The audio crackles with static at first, then the calm and confident voice of the 911 operator fills the courtroom. Maya. Her name was Maya. I try to tune it out, but the panic in my recorded voice is electric.

The tape plays in its horrifying entirety. One juror covers her mouth and several look stricken. I know why Cara is doing it, but I hate it. I hate that I sound like such a victim. I was a warrior. I fought for my life. How can I sound so small?

In the silence that follows I hear sniffling from behind me and I'm again seized by the desire to turn and face my friends, the only jury that matters.

"Detective Troy, explain to the court how Seelie was found," Cara says when the tape ends.

"She was in a locked room on the first floor of the barn."

"And you saw her?"

"Yes."

"Describe her injuries."

"I look like a doctor to you?"

Cara just cocks her head and waits.

He sighs. "She was bleeding, they took her to the hospital."

"In addition to the rubber mallet, were any other weapons found?"

"A hunting knife." He folds his arms and glares at the lawyer.

"One that is consistent with the wounds Shane Mayfield inflicted on Ms. Stanton?"

"I'm not an expert."

"Was the knife swabbed for DNA?"

"Yes."

"And whose was there?"

"It was mixed. There was DNA from both the victim and the defendant on the knife."

"But you concede that the knife could've been used by Shane to stab Seelie in the leg and cut open her face?"

"It's possible," Troy says. "Anything's possible."

"Like it's possible that Seelie hit Shane only after he viciously attacked her with a knife, correct?"

"Objection!" Blakely leaps to his feet.

"Sustained."

Cara nods graciously, changes tack. "Shane Mayfield has a history of substance-abuse problems. What drugs was he using on the day in question?"

"The autopsy showed marijuana and PCP."

"And can you enlighten the court to some of the effects of PCP?"

Something shifts in Troy's face like he's been given a gift. "It's a hallucinogen. If he was on PCP he wouldn't have known what was going on. He wouldn't be responsible for what he did."

Cara turns to the jury as if they're in this together and shakes her head like she can't believe what she's hearing. "Let me get this straight, Detective. You're saying, as an officer of the law, that someone under the influence of an illegal drug is not responsible for his crimes?"

"That's not what I meant," Troy snaps.

"Okay," Cara nods, satisfied. Troy fell right into her trap.

"Is it true that people taking PCP are prone to paranoia and acts of violence?"

"They can be."

My heart breaks for Finn, who must be hearing this as an indictment of himself. I think of the text I sent Cara last night. This would be the perfect time to address it, but instead she asks, "And is it also true that PCP was originally developed as an anesthetic?"

"How should I know?" Troy asks as Blakely gets to his feet.

"Objection," Blakely says, throwing his hands up. "Relevance?"

"Counsel?" Judge Ballard looks at Cara for an answer.

"The anesthetic properties of the drug explain why my client was required to use such force in subduing her attacker," Cara says.

The judge nods. "Overruled."

"Doesn't change the fact that she beat him to death with a hammer," Troy says.

"The jury will disregard that comment," Judge Ballard says, looking annoyed. "Detective, respect the rules of the court."

"I have nothing further, Your Honor," Cara says and returns to the table. She seems pleased, which gives me hope.

"Will the prosecution call any other witnesses?" the judge asks.

"No, Your Honor, the state rests." Blakely looks peeved as Troy saunters off the stand.

The judge addresses us now: "Defense?"

Cara pats my leg beneath the table and rises. It's time.

"The defense calls Cecelia Stanton."

55

The view from the witness stand is terrifying.

The entire room is staring at me: jurors, lawyers, and every face in the gallery. All looking at me and hearing that awful 911 call playing in their heads, I'm sure of it.

I sit down on the straight-backed wooden chair that's every bit as uncomfortable as the benches that all those staring bodies fill. A glass of water sweats on the ledge near my knee, but I don't touch it. I almost expect the microphone that's angled toward me to echo the ferocious pounding of my heart.

The court clerk asks me to raise my right hand. She does the same and says, "Do you solemnly swear that the testimony you are about to give shall be the truth, the whole truth, and nothing but the truth?"

"Yes." The word echoes loudly in my ears.

The whole truth.

Nothing but.

Cara gets to ask questions first because I'm her witness. "I know this is difficult for you," she says.

That's an understatement. I take a big breath through my

nose and exhale. I find the faction in the sea of faces and make them my lifeline.

"Seelie, can you explain what happened on October twenty-first?" Cara asks.

"On October twenty-first, I went to work after school, like I do every Friday," I tell her, and remember that I'm supposed to look at the jury. When I turn, they're all watching me. "I was alone. It was nice out. A perfect day for riding."

"Except something spoiled it, didn't it?"

"Yes. Shane Mayfield showed up."

"Were you friends with Shane?"

"No. He was older than me. And he was a bully." My voice sounds like it's shaking my brain. It takes everything I have not to look at Trevor, who is so much like his brother, and is so broken by his loss.

"What was Shane doing when you first saw him?"

"Standing near the fence, staring at us. At me and my horse," I clarify. "Like he was in a trance."

"What did you do?"

"I gave him the finger." Cara insisted I include this detail and it makes one of the jurors grin. "And then I rode into the woods."

"You made it clear you didn't want to visit with him?"

"Yes."

"But Shane didn't care what you wanted, did he?"

"No."

"Tell us about the attack," she says.

Blood roars in my ears. I steal a glance at my friends and Lyssa nods encouragingly at me.

"He was hiding in the hayloft," I tell the jury. "I'd heard

a noise and thought it might be an animal or something. Sometimes we get cats up there and I wanted to make sure it was okay. The light wasn't working, so it was hard to see."

I'm not aware of how soft my words are until Cara gently asks me to speak up.

"He was hiding in the dark. He grabbed me and slammed my face into the wall." My cheeks burn. I don't want to tell this. "He had a knife."

I close my eyes, feeling the courtroom spin. I can't do it. I can't say it out loud.

"What did he do with the knife, Seelie?"

"He cut me." I touch the savage scar that crosses my face. Each heartbeat projects kaleidoscopes of light onto my lowered lids, but I force myself to go on. "He kept yelling at me not to look, but I couldn't help it and it's like he tried to cut my eye out. I tried to get away but he got me on the ground and was choking me. His knife was almost in my ear." I touch the hollow below my ear where Lyssa kissed me last night and that memory helps crowd out the bad.

I open my eyes. I find Lyssa's and hold on for dear life.

"And then he stabbed you?" Cara asks, because in her time line that's what happens next.

But it's not the truth.

"And then he raped me."

The courtroom erupts into complete chaos. Judge Ballard pounds his gavel, bellowing for order. Cara's cat eyes are wide with shock and Blakely is apoplectic, screaming his objections over the buzz of the gallery. To my left, the jurors are exchanging glances and waiting to hear more. Mrs. Mayfield and my mother wear matching looks of stunned horror and Lyssa's face radiates pride like I'm her Cicatrix come to life.

In the din, I am unburdened.

"Order!" Judge Ballard cries and slams his gavel down. Gradually the bedlam quiets. Ballard's face is flushed. "Counsel, why was this not disclosed in discovery?"

"Because I had no idea, Your Honor," Cara says. I feel bad for her, but it had to be this way. This was what I learned on the Internet the night Ashlyn left me alone: If I told Cara, she would've been legally bound to tell the prosecution, who would tell the Mayfields, who would tell everybody, and it wasn't their story to tell. This way I got to control it. It might get struck from the record, but it doesn't matter. The jury heard the truth.

"The court will recess early for lunch. Proceedings will resume in one hour. Bailiff, please sequester the defendant," Ballard says. He points with his gavel to Cara and Blakely. "I want you two in chambers. Now."

I'm ushered out a side door into a windowless room by an armed bailiff. This wasn't a scenario Cara prepped me for. The fact that I might get into trouble for telling the truth never crossed my mind until now. I want to ask the bailiff what's happening, but his gun and the handcuffs hanging from his belt silence me. He stands in the doorway and doesn't talk to me.

I drop into one of the chairs, grateful that it's padded, and fold my arms on the table and put my head down. All the adrenaline that flooded me on the stand is gone and I feel like I could sleep for a week.

"You can't go in there, miss," the bailiff says and I bolt upright.

Lyssa is there, along with Finn, Ashlyn, and, oddly enough, my mother.

"I know," Lyssa says, but she's focused on me. She holds up a bag. "I just brought her something to eat."

The bailiff takes the bag and rifles through it, then puts it on the table.

"Thanks," I tell her.

"You really can't be back here," the bailiff says, resting his hand on the butt of his gun.

"I know, we're going," Lyssa says. She gives me a long look, grins, and then goes. Ashlyn gives a little wave and Finn flashes me a goofy thumbs-up. My mother stands there like she doesn't know what to do and the bailiff moves her along.

There's a turkey sandwich, chips, and a juice box in the bag. Just like kindergarten. I tip the bag and shake out a napkin. Drawn on it in blue ink is a peg-legged parrot, the words *YOU'RE DOING GREAT MATEY* captured in a word bubble near its beak. I smile, fold it up, and slide it into the empty pocket of my pants.

56

I'm back on the stand after lunch.

"Let the record show that I am allowing the defendant to continue her testimony," Judge Ballard says. "Because neither party was aware of the rape allegation, neither party is at an advantage. Ms. Dewitt, the witness is yours."

Cara stands before me, angling herself so the conversation is between us and the jury. "Why didn't you tell the police you were raped?"

"I was embarrassed." More truth. "Also, no one asked."

She seizes on this. "At no point in your interviews did the police ask if you had been sexually assaulted?"

"No."

She lets that sink in with the jury, then says, "What happened next?"

"I fought back. I had to. There were tools and stuff under the hay and I found a mallet." I inhale deeply and gather myself, focusing on the words and not the memories. "I hit him. I had to. He stabbed me and he would've killed me. I had to save myself."

"You feared for your life?"

"Completely."

"Thank you, Seelie. You've been very brave. I have no further questions at this time."

Blakely parks himself behind the lectern and glowers at me. "Ms. Stanton, you have already established yourself as a liar before the court—"

"Objection!" Cara cries.

"Sustained," the judge agrees.

"Fine. If I may draw the court's attention back to the order of events, it would appear that the victim only stabbed Ms. Stanton in the leg after she hit him with the hammer. Is that correct, Ms. Stanton?"

"No, he stabbed me after he cut my face and raped me." I try to keep the edge out of my voice. I have to remember his job is to make me explode. "When I was trying to get away."

"But you hit him in the head before he stabbed your leg, correct?"

"Yes, after he raped me," I say to the jury.

"So you claim," Blakely says dismissively. "But there is no evidence of this supposed intercourse. Why should the court believe it happened? There was no mention of it to the police, or apparently to anyone else. It is only now that you bring it up, months after it can be corroborated. It's nothing more than a convenient story you cooked up hoping for sympathy."

"Objection, badgering the witness," Cara says. I can see my anger reflected in Lyssa's face behind her and I make my decision.

Go big or go home.

"Sustained," the judge says. "Counsel, watch yourself."

"I can prove it," I say quietly. I know I'm not supposed to

talk unless I'm answering a question, but I've already come this far. Cara looks at me quizzically and I wish I could tell her I'm sorry for this second bombshell, but instead I just pull the folded papers from my pocket and hold them up to the judge, because I don't really know who best to give them to. He unfolds them and reads, a wrinkle of confusion creasing his brow. I turn to the twelve strangers seated in the jury box and tell them my biggest secret: "I was pregnant. From the rape. The papers are the DNA analysis of the baby. If you compare it to Shane's, it will match."

There it is, at last. The whole truth and nothing but.

The courtroom erupts again, but the crack of the gavel silences the commotion before it can get much momentum. "There will be order in my court," the judge growls. He looks down at me. "Young lady, this is not a circus, nor is it television. You cannot spontaneously present new evidence simply because it suits your purposes."

"It's the truth, though. I'm just telling the truth." For the first time today I feel like I might cry.

"The jury will disregard this evidence as it cannot be substantiated at this time," the judge says, rattling the papers from Cranston Laboratories that the abortion clinic was so helpful in procuring.

All for nothing. I divulged the worst part of the truth for nothing. I knew the deck was stacked against me and I still let myself believe that the truth would matter, that it would save me.

Blakely looks vindicated when he resumes questioning me. "Ms. Stanton, how is it, if you were so traumatized by this experience, that you stopped long enough to take a 'selfie' before calling the police?"

The sarcastic finger quotes he hooks around the word *selfie* jar me out of my shock. This isn't over.

"I was trying to see how severe my injuries were," I tell the jury. Cara warned me this would probably come up. "I was scared my eye was gone."

"I see. And when the police arrived, why didn't you tell them you had murdered Shane Mayfield?"

"I didn't murder him."

"You caused his death, did you not?"

I look at Cara for help. Her full lips are pulled into a taut line.

"He attacked me," I say. Blakely looks like he's about to take an antelope down for the kill.

"And you killed him for it, didn't you?"

Cara objects, but the judge overrules it and Blakely continues.

"You picked up that hammer with the singular intention of killing that young man, didn't you?"

"I was protecting myself." I feel faint. It's way too hot all of a sudden.

"You're avoiding the question, Ms. Stanton. Did you or did you not kill Shane Mayfield on the evening of October twenty-first?"

"Yes, I killed him," I say and a black hole opens up to swallow me. "I had to."

"Then I have no further questions."

57

When it's time for closing arguments, Blakely approaches the lectern like he's about to accept an Academy Award.

"I would like to thank the members of the jury for their service today," he says, smiling a smarmy used-car-salesman smile at the jury. "You have sat through a fairly, shall we say, theatrical trial today. I ask that you not let the drama of the day's proceedings cloud your judgment. It has largely been misdirection, because the defense has no real case. They have attempted to put the victim, Shane Mayfield, on trial. They point out that he's bigger than her and that he has a history of substance-abuse problems, as if that justifies the brutal attack that robbed him of his very life. But it does not justify it. It cannot. Everyone deserves the protection of the law, regardless of whether or not they're under the influence of mind-altering substances. Shane was like all of us. He had friends, a family. He loved and was loved in return. He might not have been perfect, but I challenge each one of you to find me someone who is. I can tell you who is far from perfect, though, and that is Cecelia Stanton."

He stabs a finger in my direction without turning. I feel like I'm watching this from somewhere far away.

"I have been tasked with proving, beyond a reasonable doubt, that Ms. Stanton willfully and intentionally killed Shane Mayfield. Ladies and gentlemen of the jury, there is nothing there for me to prove because you heard it from her own mouth: She knowingly killed that young man in cold blood. A gifted athlete, a fine young man, cut down in the prime of his life, all because of the strident overreaction of one girl." He shakes his head, like he can't believe what the world has come to.

"I know it's hard not to sympathize with her, what with the bombastic rape allegations, but I ask you to consider this: We have no proof of rape. For all we know, they engaged in an act of consensual sex and she regretted it. But it's irrelevant because our victim is not on trial for rape. Our victim is not on trial at all; Ms. Stanton is and all we know for sure is that she attacked the victim only after the sex act was complete. After. Not during. She could've allowed him to leave. Whether it was rape or a regrettable consensual encounter, she could have let him leave. Instead she chose to pick up a hammer and bludgeon him to death. Not until he was incapacitated, but until she knew beyond a shadow of a doubt that he was dead. She wanted revenge. She picked up that hammer with every intention of malice. She knew what she was doing. That is why the only thing you can reasonably do is find her guilty of murder."

Cara scribbles a note on the yellow legal pad—*trust me*—and squeezes my shoulder when she stands. It brings me back from the faraway place. She bypasses the lectern to stand directly before the jurors.

"A man is dead," she says solemnly. "And my client killed him."

I sit up straighter. What is she doing? This isn't how this is supposed to go. Cara lets the silence hang like a noose. The jurors look at me and all I can see are the guilty votes in their eyes.

"At no point have we denied that Mr. Mayfield met his death at the hands of my client. Don't forget that you're not here to decide whether or not she killed him. That is undisputed. What you're here to decide is whether she was acting within the realm of self-defense, if she was legally justified in using lethal force to protect herself."

My face is hot and I desperately want to turn around. This would be so much easier if I could just be sitting on that uncomfortable bench, sandwiched between my friends.

"When you look at that girl, you're not seeing the whole picture," Cara says. "You're not seeing the bruises that ringed her throat where Mr. Mayfield choked her. You're not seeing her black eyes or her swollen nose. You see the scar on her face, but you don't see the one on her leg that forced her onto crutches and a cane and continues to require ongoing physical therapy. You don't see the nightmares that keep her awake. There are scars she bears that I don't know about, that no one does—damage that Mr. Mayfield has done to her sense of self and her place in the world. He upended her entire universe. And not because he was high. That is not an excuse for his behavior, no matter what the prosecution would have you think. Drugs did not pick up a knife. Drugs did not strangle her. Drugs did not rape her. Shane Mayfield, and Shane Mayfield alone, did those things."

I turn around, just for a second; I can't help it. She did what I asked and I have to make sure it mattered. Finn's face is a mess of emotion: relief, remorse, and something I can't name. I can only nod at him and hope he knows it means forgiveness.

"At the beginning of this trial I told you we were looking at a story of survival." Cara's voice is soft, meant only for the jury, and they hang on her every word. "At just seventeen years old, Seelie made the choice to survive. She will forever bear the scars of that day, but she is alive because of her bravery. Had she killed Mr. Mayfield when he was attacking another woman, she would've been lauded as a hero, not put on trial. Do not take away that heroism just because it was herself that she saved. She stood up for herself when it mattered the most, and now she needs you to stand up as well. Convicting her would be nothing short of a travesty. Thank you."

She returns to our table and the judge gives the jury their instructions for deliberation.

And then we wait.

And wait.

///

Hours pass before the jury reaches a verdict. Hours in which my life rests in the hands of twelve strangers. It seems to take far too long, at least until everyone is back in the courtroom and then it's all happening much too fast.

"Who has been appointed jury foreman?" Judge Ballard asks once everyone is settled.

The heavy Latino man stands up, holding a paper. "I have, Your Honor."

"And has the jury reached a verdict?"

"Yes, Your Honor."

My heart climbs up my throat.

"Please hand that verdict to the bailiff," the judge says.

The man gives a folded paper to the same bailiff who let Lyssa bring me lunch, who then hands it up to the judge. The judge spends an eternity reading as my heart tries to break free from the prison of my ribs. My knees piston up and down of their own accord and Cara has to put a hand on my thigh for me to even notice. Does it always take this long for them to tell you what they've already decided about the rest of your life?

"Will the defendant please rise," the judge says in a way that's not a question.

I stand on liquid legs, Cara by my side. I search the judge's face for any hint, but find nothing.

"The clerk will read the verdict," he says, passing the slip of paper to yet another person who will know my fate before I do.

I waver on my feet. I'm not ready for this. Cara told me what will happen if they say guilty. I'll be put in handcuffs right here in front of everyone. I clasp my hands behind my back to hide their trembling.

The court clerk is a hatchet-faced woman with a gray bob and glasses. She studies the form for a moment, then speaks in a clear voice that needs no microphone.

"In the case of the Commonwealth of Massachusetts versus Cecelia Stanton, the jury finds the defendant not guilty of any charges."

Not.

Guilty.

Holy shit.

It takes a minute for it to really sink in and the courtroom buzzes around me.

Over the sound of weeping and rage from the other side of the court, I hear familiar voices cheering behind me. I turn and my friends are on their feet, clapping and grinning like they just won the lottery. Rick has his arm around my mom, who is inexplicably crying. Judge Ballard pounds his gavel again and it doesn't even matter that it's my friends making the most noise, because we did it.

We won.

EPILOGUE

The case gets national attention in the days following the verdict. Requests for interviews come in from major news shows and *People* magazine wants to do a feature on the case.

I surprise everyone by agreeing.

There are two reasons I do it. One is for Cara. After everything she's done for me, she deserves the attention. She made no money from defending me and that doesn't sit right with me. I figure the least I can do is pay her back with publicity.

The second reason is harder to explain. I guess I just don't want to hide anymore. The secrets and lies hurt me every bit as much as Shane did. If something like this happened to me, it's happened to other people too. Maybe if I can conquer my fear of being a spectacle then I can help someone else who might be in the same boat. That's my hope anyway.

Cara insists, in the dying wake of the media frenzy, that we attend the Winter Gala, where the local news will be covering a speech given by the governor in honor of the town's seventy-fifth anniversary celebration. She thinks it's a fitting end, a way of showing that I'm still a normal girl doing normal-girl things.

As if I would ever, in a million years, normally go to the godforsaken Gala.

But I do it. For Cara.

And I have to admit, it's actually kind of nice.

The town has set up two huge, heated white tents on the

common. White fairy lights twinkle in the trees and in the tents. The smaller of the two is filled with high cocktail tables and a sprawling catered buffet. The school's jazz quartet plays from a low stage and people mill about in their finery, carrying wine glasses and little plates of food. Everyone under twenty-one has a snowflake stamped on their hand and is given stemless glasses of sparkling cider, although I'm pretty sure most of those are getting swapped out for champagne when no one's looking.

The other tent is split into two sections with a DJ booth in the middle. One side has a wooden dance floor and the other has been turned into a temporary ice-skating rink that is already swarming with teetering kids on skates.

I'm wearing a long, beaded navy dress that Cara had delivered to my house with a note that said, *All girls deserve a princess dress, even warriors.*

How could I not wear it?

"Dude, these are awesome!" Finn says, presenting me with a martini glass full of mashed potatoes smothered in bacon and sour cream. He's holding a mostly empty one in his other hand.

"He already had three," Ashlyn tells me, taking a bite of scallop. Her shimmering dress looks like it came straight out of Daisy Buchanan's closet and a peacock feather is tucked into hair that looks dyed to match the plume. The others are decked out too, Finn in a ridiculous white tux that he's somehow pulling off, and Lyssa positively stunning in her three-piece gangster suit, hat and all.

"Thank god there's food here," Lyssa says. Her plate is piled with macaroni, some kind of rice balls, and little burger sliders. She's like a black hole, but damn if she doesn't look amazing anyway.

"Oh, it's not that bad," Cara says, sweeping in behind us. Her knee-length gold flapper dress glitters under the lights as she surveys the faction over a sparkling flute of champagne. "My, don't we clean up well?"

Finn preens. "Did you expect otherwise?"

She laughs. "I suppose not."

"Thank you for the dress," I say, even though I already thanked her by text when it arrived. The lines of the bodice actually make me look like I have a real waist and I feel a little bit like Cicatrix in it, all brave and daring curves. Plus, it weighs a ton, so it's sort of like wearing armor. "You really didn't have to do that."

"It looks fabulous, and yes, I did. I know you enough by now to know you would've bailed on this the first chance you got," she says with a knowing smile.

"They're not here to interview me," I remind her. "The press is only here for the governor."

"And some token shots of the festivities, which you will be in, my little media darling," she says, touching my nose with the tip of her gold-polished finger.

I stab at her hand with my fork and she laughs. In the course of all the interviewing, we have moved beyond a professional relationship and are something more like friends now. She's talked to me about college and law school and promised to help in any way she can if that's something I want to pursue.

Cara waves to someone and it takes me a minute to recognize

Maria Morales as she makes her way over to our group. She looks different all dressed up.

"Congratulations," she tells me, smiling widely. "I'm glad Cara was able to take care of you."

"I think she mostly took care of herself." Cara laughs. "I keep telling this girl she should be thinking about law school."

I don't know if law school is what I'm going to do, but I like the idea of having someone out there who thinks I could if I wanted to. What I do know for certain, though, is that I'm done with high school. I signed up to take the GED and am looking at colleges. I'm not stupid enough to think the not-guilty verdict is going to make everything okay at school. The jury of those peers definitely still believes I'm guilty and I'm done trying to prove myself to people who don't matter. Mom accused me of trying to run away from my problems, but that's not it. I'm just ready for the next step, wherever that may lead.

When the governor takes the stage and begins rambling about the particular beauty of small-town charm, we take that as our cue to stop acting like adults. Finn ducks off, leaving the rest of us to raid the dessert table. I almost die of fat-kid delight when I see the elaborate rainbow display of French macarons. We take way more than we should, plus cake, and four little cream-puff swans. Finn meets back up with us as we're ducking into the big tent, and passes out cups of cider.

Only it's definitely not cider.

"Did you not see Officer Morales back there? I don't need to get in trouble for underage drinking," I whisper, looking around for anyone noticing. Kids shriek with joy as they career around the ice and the dance floor is being cleared for the pageant. No one is watching us.

"You won't," he says.

"You won't," Lyssa agrees. She raises her glass, looks me square in the eye. My stomach somersaults beneath the intensity of her gaze. It's a good flip. "A toast, for being your own hero."

"To Seelie!" Finn says, clinking his glass into Lyssa's and downing a gulp of the champagne. We all touch glasses and drink. Lyssa's eyes never leave mine.

I raise mine to the middle of the group. I peel my eyes from Lyssa's, look at each of them in turn. My heart swells with love for these three people. "I couldn't have done any of this without you. Any of it."

I look at Ashlyn, who has tears in her eyes. "I know things got bad for a while, but I can't fault you for standing by your beliefs. You'll always be my sister." I touch her glass with mine, then turn to Finn.

My throat is tight, but I smile at him. "None of this was your fault. None of it. Being friends with us is kind of like the Mafia. Once you're in, it's for life." I clink his glass. "But that also means we'll break your knees if you screw up again."

Everyone laughs.

At last I turn to Lyssa, rest my glass against the edge of hers, and gaze up at her. Heartbeats pass and there's that happy little twist in my belly again. She grins down at me, waiting. "For Cicatrix," I finally say, but what I really mean is, *I love you.*

She knows.

She always did.

"To us," I say, and we drink. We watch Madison and Ryan

get crowned Winter Queen and King and we dance and we laugh. We have been through hell and bear its scars, and the fault lines aren't completely closed, but we're together and that matters.

At the end of the night we find a plastic crown hanging from the passenger-side mirror of Lyssa's Jeep, with a note: *You earned it this year.* Cherries on the *i*'s.

I pass the cheap symbol of Amesford royalty onto a squealing freshman girl who runs by with a pack of friends and we call it a night. We drive back to Lyssa's and we talk late into the night about everything and nothing. We settle into new sleeping arrangements.

We carry on.

It's all we can do.

ACKNOWLEDGMENTS

A huge thanks to Mari Kesselring and the rest of the Flux team, without whom this book wouldn't even exist.

Writerly thanks must also go to Stacey Doherty for her invaluable feedback on the earliest draft (If only all CPs could use *Buffy* references as shorthand!) and to the Electrics for being such an awesome debut group. Book people are the best people!

Further thanks and shout-outs to:

Erika Madden, for gifting me my official "tea while I'm writing" mug (it was a critical part of my station!) and for fangirl talks at the barn—they're a very large part of why this book is YA.

Madison Dungey, for being my fan even before I wrote this book. I never thought I'd be part of someone's OTP!

Ashleigh, Liv, and the rest of the barn girls, current and past, for proving that horse girls are tougher than most.

The NBHS Library Cult (aka The Poppies), for renewing my faith in your generation's geek-literacy and general awesomeness.

Lar Lar, for the sometimes-questionable decision of bringing me into this world but not taking me out.

Chris Larivee and Miranda Treat, for entirely too many things to list.

And lastly Adam, for being best husbando.

ABOUT THE AUTHOR

Mischa Thrace has worked as a teacher, a horse trainer, a baker, and a librarian and has amassed enough random skills to survive most apocalypses. She lives in western Massachusetts with her husband, a one-eyed dog, and a cranky cat who rarely leaves the basement. She loves tea, geekery, and not getting stung by bees.